D1233282

The Letter

a novel by

W. GUNTHER PLAUT

McClelland and Stewart

Financial assistance of the Canada Council and the Ontario Arts Council toward the publication of this book is gratefully acknowledged.

The Canadian Publishers
McClelland and Stewart Limited
481 University Avenue
Toronto, Ontario
M5G 2E9

Canadian Cataloguing in Publication Data

Plaut, W. Gunther, 1912-
The letter: a novel

ISBN 0-7710-7164-7

I. Title.

PS8531.L29L48 1986 C813'.54 C86-094155-8
PR9199.3.P538L48 1986

Typography and assembly by The Literary Service, Toronto, Ontario

Printed and bound in Canada by T. H. Best Printing Company Limited

Sometime during the winter of 1941-42 Heydrich,
chief of the Security Police and Secret Service,
told me of the Führer's order. . . .
I will never forget that moment.

Adolf Eichmann
from his autobiography, Ich, Adolf Eichmann

Contents

	Prologue Berlin 1935	*9*
Part I	Drawing Blood Spring 1938	*15*
Part II	The Letter Fall 1938	*59*
Part III	The Chase Winter 1941-42	*109*
Part IV	Voice in the Wilderness Summer 1942	*157*
Part V	Master Agent Winter 1943	*199*
Part VI	A Piece of Glass Winter 1944	*249*
Part VII	Showdown Spring 1945	*299*
	Afterword	*331*

Prologue

BERLIN 1935

The room was dark and badly lit, not at all befitting the imposing title on the door: *Secretariat of Racial Purity.*

The clerk behind the desk belonged to the fraternity of bureaucrats who licked the boots of their superiors and lorded it over their supplicants. He was bald and dressed badly and asked the young man in front of him questions from a printed form. He was clearly bored and did not bother to hide it.

"Your name?" He made it sound as if it didn't matter.

"Heinrich Raben, sir."

"Age?"

"Almost twenty."

"Born whcn?"

"August 1915, I don't know the exact date."

The clerk looked up.

"What kind of bullshit is that! You don't know?. . ."

The young man cleared his throat. He was well built, dark-complexioned and wore his hair like the Führer. He was still standing.

"You see, sir, that's part of my story. My parents weren't married and I was taken to a Catholic orphanage. The records there never showed exactly when or where I was born, just the name of my mother and natural father. Soon after I was adopted by Manfred Raben. He simply entered August 1, Berlin, into my papers. But I doubt. . ."

"Wait a minute!"

The clerk had risen to his feet.

"Did you say Manfred Raben?"

"Yes, sir."

"You were adopted by a Jew?"

"Yes, sir."

"So get the hell out of here before I run you in!"

The young man stood his ground.

"Please, sir, I am not a Jew – that's why I'm here. My mother's name was Kuntze, and she brought me to St. Gabriel's Home for Children. Here, look."

He spread out a paper that showed the name of Erna Kuntze, religion Catholic, and the father, Adolf Stiebel, religion Protestant.

"Surely no hint of Jews there," Heinrich commented.

The clerk sat down again.

"So what do you want?"

"I want to be certified as an Aryan, that's why I came to you. I just found out I'm not a Jew, thank God."

"Well," said the clerk, "it's an unusual case all right. I'd better ask someone about it. Wait here."

He left the room and after some minutes returned with an SS man to whom he showed obsequious deference.

"Here's the chap who claims he is like us," he said.

The SS officer was not much older than Heinrich. He fit the prescription of the ideal German: tall, blond and blue eyed, features which had helped him to an appointment as a guardian of racial purity.

"Raben? Son of *the* Raben by chance?"

"Adopted son, sir, yes."

"But raised as a Jew?"

"No, sir. My adoptive father didn't believe in religion

and I know nothing about any Jewish things. I wasn't even circumcised."

"Really now!" The officer was clearly intrigued. "Go ahead and prove it."

"You mean?. . ."

"Yes, Raben, do it. Drop your pants and you'd better not be a liar."

Heinrich hesitated. He suddenly felt that he would also drop his identity and his dignity. He fleetingly wondered whether it was all worth it.

"Well?" the black-clad man with his shiny boots barked at him. Slowly Heinrich undid his trousers. They fell to the floor softly and without resistance. The man inspected him with much mirth and obscene gestures. Heinrich had never felt so naked in his life.

"All right, button them up," the officer said at last. "I want to see your records and must ask some questions."

Routine questions:

"Adoptive parents?"

"Manfred, Magda."

"Brother?"

"None."

"Sister?"

"Helga."

"Real parents?"

"No further information."

"Association with Jews?"

"None."

"High school?"

"Just graduated, Friedrich Wilhelm Real-Gymnasium."

"Desired career?"

"Law."

After an hour he was dismissed and told he would hear the decision in time.

Three weeks later he received a certificate, duly stamped and signed:

September 1, 1935

This will attest that Heinrich Raben, natural son of Erna Kuntze and Adolf Stiebel, is judged to be a pure Aryan German.

Heil Hitler!
(s) Konrad Kabbe,
Vice-Chairman
Secretariat of Racial Purity

A note was attached, instructing him to move out of his parents' home as soon as feasible.

* * *

With this certificate in hand, Heinrich Raben launched himself on a career of serving the Third Reich. He did not know that this would entail becoming the messenger of Death itself, bearing Adolf Hitler's most secret order.

PART I

Drawing Blood

SPRING 1938

1

Helga awoke in a sweat, the nightgown clinging uncomfortably to her legs. She had dreamt about her father discovering her secret and in the light of the morning her anxiety increased. What if he learned about Rolf?

The bathroom door closed with its accustomed drawn-out moan. They now lived in a spacious apartment in Berlin's fashionable west end, where they had moved after the state had requisitioned their luxurious home at Wannsee. Father had said that there was no choice; one did not argue with the government, especially not this one.

She thought of the two men in her life: her father, the great Manfred Raben, born a Jew who wanted to be accepted as a German; and the youthful Rolf Baumgarten who was one in every way, aristocratic in descent and deportment, whose position in the Nazi hierarchy was never clear to her. It had occurred to her that Rolf might be working for the Gestapo, but a casual inquiry into his work had made him lose his temper. She never asked again.

Helga was nineteen years old. She loathed her background and the people to whom, so the Nazis insisted, she belonged. Overprotected at home, she had become a rebel with an amorous cause. *Nazi officer cashiered for blood pollution with Jewish bitch* – she could almost taste the headlines.

Yet she felt no anxiety. Do I love Rolf? she wondered, and knew the answer. You won't like it, Dad. But I've got to show you I'm no longer a child. I'll show you, however big you are.

Her father, short, solidly built and solidly anchored in his convictions, a coldly calculating man in the prime of life. Head of German Machineries, manufacturers of auto and airplane parts. "The Jewish Krupp," she heard her classmates speak of him, though Manfred Raben considered himself fully a German who happened to have Jewish ancestors. He thought of National Socialism as an aberration that was bound to pass. Helga had grown up as an atheist and sometimes was ready to believe that the Nazis might not be altogether wrong in their anti-Semitic propaganda. The Jewish school she was forced to attend was everything she disowned. Values she didn't understand, girls she disliked for their emotional ways. Cloying, she thought, not like us.

Heinrich, how did you manage to get into law school in 1935 and stay there? she wondered. Three long years already you've been able to attend! How? Why are you so privileged?

When she had asked him once he had brushed her off, and no other chance had arisen since. He had moved out of the apartment and she had not seen him often thereafter, something she did not regret. They had not liked each other for many years and their separation did not lessen their mutual aversion. But she envied him his apparent exception from the Jewish fate.

"Helga!" Her mother's voice. A faceless subdued parent, a mere reflection of her husband's will. Do they really sleep together? Helga wondered. She shuddered at the thought.

"Yes, Mother, I'm awake!"

She was disgusted that her mother had no opinions apart from her husband's. While Helga admired her father for being a man in every way, she disliked his being so taken with himself that he didn't seem to see either his wife or his daughter as independent persons. Well, what will you say when you find out that your darling child may lose her innocence with a Nazi officer?

They had met by chance in Berlin's Tiergarten where the snow was deep in the park, icicles bent the bushes which bowed low before the passers-by. A young Army officer sat on a bench unpacking his lunch. The sun was shining warmly, perfect for skiing, skating and sitting happily in the glow of a mid-winter's day. She paused for a moment; the bench was inviting. No, I mustn't. . .

"How about sitting down and sharing my lunch?" the officer said with charming boldness.

She shook her head. "Thank you, I can't."

He looked at her, blue eyes set wide in a strong face, slender figure, of medium height.

"Why not? I guarantee my sandwiches are good. I made them myself."

She stood irresolute for a moment. "Oh, all right," she said, "but thanks, no lunch."

Thus, in the fifth year of Hitler's reign, a relationship began that held every promise of danger and failure: Rolf Baumgarten, young Army captain, son of one of Germany's best-known aristocratic families, and Helga Raben, daughter of the country's last remaining Jewish industrialist.

They began to see each other once a week, and would meet near the big clock by the Zoo shortly after dark. Though he had never come in uniform she feared the day he would and someone might recognize her. One evening she did see a classmate not far away waiting for her date.

"Quick, Rolf, she must not see me."

She pulled him into the dusky cover of the railroad underpass.

"Hey, what's the big hurry? Can't a girl be seen with a fellow?"

She knew then she had to tell him. They sat on a bench

in the park, just as they had done when they had first met. Only now spring was in the air, the swallows were back and the first flowers were showing their heads.

"I've never told you, Rolf. . ."

She could not go on. Her palms were suddenly wet.

"Told me what?"

She tried but couldn't say it.

"For God's sake, Helga, what's so awful that you can't tell me? Are you engaged to someone? Whatever it is, I can handle it."

At last she found her voice. "No, Rolf, it's worse."

"Are you married?"

"No. I'm Jewish, the daughter of Manfred Raben, and I'm in love with you." She blurted it out all at once and began to weep. Her sobs trailed off into staccato moans.

"Five years already I'm an outcast in this country. What's wrong with me? I'm as German as you. . ."

Rolf took her hand and held it, then drew her to him and embraced her.

"Darling, it doesn't matter to me, not a damn. This Jew business is for the birds. You're my Helga. I'll handle it somehow," he said, though he had no idea how he might do it. It was one thing for Göring to declare General Milch an honorary Aryan; it was another for a 29-year-old Army captain to buck the racial mania of the Nazi state.

"Let me do the worrying," he continued. "You could get by, you know, you aren't circumcised."

His lighthearted tone failed to comfort her.

"Rolf, it's not possible. My father is too well known."

"That's true," he admitted after some hesitation. "I hadn't thought of that."

They sat still, holding hands. The darkness silhouetted Rolf's profile: strong chin, slight mustache, wavy hair. I love him, she thought. God, how I love him! I'm old enough to know my heart.

He spoke at last, responding as if he had read her mind. "Don't you know great love affairs always run into some snag? That's what makes them great."

"It won't work," she protested. "Remember, we Jews are Germany's misfortune."

"Have you forgotten where the Führer got it from?" Rolf laughed. "From a Jew, Heine, who said it a hundred years ago."

"And does that help me, or us? I can't introduce you to my father and you can't take me to your house. And your superiors, they would love it, wouldn't they? They would make you a private, or kick you out altogether. And me – they would shave my hair and exhibit me in the street. And then they'd send me to Oranienburg and put a placard around my neck: *Race Polluter.* Rolfi, darling, we've got to break it up."

But they had continued to see each other. At first they went to movies. Lately they would take the S-Bahn to Grunewald and wander in its lovers' lanes. Once, nestled in the bushes off the road, she felt herself yielding with a sense of delicious guilt; but footsteps were heard nearby and they hastily rearranged their clothing.

Helga insisted on being home by ten o'clock in order to maintain her story that she was studying with a friend. Her parents had never doubted her tale; they had not asked for her schoolmate's name or telephone number. After all, a 19-year-old daughter who was about to graduate was no longer a child.

She had been brought up in a large suburban villa and received all the advantages of a wealthy child: horses, travel, an English tutor who helped her speak the language with ease and confidence, servants who were eager to respond to her wishes. Yet, despite her intelligence and judgment, she had never emerged as a person in her own right. Her father had dominated the family with absolute authority.

"Are you up, Helga?" Mother again.

"Yes, Mother."

She lingered. The idea of going to school had become hateful. The final exams were coming and she feared she would fail. She thought about Rolf as she dressed. Just thinking of him buoyed her spirits. With all the dangers of their relationship, Rolf represented power and possibility.

2

She made a detour via Alexanderplatz, hoping to catch a glimpse of Rolf. But instead she ran into her brother. She had not seen him in six months and realized why she disliked him. Beneath the winsome façade, Heinrich was a cruel and ruthless man.

"Well, well! And what's my little sister doing in this part of town? Sort of flirting with the devil, aren't you?" He pointed at the Gestapo headquarters across the square. "Jews shouldn't get too close, you know."

"So what are you doing here? They call you a kike too."

He smiled patronizingly. "That's how much you know. You and I aren't even related. They found my birth record at the adoption agency and I'm as Aryan as they come. You should feel privileged I even talk to you."

Helga felt like spitting at him. "Maybe you should change your name," she said.

"I've been thinking about it," Heinrich responded in a matter-of-fact tone. "I can't get far with that monicker anymore."

"And how about Father's money? Does that stink too, or is it lily-white Aryan?"

"You talk too much." Now he wanted to hurt her. "Even if you were a certified German, it wouldn't help you because you were born dumb. You don't know what's playing out there. You haven't learned a thing. Not even how to wiggle your ass, I bet. I mean all the way. Or have you? Maybe I should find someone to teach you."

"You're a bastard," she hissed at him.

Helga turned and walked away, casting a glance at the gray building shadowing the square.

The few remaining blocks to Kaiserstrasse, where her school was located, seemed interminably long. From every corner the world seemed to shout *Jew, Jew!. . . This business owned by a Jew,* a placard proclaimed. *Germans don't buy here. . . . This bench reserved for Germans. . . . Jews and dogs keep off. . . .* Jews cannot be lawyers. Jews cannot be doctors in German hospitals. Jews must have Jewish names. They have no citizenship, no rights. Get out of this country and stay out!

She was in a state of deep despair when at last she arrived at school. The principal, Dr. Klappermann, a small man who had his head covered with a *Käppchen*, stood at the door.

"Good morning, Miss Raben," he greeted her pleasantly, though Helga felt an undertone of irony in his high-pitched voice. "I'm glad to see you. Won't you come into my office for a few moments."

The building was an old-fashioned residence which had recently been converted into a girls' school after Jews had been forbidden to continue attending public institutions. The principal's office was small and dimly lit; it looked like a former maid's room, Helga thought.

"Please sit down, Miss Raben." Dr. Klappermann always addressed her formally. Other teachers simply called her Raben or used her first name.

"How are you getting on in school?" he inquired. "I know this is a new environment for you, and for all of us, for that matter."

Helga shrugged her shoulders.

The principal looked into a folder that he had evidently readied for inspection.

"Miss Raben, your school record is not as good as it might be. You come late, your homework is below average and the teachers tell me you are daydreaming."

"Yes, sir," she responded demurely. "I would like to do better."

"I hope so." He adjusted his skull cap. "I have not yet told your father about your work. However, if it does not improve, I must. After all, Herr Raben is one of our important citizens, if one may still use that term. He's entitled to special consideration. We want you to graduate, but we need your cooperation."

Helga did not respond.

"I'm not sure you are aware of the situation," the principal continued. "Perhaps you don't think a graduation certificate from our school is worth very much. Of course, you can't use it to get into a German university. *Den Juden ist der Eintritt verboten.* I hear your brother is still a student. I'm puzzled by this inconsistency in the official application of their racial laws. Maybe it's out of respect for your father. However, we're concerned with *your* prospects, and they're not good."

Helga tried to focus on the man in front of her. The mention of her brother brought a bitter taste to her mouth.

She finally managed to form her words. "I'm discouraged. I wasn't a bad student at the Lyceum. But now. . ."

"Yes, Miss Raben, that's the burden we all have to bear. We once thought we could make it as Germans, but now it's clear we can't."

"Dr. Klappermann, may I be permitted to say that in my own eyes I'm still a German, regardless of what anyone says?"

"Well, I see we don't agree. I wish you were more realistic, but then, you seem to be your father's true daughter. He too continues to bank on Germany returning to sanity, doesn't he? If only he were right! I for one will not chance it. I'll be leaving here as soon as the exams are finished. Then I'm off to America. Thank God, they're still letting us go. Good luck, Miss Raben, for whatever lies ahead for you."

He rose. The room seemed even darker. She thanked him and left. Klappermann had touched on matters Helga had tried to hide from herself. Would she be able to talk about them to her father?

She passed the day worrying about the exams. She'd do well in English and German literature, and adequately in history and geography. She'd have to be very lucky to scrape through in the sciences. Hebrew, of course, was a total loss. She had simply resisted it. If it had been taught as a foreign language she might have tried to learn its secrets, but they presented it as "their" language and that automatically made her a rebel.

That week there had been no word from Rolf. She was unable to study; she read but could not concentrate.

"Aren't you feeling well," her mother asked, "or is it the exams? They bother you, I know."

"I hate the school," Helga admitted, "and the long ride and walk through that horrible quarter of town."

"I know, dear, but what can we do? Maybe we should get a tutor for a few weeks."

Helga declined. The idea of failure evoked a sense of bittersweet anticipation, like scratching one's skin until the scab came off. Yet the thought frightened her.

A note was delivered to Captain Rolf Friedrich Baumgarten by a nondescript-looking man in a grayish suit with wide shoulders and flaring pants. Ordinarily this would have qualified him as a stylish dresser, but his trousers were not creased and his shoes not polished. Rolf, who liked to analyze people by their clothes, concluded that the messenger suffered from some character flaw. Not surprising then that a man forty to fifty years of age, who had probably come by bicycle, should be no more than a menial go-between in the bureaucracy.

But when he looked at the letter he realized he had misjudged the messenger. No underling would have been entrusted with a message marked *Top Secret.* He carefully opened the envelope. No haste must be exhibited lest the messenger think him anxious. Whoever sent him would inquire after Baumgarten's reactions, and such matters found their way into one's personnel file.

The paper he extracted bore the initials H.H., the first time he had received a personal communication from the all-powerful head of the national police force.

> *You are requested to attend a special planning conference at my office the day after tomorrow. You are not to wear your uniform. No mention of*

this meeting is to be made to your superiors in the Army, or to anyone else, either before or after the meeting.

Heil Hitler!
(s) Himmler
Reichsführer SS

Rolf was more relieved than he cared to admit. As long as he was a liaison officer, assigned by the Army to the Gestapo, he was under Himmler's command, and for a moment he had feared that his relationship with the young daughter of one of Germany's best-known Jewish families had been exposed. The consequences would be drastic; his military career would be in ruins.

It would be a terrible blow to his mother. Her sense of propriety had lately increased to rather annoying levels. She was at pains to let him know of his important and noble family connections. Her father was General von Friedrichsruh, who had the misfortune of being born at the wrong time: too young to have an heroic record in the Franco-Prussian war and too old to receive a combat assignment in the Great War. He was conservative, of the old school, and had given solid and predictable service to Bismarck and the Kaiser. His vivacious daughter had rebelled against the confining traditions of her Junker class and had, much to her parents' distress, run off with a wealthy and obscure commoner from Riga who had the good grace to die shortly after Rolf was born.

By grandfatherly decree, Riga was designated out of bounds for Rolf who had no further relations with his father's family. His mother was properly re-educated to the values of her class and consented to marry a poor but well-connected Bavarian count, von Bumm, who had no compunction whatsoever to spend the deceased Baumgarten's fortune rather freely.

Rolf disliked him intensely, but he admired his mother for having fallen in love with an unapproved partner, even as he had. Of course, there was a difference. Formerly the disapproval came only from the family, now it also came from the state. The difference was palpable and dangerous. He decided that he would make no contact with Helga, at least not until after the mysterious conference with Himmler.

In the opening gambits of the meeting it took Himmler only a few moments to establish his authority. Schoolmasterly and pedantic, given to slight corpulence, he had piercing eyes which his rimless glasses enlarged. His facial features were as un-Aryan as the Führer's, which somehow muddied the proverbial emphasis of the SS on tall, blue-eyed specimens as the purveyors of Germany's ideal racial strain. It also made Rolf, dark haired and with olive skin, more at ease.

Rolf Baumgarten was clearly low man on the totem pole of the small assemblage. All were in civvies, except Himmler. Brief introductions were made: Müller, from the Ministry of the Interior; Deimlich, the only one Rolf had met, a deputy of the police administration; Schwalmbach, connected with the Secret Police; Dr. Stramm, who represented the Propaganda Minister; and Julius Streicher, Germany's leading Jew baiter whose journal, *Der Stürmer*, specialized in pornographic descriptions of German maidens being violated by thick-lipped, hook-nosed Jewish lechers.

Rolf took an instant dislike to Streicher and imagined what it would be like if he himself were to be excoriated by the journal. He wondered whether the man experienced orgasm when he wrote his luscious tales of fornication.

"*Meine Herren*," Himmler began, "this meeting is being held on orders of the Führer himself. The reason for the secrecy will become self-evident."

He paused and looked at each participant.

"No report will be issued. Your immediate superiors, if they inquire, are to be put off. Tell them you are under orders to communicate on this matter only with your chief who in each case knows that something is afoot. He will hear the news directly from the Führer. Dr. Goebbels and Field Marshal Göring are already acquainted with our project, which has their full and enthusiastic support. As you may conclude from Mr. Streicher's presence, the Jews are the object of our discussion."

Streicher glowed with anticipation. Himmler polished his glasses and spoke again.

"I need not tell you that from the beginning of his crusade for Germany the Führer has considered the Jews his greatest obstacle and implacable enemy. He once told Major Hell that he would love to string them up one by one in every public square and cut them down only when they began to stink. He wanted Germans to detest forever the very smell of the Jewish plague. The tragedy is that our good German citizens still haven't fully grasped the Führer's vision. So we must help them, and this is why you are here."

He took off his glasses and polished them again, as if to see more clearly what lay ahead. He looked vulnerable without them; he seemed to need their protection to fortify his authority.

"The Jews are now effectively disconnected from German life. There are still some businesses which have not as yet been Aryanized, but that will be taken care of in a short while. We are a little behind schedule in Austria, which is understandable. After all, it's only a few months since they became part of us.

"In effect, we have already ghettoized the Jews inside the Reich. Not by walls, at least not yet. So far merely by our will. The German people have gone along with us, though without real enthusiasm. We have taught them to dislike Jews. We are succeeding in making Jews despicable in their eyes. Now we have to make them repugnant to the German soul, so that our people will rejoice in their expulsion and, if the time should ever come, even accept their extermination. To that end, we must teach them to have no pity for these subhuman creatures. I am beginning with my own SS. The highest morality is to be strong in the face of debilitating pity.

"But first things first. The Jews still believe that each step in their disenfranchisement is the last. That's why the majority are still here, hoping for us to relent or even disappear. In this, of course, they are abetted by their fellow Jews in other countries."

"Like Rosenfeld, that swinish cripple," interjected Streicher. He was referring to Roosevelt, whom *Der Stürmer* always called a Jew, claiming that Rosenfeld was really his name, proving thereby his racial descent. Himmler did not react and overlooked the interruption, rather pointedly, Rolf observed.

"To come to the point," Himmler continued, "we will now plan to shock the Jews to such an extent that they will pack up and leave us. The problem is that there are so few places they can go. The weak-kneed democracies haven't the guts to admit that they too don't want Jews. The Führer is convinced, and naturally I concur, that if we killed all German Jews tomorrow, the world would cry a few crocodile tears and secretly say 'Thanks' and 'good riddance.'

"So our first step is to make it finally and unmistakably clear to the Jews in our Reich that they have no future here, not tomorrow, not ever again. Our message must be unambiguous: leave our sacred soil or suffer the consequences. If you stay, we will ghettoize you physically, put you in concentration camps and eventually help you to meet your Jehovah face to face. In the process, of course, we will take your precious possessions."

"Bravo!" shouted Streicher, saliva dribbling from his lips.

"All we need now is a proper occasion. A public scandal or a murder of some prominent person that we will lay at the Jews' door, or the burning of some building that we want to get rid of anyway."

He looked at Müller, a small smile creasing his face. "I'm sure the Field Marshal would be most helpful."

Müller sat stony-faced. It was not considered good form to allude to the rumor that Göring had planned the burning of the Reichstag five years before. Himmler next turned to Deimlich, the man from the police force.

"We will organize a public outcry against the Jews, a veritable orgy of destruction, arrests, confiscations and the like. I will take care of details. I want your people to stay out of sight. A day later they can spring into action and help them clear up the mess."

"May I ask what you have in mind?" asked Deimlich.

"The popular fury will be directed against all Jewish property in Germany. I will be responsible for mobilizing members of the SA, who will see to it that all their synagogues are devastated. They will also destroy Jewish shops, anything that is visibly identified with Jews. The SS will take care of mass arrests. The action will have a dual purpose: to inure Germans to the destruction of the Jews, and to convince every last Jew that he has lost any hope of being protected by the state, that he is fair game and therefore should flee at once. Anywhere. We'll lay no obstacles in his way. We'll even let him take a few of his ill-gotten goods, for if he is destitute no nation will let him in. As it is, he's not exactly welcome in any place I know of. Not even in Palestine where the Arabs and British will greet him with barbed wire."

Himmler turned to Stramm.

"*Herr Doktor*, your chief already knows what we hope to do. We need a concerted campaign on the radio and in the press which will focus on the Jews as the last obstacle to full economic prosperity and racial salvation. He has deputized you to sensitize our people and prepare them for the day of destruction. As for *Herr* Streicher, I know I can count on him."

Finally he addressed Rolf.

"You, Captain Baumgarten, are here for information only. You are to do nothing and confide in no one. If one of your superiors inquires and sticks his nose into our business, let me know at once and I will handle it. If all is quiet on your front, so much the better. When the day comes you will report to General Keitel and tell him of the Führer's objectives. Is that clear?"

Himmler did not wait for Rolf's assent. He rose, everyone following suit.

"Heil Hitler!" The outstretched arm, the meeting was over. Armed SS men guided the visitors to a back door, whence they left at five-minute intervals. They said nothing to each other lest they be overheard. The conspiracy was under way and began with silence.

Rolf stepped into the crisp morning air. A cool wind was blowing and he bent his slender frame to face it. He was a good-looking man with classic, almost too regular features. As he looked at the passers-by he wondered who amongst them would become a victim of Operation *Schluss*. The thought left him troubled. He had never hated Jews; his mother had always forbidden anti-Semitic expressions. "That sounds better in a plebeian mouth," she would say. Judged by that standard, her new husband was a thorough plebeian. Words like *Scheissjude* rolled from Bumm's lips like pearls of wisdom. Rolf's dislike for Bumm went up a notch every time he uttered samples from his storehouse of epithets.

And now, Rolf mused, he himself was part of a plan to drive the Jews from Germany.

He went to his rented room and wrote a brief note telling

Helga that she and her people should leave the country and that their relationship had to end. He addressed it *poste restante* and signed it "R" as he had done in earlier communications. But when he took the letter to the mailbox it weighed like a stone in his pocket. The sun was bright with the same glorious warmth it had dispensed six months before when he and Helga had met. For a moment he stood irresolute. Then he took the note and tore it to pieces.

4

At Cafe Bauer, Manfred Raben sipped his coffee and glanced at the Swiss paper. The cafe still kept a small collection of foreign journals on hand for its second-floor customers who did not mind spending a little extra money on their beverage or ice cream. They were mostly Jews these days who came to scan the European press for any sign of hope, some news that might reveal chinks in the Nazi armor. Raben was to meet his daughter here after school.

The *Neue Zürcher Zeitung* had a story about Nazi subversion in Czechoslovakia and predicted a major crisis over alleged crimes against Germans in the Sudetenland. Manfred was relieved that for once the Jews were not blamed. He became so absorbed that he was startled to find his daughter standing next to him. She looked fresh and fetching in a light-blue jersey which blended with her blond bobbed hair and blue eyes. Who would know her ancestry if the racial sleuths hadn't ferreted us out? he thought.

He ordered a *Sachertorte* for her, which was her favorite delicacy since she was a child. She ate it slowly, as if to delay the crucial question.

"Vatchen," she said finally, "I'm worried. Tell me honestly, do you think we have a future here? Dr. Klappermann, our principal, is leaving for America. What do you think will happen to us?"

Her father shifted uneasily. The question was one he had tried to avoid. On a few occasions he started to discuss it with associates, but found them vague and noncommittal. He also discovered that he had no real friends with whom he could share anything except business propositions. In his social life he had avoided Jews and had cultivated men for their business prestige. Lately they had restricted their relationship to non-personal contacts. Even his lawyer, who had been his comrade in the last war, had become distant.

"Vatchen?" His daughter's question rose once more from the pool of reverie.

"Yes, Hilli, I'll try to answer your question. It's not easy. Besides, there is no guarantee for prophecies."

He ordered another coffee and continued when the waiter had left.

"You see, if I were just anybody, if I were not Manfred Raben, industrialist, things would be simpler. And worse, of course. My business would have been taken over and we might be forced to make a decision no one should have to make: to leave this country where our family has lived for over four hundred years. We would be strangers everywhere else."

"And aren't we here? You among the Aryans, and I among the Jews."

"You're very perceptive, Hilli. Strange as it may appear, your mother is the only one who seems to have an anchor point. She prefers to be a Jew. She's now going to some Jewish cultural events and even thinks of studying Hebrew. If it were left to her, she might even be ready to emigrate."

He looked around to be sure they were not overheard.

"We would not be poor, we have money in England, though it would be a radically different existence. Besides, that's not the issue. Is there a future for us *here*? Five years ago, when the Nazis came to power, I would have answered with a clear yes. Now I'm not sure. Then I thought they'd last a year, two years at most. Obviously I was wrong."

He paused and looked at the traffic below and at the people pursuing their business.

"The German people have disappointed me, their churches disgust me. Except for a few bishops like Faulhaber and von Galen, they are silent as the grave."

Manfred Raben looked at his watch, an old-fashioned pocket piece that opened quietly and closed with a definite click.

"I must be on my way. You're unhappy that I have not answered you precisely. To be frank, I too am not happy with my lack of clarity. That's why I have put off a decision. I think I'll give them another half year. If things get worse we must face the music. We'll leave, hopefully for a short time only. A half year, Hilli. Meanwhile, apply yourself and get your *Abitur*."

He did not inquire how her studies were going.

Spring was in full bloom when Helga learned that she had failed. On the way home, with the dismal result in her pocket, she made a detour to the post office on Pestalozzistrasse. Anything to delay confronting her parents with the dreadful news. There was a note from Rolf: *Tomorrow night. Usual time and place.*

She arrived home in a defiant mood.

"Well, how did it go?" her father greeted her. "Is it good or bad news?"

Helga's defiance drowned in a flood of sudden tears.

"I'm sorry," she sobbed. "I tried but I couldn't. It was Hebrew that sank me."

Magda began to cry, but Manfred remained strangely calm. "I'm not really surprised," he said, "but I am disappointed, very disappointed."

He rose and paced the floor. "Now that you have failed, and failed us, I might add, I think we are entitled to the truth."

Helga dried her face. A new anxiety swept over her.

"You are not stupid, Helga. You're just as intelligent as most other girls in your class, I'm sure of that. You were a good student at the Lyceum. Your whole demeanor has changed in the last months. Is some outside influence responsible?"

"I don't know what you mean," Helga said.

"Are you seeing someone we don't know about?"

She hesitated, unable to decide whether to tell the truth.

"I take it there is a romantic involvement. Who is he and how serious is it?"

"You are right, Vatchen," Helga said, regaining her composure. "There is a man. I met him at Rot-Weiss, at the tennis matches early in the spring. Someone introduced us. He's a half Jew, I think, and I've seen him off and on. Am I in love? I don't think so. I admit it didn't improve my studies, but that's not the reason I failed. I'm discouraged about our future in Germany."

"What's the young man's name?" her mother asked. "Do we know the family?"

"Rudolf Mannheim," Helga said quickly. "As for his family, I don't know much. His father died in Riga, I think. He's waiting for his visa to the United States."

"All right," said her father. His words had an edge of finality."I may send you to England for a few months, to let you have a taste of what it's like to live in a foreign country. And while you're beautifying their scene, things may turn around here. The Army is not happy with the Führer's saber rattling. They don't want to go to war if they don't think they can win, and especially not over the Sudetenland for which they don't want to sacrifice the country. If Hitler goes on this way, the Army may turn against him, and that would be the end of the Thousand-Year Reich. Yes, England might be a good cooling-off place for you. I'll phone Mother's cousin in London and also a business affiliate. You could leave next week."

* * *

Clouds hung heavy in the sky the next day when Helga had her date with Rolf. She had hoped for a balmy evening, perhaps a walk in Grunewald. But by the time she met him in the shadow of the underpass, near the clock at the Zoo station, it had begun to drizzle. They took the train to Friedrichstrasse and sat in a small cafe off the beaten track.

"And now I'll be shipped off to England," Helga poured out her tale. "I may never see you again. What are we to do, Rolfi?"

He looked at her. She was vulnerable and forlorn. A surge of compassion swept over him.

"Perhaps times will change. I want you here, near me, but you must do what your father says. Go and take your parents with you."

"Father wants to wait. Oh, Rolf, I'm so lonely when I'm not with you. I want you. . ."

He looked at her intently, took her hand and kissed it. The voices of pool players punctuated the stillness.

They left the cafe and walked north, the long stride of the soldier and the hurried beat of a woman's shoes.

"I know a place where we can rent a room for an hour or two."

Helga did not ask how he knew. It did not matter.

A row of dingy houses in a badly lit street hovered by the canal. Rolf was not sure of the address. When he took his chance and rang a bell, the concierge looked at them and motioned: "Next door."

They rang several times before a slovenly woman answered.

"For how long?" she asked as if she were selling a subscription to a journal. "The cost is two marks an hour. I can show you the room."

Helga wanted to run away from the squalor and stale odor of the house, but Rolf was already halfway up the stairs. She stumbled after him.

The room was neat: a bed, two chairs, a chest with a wash basin and pitcher. Through the grimy window the canal could be dimly seen, its ripples mingling with the streaks on the pane. Raucous laughter came from a nearby room. Rolf paid four marks. The door closed roughly and he turned the key.

"Oh, darling, is this the way it will be with us?" Helga threw herself at Rolf. "Are we already in the charnel house?"

He hugged her tightly. "All will be forgotten once we have each other."

He kissed her eyes, her cheeks, her neck. He fumbled with her jersey.

"I'm afraid," Helga wept. "Be careful, we have enough trouble."

He reassured her and was gentle. She cried, then her tenseness gave way to the glory of love for which she had yearned. She hungered for him as a starved person hungers for bread. The room was forgotten; they lived in another world.

They kissed a brief farewell at the station. She was not to write him from England. He would be in touch with her at her cousin's home, using a woman's signature without a return address. Should she ever come back to Berlin, the old postal drop would still be usable. But no message was to be sent, only the word *Canal*.

Three days later Helga was on her way to England.

In midsummer it became obvious that Hitler was prepared to go to war over Czechoslovakia. At Gestapo headquarters, where Rolf now had an office, officials debated the tactics of a two-front war, although it was the Army's business, not theirs. How long would it take to smash the Czechs? Could the Western line be held against the French Army until Prague was secured? What would happen if the Russians also moved on Germany? Rolf duly reported back what he heard, and the Army people bitterly resented the interference which they feared was a potential power grab by the SS.

Rolf had met Reinhard Heydrich, Himmler's deputy and head of the Gestapo as well as the Security Division, commonly known as S.D. Heydrich had been delegated to prepare detailed plans for a nationwide pogrom against the Jews and to execute it at the proper time. He was a career *Wunderkind*: at thirty-four he had risen to the top of the heap. Work had thrown him and Rolf together and they disliked each other instantly. Rolf found the S.D. chief crude and cruel under an elegant façade; in turn, Heydrich thought of him as effete, a somewhat degenerate descendant of a defunct German nobility. "I could kill a Jew with my bare hands if I had the chance," Heydrich once boasted, his eyes glistening as he visualized this exciting possibility.

It was commonly known that Heydrich had been dismissed from the Navy because he refused to marry a woman whom he had seduced. A heavy drinker, he frequented the notorious Salon Kitty where seduction was not necessary.

It was also a matter of record that the blond, pale-eyed Heydrich had a Jewish grandmother called Sarah who shed her faith at the baptismal font but could not thereby cleanse her Jewish taint. This connection was deemed important enough for Himmler to bring to Hitler's attention. By this time Heydrich's anti-Semitic passion was well known, and Hitler shrewdly reasoned that not clearing his name officially would force Heydrich to remain an uncompromising persecutor of Jews, to be entrusted with special tasks.

Rolf found himself exposed to men who had power and loved it for its own sake. It was different when he reported for the weekly briefing session at the Army offices. The new man there was General Franz Halder, who had taken the place of Ludwig Beck, the general who had resigned his position because he found Hitler's policies both adventurous and repugnant.

Halder appealed to Rolf from the beginning. While the briefings were usually held by a Colonel Kinz, Halder appeared from time to time and added observations which struck Rolf as coming from a world diametrically opposed to that of Heydrich. The S.D. chief was brash, Halder was reticent; the former used gutter language, the latter spoke with a touch of literary elegance. Rolf heard no overblown phrases from Halder. "Blood and soil," "German destiny," "Jewish conspiracy" – stock expressions in Heydrich's vocabulary – were absent from the general's speech. There were in fact moments when Halder seemed to be in direct conflict with the Führer's bellicose Czech policy. Hitler had set October 1 as the date by which the Czechs had to accept his terms, else he would use force; Halder implied that he believed this strategy to be potentially disastrous. In his view, Germany was not ready to take on the nations that would certainly support the Czechs.

In early September 1938 Rolf was summoned to the general's inner office. Halder's uniform collar was unbuttoned, he was smoking and offered Rolf a glass of brandy and a cigar. Clearly it was to be an informal meeting between the chief and a lowly liaison officer.

Halder had known and greatly admired Rolf's grandfather and called him the ideal German soldier. "We need more like him," he said. He became personal. Was Rolf happy in his dual role which gave him no clearly defined task except to be on hand for special reporting?

Rolf was wary; he did not know where the general was leading him.

"*Herr General*, I'm an officer and serve where assigned. I've never considered my personal feelings to be of significance. In this respect anyway," he added, thinking of Helga.

"Of course," Halder agreed. "That's to be expected. But I wasn't really inquiring about your personal happiness. Let me put it differently. I hear you are now reporting to this chap Heydrich. Do you find him agreeable and compatible? If you are not fully at ease over there, I'll be glad to reassign you. In that case your personal record will show only that you're honest and reliable. Well?"

Rolf decided to take the chance.

"Sir, you are my superior and you order me to speak my mind. May I assume that what I say will be heard only by you, *Herr General*?"

Halder nodded assent and poured another brandy.

"You see, sir, I'm in a difficult position. I'm a junior officer, yet from time to time I become privy to highly sensitive information. No one has really specified what I am to report."

He drank the brandy. The critical part of the answer seemed to require some additional support.

"However, lately I've participated in sessions over there when everyone was sworn to secrecy. At one rather extraordinary session I was specifically singled out and informed that I would be told when to report, and then only to General Keitel. I felt highly uncomfortable with everything that was planned."

Halder stood up and faced Rolf.

"Good. You've gained an admirer in me, Baumgarten. I would feel just like you if the roles were reversed. So I will personally give you instructions on what to report to the Gestapo and in turn you'll tell me everything I need to know. On a one-to-one basis. I'll instruct my staff to give you direct access to me when you have something to convey. Don't hesitate to relate little things. They sometimes make the difference."

Rolf realized that the conversation had taken on a conspiratorial tone, and he had no doubt where his loyalty lay. He was an Army man; the general was as attractive as Heydrich was detestable.

Only much later did Rolf find out that at the time of their conversation Halder was involved in a plot to overthrow Hitler. Had the September crisis not resulted in Chamberlain's surrender at Munich, had the British and French stood firm in their support of the Czechs, the generals, under the leadership of Halder and Beck, would have revolted. As it was, the Western powers did not have the courage to call Hitler's bluff, and the rebellion proceeded no further. But neither was it discovered.

* * *

At Alexanderplatz the mood changed from tenseness to exaltation. The surrender at Munich proved to Himmler and Heydrich beyond a doubt that not only was the Führer guided by supernatural powers toward external victories, but also that there would be no further need to worry about foreign reaction to any internal policy. The West was degenerate and cowardly, and the Jews were the last people they would wish to protect. The West was at heart anti-Semitic like the Germans, said Himmler, except that its leaders did not have Germany's vision and will to solve the problem once and for all. The time was now ripe to work out the details of Operation *Schluss*. Heydrich was put in charge; the word to start was to be given by Göring; the pretext would be determined by Goebbels. The time for action was set for the second week in November.

Rolf inquired from Heydrich when the Army was to be informed.

"Tell Halder what we're up to, but tell him not to squeal. He's to keep his men out of the way. It's none of their goddamn business, the SA will handle everything. Besides, by the time you get to your boss, Goebbels may already have given him the low-down."

Rolf commented no further. He had long before made up his mind not to tangle needlessly with the S.D. man. He could not match Heydrich's ruthlessness.

"And as for you, dear captain," added the S.D. leader with ill-concealed irony, "I suggest you leave town for a few days when the *Aktion* takes place. You wouldn't want your refined taste to be offended. It will be a great time to give your girl friend a tumble, and if she's not around I could loan you one."

Rolf was not amused. The detestable Heydrich had come uncomfortably close.

7

The British awakened Helga's latent interest in politics. Her mother's cousin was a widow who had left Germany in 1935 after her husband had been arrested and a few weeks later his body had been returned to her in a plain box. A note was attached to it:

> *Coffin contains remains of Markus Kostler, Jew, who died in Sachsenhausen Concentration Camp on May 31, 1935. Coffin has been officially sealed and may not be opened.*
>
> *Heil Hitler!*
> *The Commandant*

The signature was illegible and it did not matter. Jettie Kostler had little in earthly goods, and the insurance company refused to honor her husband's contract. The cause of death had to be established beyond a reasonable doubt, they claimed, and since suicide which would vitiate the policy could not be ruled out, payment could not be made. Sorry, this was the law.

The widow did not stay on to fight a hopeless case and grasped the opportunity of a job offer in London by a firm with which her husband had done business. She had no marketable skills; housewife had been her full-time occupation. She became a stockroom clerk, lived in a modest flat in Hampstead and continued her life-long practice of Sabbath visits to the synagogue. She had no children and, considering her circumstances and the times, was glad of it. Still, she was lonely. Though her command of English was adequate, she had difficulty making friends. At fifty, alone in the huge city, she found herself to be an anonymous occupant of an indifferent living space, providing her with existence more than with life. Therefore, she was delighted when her cousin's husband wired her and suggested the temporary visitor from Berlin.

Jettie Kostler received Helga with open arms and soon enveloped her with the kind of affection her young guest had never experienced. Helga felt at home immediately and supplemented Jettie's meager means with the funds her father had managed to export. The manager of INCOR, a business affiliate of German Machineries, introduced her to a circle of young people at London University. She had forgotten what it felt like to mix freely with both Jews and Gentiles and enjoyed the ease of the gatherings. Uniforms were absent from the streets, the Bobbies carried no arms and people liberally criticized the Prime Minister. It was a new world and very attractive.

But when September came, the mood of the country changed. Suspense was followed by apprehension and dissolved into anger. She began to read the dailies, something she had not done at home. Names like Henderson and Chamberlain became familiar; Godesberg was suddenly an important town; Masaryk, Beneš, Daladier and Mussolini came to play in a drama that was hurrying to an unknown climax. When it ended, Czechoslovakia lay dying at the feet of the anti-hero, and Helga knew that the hectic month had taught her more history than she had ever learned at school. She also discovered that she identified with the British, and when Jettie suggested that she go with her to synagogue to pray for the country, she agreed.

Though she understood little, she was attracted to the stately proceedings, much to her own surprise. The prayer book had a translation but she had no idea what its instructions conveyed. Still, she was impressed with the seriousness of the ritual; the formal dress of the men with their top hats; the cantor's somber intonations; the cadences of Hebrew that had passed her by in school. Were these her people after all? She was astonished at the very question.

She reminded herself that she was an atheist and that being a Jew was something of dubious value. What was it then that appealed to her and made her go every week from then on without her aunt asking her?

* * *

A typewritten letter on undistinguished lined note paper came addressed to "Helga Kostler":

> *Fall has been beautiful but lonely. We still stroll along the canal and wonder how you are. Walked by the old synagogue the other day but had bad feelings about it and don't think I'll ever be able to go in again. I am trying to tell Dad to quit his little store, there's no future in it. He's not quite ready yet, though I think he soon will be, whether he likes it or not. Hope you have fun and still remember your school chum. Wish I were with you.*
>
> *Leni*

She pondered the note. There was no doubt that Rolf had written it; a woman's signature had been agreed upon. The reference to her father was also clear; Rolf told her that her parents had little time left. But the synagogue hint left her puzzled. Why would one no longer be able or willing to go in?

When she wrote her family she tried to convey something of the mood in London. She missed them, she wrote, though Aunt Jettie was a dear. Why would they not come, at least on a visit? She gave filial reasons for her urgings and hoped they would read between the lines. She also told them she was taking a course in dental hygiene and liked it a great deal. Do come, she concluded, you really must see me in my new environs. She did not write about her visits to the synagogue; Father would not understand.

Manfred received his daughter's letter with mixed feelings. He was relieved to find her happy and adjusted, but at the same time he did not want her to plan on staying. As he saw it, Hitler's unexpected success in Munich had reduced his bellicosity and had spread a mood of triumphalism across the land. Perhaps the Jews would now get a reprieve. With a man of notably mercurial temperament, everything was possible.

Yet the Aryanization of Jewish businesses had proceeded apace. The Rabens' last Gentile maid had left and Magda now had to run their home with the help of a young Jewish woman from a Bavarian village who had come to Berlin to await her visa to the Dominican Republic, one of the few countries prepared to rescue her. She did not even know exactly where it was. Manfred's two closest associates, both half Jews, had emigrated, leaving behind most of their possessions. One had gone to South Africa, the other to Belgium.

Czechoslovakia was breaking up, and everyone was shifting into war production. Manfred's factories were now running on a 24-hour schedule, profits were greater than ever. He felt he was leading a charmed life.

His son came on one of his infrequent visits. With some embarrassment he told his parents that he had made application for a change of name. As long as he was known as Raben, everyone would dub him a Jew, he explained, which was grossly unfair, wasn't it? He hoped his parents wouldn't mind. He would continue to consider them his parents and if the need arose he might be in a position to protect them.

Manfred was alarmed and, to his own surprise, annoyed.

"And how would you do that? You haven't joined the SA, have you?"

"No, Father, I haven't. They're thugs, scum of the earth, and they're on their way out. The SS are keeping them under control."

"You seem to be well informed," said Magda.

"Well, yes," he replied with some hesitation. "As a matter of fact, I have spent some time with Heydrich's Intelligence operation. Fascinating. I'll probably join them full-time after I finish exams."

The room was silent. Double windows dampened the sound of automobiles coming to a screeching halt at the nearby semaphore.

"You are your own man, Heinrich," Manfred said at last. "I will not judge your action. I'm sorry that our name which has been honored for centuries will die with me. And I hope we'll never have to call on you for help."

"Father, I'm no prophet. But I think you will. You have my address."

8

In Paris a young Polish Jew, Herschel Grynszpan, read a letter from his parents in Hanover:

> *We are now stateless. The Poles have taken away our citizenship papers and the Germans want to take away our residence permit. We may have to leave, but as stateless persons, where could we go?*

A few days later *Le Monde* brought further news. On October 28 the Gestapo had rounded up thousands of Polish Jews and dumped them at Zbaszyu, the Polish border. There, the paper reported, they existed in utter deprivation, suspended between two nations that had one objective: to prohibit these Jews from entering their countries.

Herschel Grynszpan had received no further word about his parents. His agitation grew until he could neither sleep nor think of anything else. Every day he scanned the press for news. What there was read like the reportage of a soccer match, minus the pinch of emotion one might find even on the sports page. No one seemed to care. How could he arouse the world's conscience? What would it take to let people understand that Jews were human beings, not animals shipped in boxcars to the stockyards?

Grynszpan wandered the streets of Paris in despair. When

he passed a gun shop he made a sudden decision and bought a revolver. He took the Metro to the German embassy. When the door was opened he asked to speak to the ambassador. He trembled, he could hardly see.

Von Welczeck asked his Third Secretary to inquire after the visitor's wishes. Moments later, Ernst vom Rath lay mortally wounded. Grynszpan had mistaken him for the ambassador.

The shooting was news around the world, for young Grynszpan told the reasons for his desperate act to the police, and did so with dramatic urgency. The press was sympathetic.

Heydrich learned of it in Munich, where he had gone with all major party chiefs to celebrate the anniversary of Hitler's *Putsch*. He was delighted; a splendid pretext for the Jewish razzia was at hand. Hitler agreed at once to fix the date of the pogrom for the night of November 9/10. Germans would "rise spontaneously" to avenge a noble servant of the Reich. Keep the objective in mind, he told his staff; unsettle the Jews so they leave the country in a hurry. Germany must be *judenrein* in six months.

* * *

At supper time Rolf answered his telephone.

"You're to report in half an hour, Captain. Urgent. At Alexanderplatz."

"You mean now?"

"In half an hour. Heil Hitler!"

When he arrived in Heydrich's office the S.D. chief was absent. Müller conducted the briefing for the men who had been summoned. He had thin lips that hardly parted when he spoke, which gave him the nickname "Hissing Snake." An SS recruit from the police force in Bavaria, he admired Heydrich for his lack of moral scruples.

"I have a telegraphic message from the *Obergruppenführer* in Munich," he hissed. He waved the paper. "We are to organize a nationwide *Aktion* before daybreak. All synagogues in Germany are to be burned. Smash and devastate Jew-owned shops and businesses. Arrest as many prominent Jews as you can get your hands on. Smash their apartments and ship them off to the nearest concentration camp. Captain Baumgarten, let General Halder know the plan has the Führer's approval. Dr. Goebbels has given the go-ahead in his name."

"Will the *Aktion* be just for tonight?" someone asked.

"Tonight for what is to be known as a popular spontaneous reaction to the crime engineered by international Jewry. But the arrests can continue for a few days."

Müller read from the telegram:

> *Only measures which do not constitute danger to German life and property are to be undertaken. Synagogues must not be burned to the ground if there is danger that surrounding properties may be jeopardized.*
>
> *Businesses and private dwellings should be devastated, but looting is forbidden.*
>
> *As many Jews as possible, and especially rich Jews, should be arrested, as many as our prisons can accommodate.*

"We are to notify the nearest camp where they'll be shipped," Müller continued. "So get going and notify your sections. Then let's meet again on Friday morning to review the *Aktion*. Shall we say ten o'clock?"

They rose, but Müller detained them.

"I want you to understand that police and Army are to stay out of it. I'll take care of the police, and you, Captain Baumgarten, will bring this urgent matter to the general's attention. Heil Hitler!"

* * *

The Rabens were awakened at four in the morning by loud knocks at the front door.

"Open up, *Scheissjude*, or we'll bash in your door and your head!"

Three men stood outside in civilian clothes, their lapels bearing the insignia of Party membership. A short, fat, bald man with no discernible neck commanded:

"You're the Jew Raben?"

Assent.

"Get dressed. I give you five minutes."

Manfred tried to delay the inevitable.

"Where am I going? On whose authority are you acting?"

"You'll find out soon enough. And one minute of your five is already gone. As for authority, *Scheissjude*, I have it right here, in my German boot." He lifted his foot and kicked Manfred in the groin.

Raben doubled up with pain and fell to the floor.

The fat one kicked him in the head. "*Los!* You've got three minutes."

Magda lurched forward to help her husband. A tall, blondish member of the threesome restrained her and, in so doing, touched her breasts.

"Hey," he exclaimed, "look at this! Prime Jewish tits, free to squeeze, no charge."

"Johann," said the third one, a scrawny figure with a sour face, "remember the instructions. Leave her alone. Next thing, you want to fuck her. Not with a Jew bitch. It's like sleeping with swine."

When Magda fainted, they let her lie crumpled up on the floor and vandalized the house. Except for the hallway, the orgy took place in the dark. Manfred had pulled on his trousers and a jacket. When he tried to tend to his wife, they tore him away and kicked him down the stairs. The last he saw of Magda was a disjointed heap of flesh, a discarded doll, half naked and still.

Outside, the sky was an eerie red. All over town synagogues were burning. SA men surged along Kurfürstendamm, smashing windows and looting, oblivious of the pious rules laid down for the night. The streets were littered with shattered glass.

"Sight-seeing tour," said the bully sitting next to Manfred in the back seat. "Johann, drive to Oranienburgerstrasse. Let's see what the people have done with that divine whorehouse." He was referring to the city's largest Jewish house of worship.

Though it was five o'clock in the morning, the crowds were so thick that the car could not get through. Word of the pogrom had spread like wildfire and had dragged thousands of voyeurs out of their beds. They watched the flames leaping from the vaulted windows of the great synagogue.

The threesome delivered their cargo to Alexanderplatz. Manfred Raben was hustled into the cellar with a hundred other victims. He thought he glimpsed Heinrich among the guards, but he could not be sure.

SA Mann Johann Stempfer had no trouble remembering the Raben address. At 6:00 a.m., finished with his assignment, he returned to Leibnizstrasse, raped Magda and beat her into unconsciousness. It was light now and he took his time searching the house for valuables. There were enough watches and rings to reward his manly diligence.

* * *

Rolf Baumgarten was among the spectators. He had remembered to stay out of sight in his official uniform and had dressed in civilian clothes. The crowd had streamed toward the great synagogue on Oranienburgerstrasse, which was already in flames when he reached it. Men and women stood roaring their approval. An elderly Jew was dragged from the burning building. In the eerie light Rolf saw that the man's clothes were singed by the flames and his white beard blackened with soot. Two brownshirts stood him against the wall and cut off his beard, to the merriment of the mob.

"Cut off his pecker too!" someone yelled.

Instead, the SA men took the Jew and hanged him by his arms from a lamp post in front of the synagogue. A young boy ran up to him and spit in his face.

Some people turned and walked away silently. The merriment had vanished. Rolf left with them, sick at heart.

* * *

On Friday morning Heydrich presided at the briefing session.

"A great success in every respect," he proclaimed. "We did our work well. Our organization was first-rate. The mop-up is now in the Field Marshal's hands. I hear he has more surprises for the Jews, like paying with their own money for the damage they suffered. Also, I've suggested to Dr. Goebbels that the Jews clean up the mess. After all, they drove the German people beyond the point of endurance."

"What was the damage in the whole Reich? How many dead?" asked Müller.

"I'll read from my report to the Field Marshal:

> *The full extent of the devastation of Jewish stores and homes cannot yet be precisely assessed in figures. So far we know that 815 shops have been destroyed, 119 synagogues burned and another 76 completely destroyed. 20,000 Jews were arrested. 36 were killed, another 36 seriously injured. All of the killed and injured were Jews.*

"I hear that there were some rapes," Heydrich continued. "Major Buch will deal with that if they were party members. Finally, I want to commend police and Army for staying out of the way. This cooperation augurs well for the difficult but glorious days ahead."

PART II

The Letter

FALL 1938

When the events of Crystal Night became known in England, a wave of indignation swept the nation. The true nature of Nazism now stood exposed, the papers said. And if Hitler was shown to be irrational in domestic affairs, would international relations be far behind? Rearm, counseled Winston Churchill, the Tories' dissident bulldog orator. War became a word which people once again heard and spoke as part of their daily conversation.

Helga followed the events with deep anxiety. Rolf's letter became all too clear now. She was glad to be far away from the raging mobs, yet felt guilty for enjoying the carefree life of a student in London. Were her parents affected by the Nazi orgy? she wondered.

On November 11 she telephoned them. There was no answer. She called German Machineries and learned only that her father had not come to the office. She tried again during the following days but obtained no further information. No, Mr. Raben had not returned to work. No, we don't know the reason. Sorry, said the telephone operator, we cannot put the call through. We are terribly sorry, we can't give any reasons. . . .

Helga feared the worst. She did not know Heinrich's address, and contacting Rolf was out of the question.

A week later a letter came from her mother:

Father is away on business. Hopefully he will come back soon. There have been some changes. We may have to rethink our plans and soon have a reunion if things go the way I hope. But you can never tell with Father. As soon as he comes home we'll decide how to handle the situation. Winter is around the corner. People are talking of Christmas, but I think we'll forgo the tree this year. Haven't seen Heinrich lately, he's probably busy in his new job. Stay safe and healthy.

Love, Your Mother

The message was clear. Father was in prison. Did her mother want her to come home? "Stay safe" could mean she ought to remain where she was – this was Jettie's interpretation. Helga read it as a general good wish.

She responded in a style of concealment that would pass by the censor should the letter be opened.

There was no answer. Instead, a telegram came from her brother:

Drastic changes at home. Regret essential you come home. Advise travel plans. Will meet you at station.

Heinrich's sudden appearance on the family scene was an ominous sign. Father was in trouble, or worse. Mother needed help. Helga took the first boat to Hamburg and the *D-Zug* to Berlin.

She looked for her brother and did not find him in the mass of people thronging the station. When he suddenly stood before her, she did not recognize him at first. He wore an SS uniform, his hair and new mustache shaped like the Führer's.

"I'll explain everything," Heinrich said, "but not here, and not at home either. There's a cafe around the corner where we can talk."

They passed the front room where two pool players stood enveloped in clouds of cigar smoke and found a dimly lit booth in the back.

"Steel yourself, Helga. I wouldn't have asked you to come, but I had no choice. For obvious reasons I cannot be seen involved with our family. I think you get the point, even if you don't approve. What I'm about to tell you I have secondhand."

"Have you seen our parents?"

He did not answer.

"Why don't you say something? Tell me already!" Helga burst into tears.

"Father was arrested in the morning hours of November 10."

Heinrich said he had glimpsed him at Gestapo headquarters but could neither reach him nor do anything for him. The house was vandalized. Mother had moved out for a few days, he did not know where.

Father had been taken to Sachsenhausen. He, Heinrich, did not dare to intervene, but after two weeks the old man was released. He heard he had changed drastically. Aged decades. And when Father went to the office he found an SA man sitting in his director's chair. "German Machineries is now truly German," the man said and told him that a new management was taking over. The factories were being sold to Göring Kraftwerke at a sales price fixed by the buyer. It was a pittance from which were deducted the punitive damages all Jews had to pay for the Crystal Night destruction. Father agreed, on the condition that what was left be transferred to England. All in all he received less than ten percent.

"Mother, I am told, was even more changed than Father. She took to bed and was totally withdrawn and cried incessantly. No one could do anything for her. Yesterday morning I was called to the house which was still in its devastated condition. The concierge had my address. When

I opened the front door, the apartment reeked of gas."

"No!" Helga screamed, oblivious of her surroundings. "They're dead!"

"They were lying on the kitchen floor, their hands clasped."

Helga was frozen, her soul cold with anger. At last she asked Heinrich in a voice she could hardly recognize: "And what did you do all that time?"

"I told you, I couldn't see them."

"Why? Because they were no longer your parents?"

She looked at her brother in his new black uniform with the shiny buttons, the death's head insignia and the swastika armband. She despised him for going over to the enemy.

She would avenge her parents, she swore to herself. The SS man opposite her was a detestable stranger.

"The funeral is tomorrow at noon," said the stranger. "At the old cemetery on Schönhauser Allee. It's Jewish. We have no choice. No one else will take them."

"I prefer it that way," Helga said in a voice so distant it seemed to belong to someone else, "and I think that they too would want it. After all, they died because they were Jews."

She rose abruptly, faced him and spit on the ground, splattering his boots. Then she turned and walked away.

* * *

On entering the cemetery gates Helga found only a few dozen people in attendance. She passed by the tombstones of famous Jews. When she reached the mourners assembled for the graveside service, she noted the absence of all of her father's business associates. A maid and a gardener who had been in the Rabens' employ were present, and a dozen workers from the factory. A few cousins from her mother's side. Father's family was small and either were dead or had left the country. Grandma in Thuringia had died the year before. Her brother standing across the street made her angry again.

She was introduced to the rabbi, a tall, slightly stooped, elderly man whose name she did not grasp. "We are all one in our suffering," he said, "God has made us one, and we are being forcibly reminded that we are. In former days the way one died determined whether one could be buried in the cemetery proper or had to be laid to rest near the fence. Not today. Many have chosen death as a last assertion of their dignity. In Jewish history this happened before. Eight hundred years ago, in the Rhineland, our forebears did the same when the Crusaders roamed the country looking for victims whom they could kill at smaller risk than the Saracens. Manfred Raben," the rabbi said, "was a great industrialist and pioneer. An asset to the nation and now a great loss." He would intone the ancient Psalms whose vision included believers and non-believers. "After all," he concluded wistfully, "we all face the challenge of faith and doubt. May they rest in peace."

The cantor sang. To Helga the simple chant was reassuring. Dearest parents, she thought, you have brought me up as a German. But they have made me a Jew. And I will be one.

* * *

Helga spent the week cleaning out her parents' apartment and in the late afternoon sat by the window in a dingy cafe at Alexanderplatz which was near the Gestapo headquarters. She hoped she might spot Rolf in his Army uniform among the sea of brown and black.

She wrote him a letter as agreed, "Canal."

On the following Tuesday she thought she saw him. She hurried after him but realized it was not Rolf after all. The next night she went to the Zoo station and waited. They had always met here on Wednesdays.

The November wind made her shiver, despite her winter coat and cap, the same outfit she had worn ten months before when she had first met Rolf. Only then she was carefree, a school girl; now sadness and bitterness had changed her features and demeanor.

Helga looked up and down the street for the slender Army officer, but he was nowhere to be seen. Suddenly a man in civvies stood by her side, a gray fedora pressed low on his brow. When she looked at him in the dim light, she could hardly keep herself from embracing him. Rolf had come after all.

They walked separately to the S-Bahn, sat apart and left the train at the Friedrichstrasse station as if they had had a previous understanding. They went to the same flop house on the canal. This time they rented the room for the night.

Their passion left no room for words. Helga clung to Rolf as a drowning person clings to a raft. He represented hope in a hopeless world, decency in an immoral town. She loved him and he matched her desperate ardor.

Helga poured out her heart. She told him of her parents' suicide, of her need to anchor herself. He told her of the events of Crystal Night.

"That night I knew. I abhorred everything about Nazism, its inhumanity, its senseless anti-Semitism."

He lay there, reminiscing about his upbringing, the respect for law and order that had been so much a part of it, and the lawlessness that had now infected the nation.

"You know I'm no Nazi. I'm an Army man and there are others like me who think as I do."

"But suppose they find out you made love to a Jewish girl?" she asked.

"I've thought about it, of course, but you're worth a chance."

She hugged him gratefully.

"I was brought up to respect all people," he said. "To me Jews are no different from anyone else. I would have fallen in love with you anyway, and since the Nazis say you're out of bounds, I suppose loving you is part of my protest. What I mean is, you're Helga, and to hell with anyone who doesn't like it."

They made love again, their ardor heightened by their sense of defiance.

They talked about the future, about the parting that was imminent.

"I wish there was some way I could stay. Oh God, how I wish it! Rolfi, I'd take any chance."

They lay in silence, each weighing the possible against the improbable.

"There is a way," Rolf said at last, "but it's risky, very risky."

"Tell me what I must do."

"You'd have to leave Berlin," he speculated, "and move to another city. Probably a large one where no one would know you. I have friends with certain contacts who could supply you with a new identity, new name, new papers. They would make you into an Aryan, which you always wanted to be. After all, you're blond, you fit the standard model. I'll try and get assigned to where you live. Of course, it'll take a bit of doing, but I think it could be arranged."

* * *

Helga wrote Jettie the sad news about her parents and added that she did not know when she would return to England.

Three weeks later she had her passport validated at the Charlottenburg police *Revier*, pretending it was for emigration purposes.

"Good-bye, Miss Raben," they said, "may the future

bring you much happiness." They expressed their sympathy over her parents' death. The sergeant, an old Social Democrat, pressed her hand as he saw her out.

"Whatever others may say, I greatly respected your father. He was quite a man. I see you're going to England. Well, I just hope we won't have a war with them. God bless you."

Anyone asking for Helga Raben would now learn that she had emigrated to Britain. At her post office box she found her new papers. Hilde Schmitt, age twenty-two, born in Königsberg, East Prussia. Orphaned. Occupation: English translator. Schooling: mostly in England.

In her purse was a ticket for Cologne.

Jews were disappearing from Germany. Soon there were only memories and a few questions. "Yes, we knew Mr. Cohn. A nice man. Too bad he was taken away. No, we don't know where he is. Perhaps he went to America or even Palestine." Poor Mr. Cohn, Mr. Levy, Mr. Goldberg. Yes, it was unfortunate. But it's the law now, there's nothing we can do. . . .

She had found a vacant room on Roonstrasse, opposite the burnt-out shell of the synagogue. Looking at it, Helga was forever reminded of November 10.

She thought back on her childhood: servants, vacations, music lessons, tennis at a club which had no other Jewish members. A fair student, good looking if one went by the interest boys showed in her. Strange, she thought, sitting in her rented room in Cologne, how the Nazis have turned a spoilt child into a determined woman.

As the months went by, she assumed her new identity with greater ease. She had obtained a position as general secretary and translator, and encouraged people to call her Hilli, rather than Fräulein Schmitt. Hilli was easy to answer to, especially when Rolf came calling on an occasional Sunday.

Her landlady was broadminded. "Such a handsome man,"

she commented approvingly. With his erect bearing, springy step and impeccable manners, he fit the prototype of the career officer; and when he came, Helga dressed up in her best clothes. Together they made an attractive pair: the blond, typically Aryan woman and the aristocratic soldier. They went to restaurants and the movies, and they made love.

But between his visits she was lonely. She spent most of her time in her room furnished with a bed, an overstuffed chair which had springs that protested every time she sat down, and an armoire with a cracked mirror. There was a small potbellied stove on which she cooked her simple meals. After a while the landlady gave her permission to use the kitchen, but Helga declined. Neither in the rooming house nor at work did she want any relationship that might cause someone to ask her questions about her background. She read a great deal, went to the movies and occasionally to the symphony, and waited for Rolf.

It was summer now, and when he came from Berlin they would go by train to Bad Godesberg and have lunch on Petersberg, or travel by boat up the Rhine and revel in the beauty of the hills. Yet something was missing. The ardor of their embrace seemed to have lost the power to heal her loneliness. She wondered whether the future would compensate her for her half existence.

A month later, in mid-August 1939, Rolf informed her that he could no longer visit Cologne. He hinted of certain developments but did not elaborate. She would have to move back to the capital if they were to continue seeing each other. He said it in a manner that appeared almost offhand and shocked her deeply. When she pursued it, he denied all other meaning and urged her to come back to Berlin.

"You're Hilde Schmitt now. Unfortunately there are hardly any Jews left to recognize."

"But there are others," she said. "Employees of Dad's,

maids and gardeners, former schoolmates." She looked at Rolf. "Do you really want me there, Rolf? Tell me the truth."

"Of course I do. I want you, I need you."

Helga assented yet chided herself for her lack of enthusiasm. After all, she would be near her lover. Her firm cooperated and transferred her to the main office in the capital.

Two weeks later she arrived in Berlin, her hair dyed black and wearing a floppy hat that covered much of her face. She took a room in a workers' quarter, in Moabit, where she was least likely to be known. It was a long way from the west end to these streets which Heinrich Zille had drawn and the people Käthe Kollwitz had immortalized.

Czechoslovakia had ceased to exist. The Nazis made a pact with Stalin and sealed the fate of Poland. As the summer of 1939 neared its end, Hitler's armies were poised to strike. On September 1 his divisions crossed the Polish borders and conquered the country. France and Britain declared war but sat quietly at the Maginot Line. Germany was riding high. The mood in the country was upbeat.

Not in Poland. There the last restraints fell away from Himmler's henchmen. It was open season on Jews. German men who were husbands and fathers at home discovered how pleasant it was to maim, torture and kill. Above all, kill, by any means. They knew they were doing nothing more than exterminating parasites. For most of the killers orders from above came before moral scruples. And spilled blood called for more blood to be spilled.

In Germany men of Army age were disappearing from the streets. Civilian clothes were now seen only on older people and those unfit to serve. The Thousand-Year Reich was in full bloom. Helga joined the *Frauenhilfe*, an auxiliary corps of women dedicated to easing the lot of soldiers and families left behind.

In the spring of 1940 Rolf was assigned to the western

front. Just before he left, Helga missed her period, but the signs of pregnancy turned out to be nothing more than a temporary irregularity. Both she and Rolf determined to be more careful. In a world of unexpected happenings and strange turns, an illegitimate child would become a danger point. Helga would have to show proof of Aryan ancestry and provide birth and marriage records of her putative parents. Neither she nor Rolf felt that the chance was worth taking.

The war in the West broke out again. Denmark and Norway were occupied; in June France fell to the Germans. Hitler came away from Compiègne as the acknowledged warlord and omnipotent god of the German people. Of all the enemies, Britain alone was left and her fate was being sealed by Göring's *Luftwaffe*. Jews were being dealt with more ruthlessly than ever, and rumors circulated that their "resettlement" which was now under way had other sinister purposes.

* * *

Colonel Baumgarten – the double advancement conferred on Rolf by his chief, General Halder – returned by staff automobile from France with ambiguous instructions. He was to maintain his post as the Army's chief liaison officer with the S.D., but at the same time, and without Heydrich's knowledge, was to confer with certain Army officers. "You will like them," the general had said. "Remember our discussion? You averred that in a conflict of loyalties you would do anything to maintain the honor of the Service and of the Nation." He remembered it clearly, Rolf asserted.

"We Germans are doing well," Halder continued, "almost too well. By our quick success we'll be misled into ever-larger ventures. Some of us are worried. Talk with these two men whose names I've given you. They come from the best families, people with whom you'll feel comfortable. I know I can trust you. And not a word to that long-nosed blond miscreation whose major task in life is sniffing out Jews."

"You mean Reinhard Heydrich? I despise him."

"I wouldn't expect anything else from you. Reinhard, ha! More like Reineke Fox, whose great victories are killing helpless chickens. Men like him destroy not only people, they pervert the character of our nation. Go and see the two men, they may give you some hope."

"Would the general be good enough to fill me in on them?"

"Baumgarten, your and their grandfathers knew each other. Same class, same ideas, same ideals. You remember General von Wartenburg of the Clausewitz era? Of course you do. Can't study Napoleon's campaign without learning about the Prussian count. Peter Yorck von Wartenburg is his direct descendant. Splendid young fellow with great promise. And then von Moltke. Young Helmuth is like his famous namesake of seventy years ago, the old Field Marshal. He's the finest we have, bright, gutsy. He's got an estate at Kreisau, in Silesia, where he, Wartenburg and some other chaps get together when the war can spare them. Discussion group. Really quite unique. I've given them your name, they'll call you. If you don't like what you hear at Kreisau, quit. But first listen with both ears."

"It sounds mysterious," said Rolf.

"Well, it is. Heydrich and company want conformity, total mind control. They can't stand generals like Beck. They're afraid of Witzleben and Goerdeler. Too independent in their thoughts. Uncontrolled, very upsetting. That's why I don't want you to mention it at staff meetings, especially not at Alexanderplatz. Go to Kreisau and make your own judgments. Your grandfather would approve. After a couple of get-togethers, let me know what you think."

As his car sped along a newly constructed stretch of the

Autobahn, he tried to recapture his conversation with the chief. It had conspiratorial overtones, though nothing specific was mentioned. "Don't tell Heydrich" was in itself nothing more than a challenge to be prudent and loyal to the Army. Yet it was more; the general's tone conveyed it.

Why did he choose me? he thought. He likes me, that's obvious. Promoted me twice before I'm due. He trusts me, he knows Mother and knew Grandpa. What if he knew I had a Jewish mistress? Would he protect me, and could he?

It was getting dark. The landscape was peaceful. Cattle stood at the roadside. Here and there children waved. Rolf envied them their peace of mind. I too should be happy, he thought. We sit on top of the world. Surpassing victories, our pride restored. Yet I'm not at ease. The country is run by men I can't respect. Life means nothing, honor is a hollow word for them. Power is everything. Supermen! It's easy to be superior when you have a gun and the others don't. What did the chief say? Reineke Fox in the chicken coop. It costs nothing to be a hero that way.

He dozed off. It was ten o'clock at night when they reached Berlin. Still time to see Hilli.

* * *

Two days later he received a call from Moltke. General Halder had told him much about his young liaison officer. Would he consider spending a few days at his estate at Kreisau? Lovely down there this time of year, even a bit of hunting. But mostly conversation amongst friends whom he'd enjoy meeting. Rolf said he'd like that; the general had whetted his appetite.

He was treated with respect. Von Wartenburg was there, and some young officers whom he had never met. All were of the old nobility and the talk was so vague that he wondered why he had come down. Slowly, however, the topics became more pointed, the discussions on the nature of the German spirit more pragmatic. Now that Germany was in control of Western Europe, with only England remaining to be subdued, where did it all lead? Are we to become an eternal occupier like ancient Rome? That would in effect mean an ever-growing extension of terror. The real master of the Reich would be a man like Himmler or Heydrich, whose powers had been vastly enlarged through the new all-embracing secret and not-so-secret police in Germany and the occupied countries, the *Reichssicherheitshauptamt* or R.S.H.A., as it was referred to.

"And where does Hitler fit into all of this?" someone asked.

"The Führer is busy with conquests," Moltke answered. "He sets policies and lets his deputies carry them out."

"The trouble is," said Wartenburg, "that his fantastic successes have convinced him that he's infallible. His appetite for victories is ravenous, and to feed it he will in time sacrifice the flower of our youth. At best, Germany's men will forever be soldiers somewhere in the world. Russia will be next. Not to civilize but to oppress, control, exploit. If it comes to that, it will be a Pyrrhic victory. We'll win battles and lose our soul."

It was the first open critique of Hitler that Rolf had heard in years. Göring, Goebbels and Himmler were the butt of jokes, and everyone detested Heydrich – but Hitler was always exempt. Rolf now learned that these men seriously contemplated a Reich without the Führer, without Nazism and its philosophy.

He found himself strangely exhilarated and realized that he shared the Kreisau approach. It appealed to his innermost sentiments which now rose to the surface of his consciousness.

Past attempts to remove the Führer had failed, he learned. It was urgent to keep the flame of resistance alive. There would be other opportunities; for now, some trustworthy allies were needed. Could Rolf be counted on? they asked. He agreed without hesitation.

He was assigned a specific task. Find a proper contact in the American embassy. Isolationism was rampant in the U.S.; the German Bund was getting stronger; and Nazi admirers like Lindbergh gave Hitler's policies a glow of legitimacy. We must persuade the Americans to avoid supporting Hitler and falling into his trap. "Leave it to me," Rolf said, "I'll find someone on whom I can rely. If I fail, I'll let you know."

* * *

Luck was on his side. At a reception given by the Nuncio, Cardinal Pacelli, he was introduced to the new military attaché of the United States. Major Kenneth Driscoll resembled Rolf somewhat, dark haired and dark complexioned but without mustache. He was an Annapolis graduate who had been in the Warsaw embassy when Hitler invaded Poland and had watched in horror how the conqueror had dealt with the vanquished population. His wife's father was a United States senator whom the America First contingent had labeled an interventionist, internationalist or worse. Driscoll shared the senator's view that America had to enter the conflict, lest it allow Hitler a complete, unhindered victory in Europe, and then stand alone to face a double-pronged assault by Germany and Japan.

Driscoll had been given classified information that certain members of the German military were interested in ending the war before a power-drunk Hitler ran amok. The United States, he had been told, was looked upon by these conspirators as a political ally in their plot. "Make contact with them if you can find them," were the brief instructions from Washington.

It did not take the two men long to reach an understanding. Driscoll gave Rolf assurances that his name would not be used in any dispatches. It was suspected that German Intelligence had broken the U.S. code, and there was more than a hint that a Nazi sympathizer was working at the embassy. It was therefore risky for Rolf to be seen too often with Driscoll. Heydrich's new counter-Intelligence man, Walter Schellenberg, might be smelling a rat.

One evening, sitting on the bed in Helga's modest room, Rolf broached an idea that had formed in his mind.

"Your landlord's at home?" he asked.

"No, he's not."

"I want to share something with you that must not be overheard."

Rolf had never let Helga glimpse the realm in which he worked. Once having asked him about it and being curtly rebutted, she respected his desire to keep his private and public worlds apart. She liked to imagine that the quiet and thoughtful man who was her lover was the same kind of person when he discharged his official duties.

Their relationship had changed. Was it because it had become routine or because of Rolf's tie to the Nazi hierarchy? He worked quite obviously at Gestapo headquarters. What was an Army man doing there? Was he a party to the goings-on in that forbidding-looking building with its granite stones and heavy bars shielding the windows that made it look like a jail?

"I. . .I need your help, Hilli."

"Anything, Rolf. I'm happy to do something for you rather than the other way around."

"Well, you know I'm not a Nazi and I've never been one. Not all Germans like what's going on. I belong to them. There are. . ."

Helga understood his hesitation.

"You see, Hilli, we've got to end this war. Hitler won't stop until all Europe lies at his feet. But as long as America supports England, Germany will not win. There are men in the Army who want to end it now, before this war ruins us all by dragging on forever and destroying what little is left of our civilization – and before the Führer becomes the Messiah in the mind of the people."

He paused. Helga wondered what role she could possibly play in such an arena.

"The Americans must know that we *other* Germans exist. That's where you come in."

He listened for any sounds in the house.

"Would you consider working in the American embassy?" Rolf asked in a whisper. "There's a man there who knows me and my group. We need to stay in touch and you could be the go-between. He doesn't have to know your identity."

"Of course." Helga was quick to answer. "I'd be doing my small part to throw a monkey wrench into the Nazi war machine. But won't it attract attention? I mean, Hilde Schmitt, German national, working for the Americans?"

"On the contrary," Rolf said, and explained that it was not uncommon for Germans to work in non-sensitive positions in foreign embassies; the Nazis in fact encouraged it, hoping to obtain a few extra scraps of information and even an occasional prime morsel.

A month later, at New Year's time, Hilde Schmitt became a translator at the U.S. embassy in Berlin.

* * *

Schellenberg was a rising star in the Himmler-Heydrich empire. He had caught Heydrich's eye because of a widely publicized kidnapping plot in which he managed to abduct two Englishmen. A university graduate, he fancied himself an intellectual who combined bureaucratic efficiency with a degree of ruthlessness which his boss appreciated. A few weeks after his appointment Heydrich called Schellenberg, the equivalent of a major in the Gestapo hierarchy, to his office.

"I'm getting mixed signals on General Halder. A good soldier, no question about it. Fine record in France. But he still hobnobs with Beck, he likes Goerdeler, and the aristocrats with their monocles are crazy about him. That alone would put me on guard. When it comes right down to it, we can't trust any of that bunch. If things were going badly, they'd be the first to bail out. Miserable bastards. We should have a thorough housecleaning and give these stuck-up Junkers a kick in the balls. Now General Keitel, there's a different man. Totally loyal to the Führer, which is more than can be said about these dandies with their *von und zu*."

Schellenberg nodded eagerly. It was the first time Heydrich had raised the subject.

"Is there something fruitful that my department can do?" he asked.

"That's why I called you in. Suppose someone wanted to get the goods on me, how would he start? With my associates, whom do I trust? Why him? You get the point."

"Yes, sir. Quite."

"Who's Halder's white-haired boy? Chap by the name of Baumgarten. I've known him for some time. Rarely says anything, very private. Halder swears by him. What's so great about him? He's just thirty or so and already a colonel. Pretty fast going in the Army – not in the SS of course, we're all young. But the Army loves a well-seasoned calcified officers' corps. The older the better. Baumgarten doesn't fit. Sure, his grandfather was a general in the last war, old boy protection. But I'd like you to find out everything about him. Go back three generations – schooling, finances, Army record, girl friends past and present; whom he sees, etc. The whole business. You'll know what to do. Put a bright eager man on it and let me see the dossier.

No real hurry, but don't wait too long either. In case you haven't figured it out yet, I don't like the bastard. Something about him that makes me reach for my gun. I want to sink him for good."

"Yes, sir," said Schellenberg, swept along by Heydrich's ardor. "I have just the right man to put on your friend's trail. Not to worry, sir. We'll get the goods. If there are any. And maybe even if there aren't."

* * *

Helga had become friendly with Kenneth Driscoll, to whom she imparted whatever information about Nazi resistance Rolf was able to provide. As military attaché Driscoll had little to do these days, for the Nazis restricted his movements. It was wartime, they said, and even a neutral nation like the U.S. had to respect these necessary limitations. At noon Driscoll would come to Helga's desk and sit with her while they had lunch – the American kind, not the heavy noontime meal the Germans preferred.

"Do you mind if I call you Hilli?" he asked her.

"Please do."

"And call me Ken. Never mind that 'Major Driscoll' stuff. We Americans don't like formality, particularly not where I come from."

"Which is?. . ."

"Iowa, breadbasket of America."

She was not sure where Iowa was but she liked Ken's natural openness. In this respect he differed markedly from Rolf who by family background and Army training was reserved and reticent. Ken, she found, had a deep-seated contempt for the Nazis, for their racial nonsense and their brutal repressive methods, and he frequently expressed his sentiments. Helga, who liked him from the first moment she met him, began to accompany him to receptions at various embassies.

He was puzzled by her, and the puzzlement added to the attraction. She was young, twenty-four, according to her papers. What would move such a woman to be a violent anti-Nazi? She wasn't a Jew, yet she was outraged at the treatment meted out to these hapless people. If there were many Germans like that, all was not lost. He faithfully transmitted his impressions to the ambassador and to Washington. They were, however, interested only in his analysis of dissidents in the Army; they were disinterested in his reports on the killing of Jews in Poland and the deportation of German and French Jews toward unknown destinations in the East.

He informed his superiors of the Nazis' major objective regarding the U.S.: to keep America out of the conflict as long as possible, until the Russians would be disposed of. Yes, their very allies, the Soviets, would be next to feel the boot of the *Wehrmacht*. That's what his contacts told him. Then it will be America's turn. The earlier the U.S. gets in, the German dissidents feel, the better chance they have. And the less formidable Germany will be.

Helga became expert in translating diplomatic jargon, learning high-level double-talk. New words appeared in dispatches and much of what was not made public was supplied by Rolf. *Einsatzkommando* meant special unit for the extermination of undesirables; and *verarbeiten* became the code word for such killing.

Rolf was frequently away now and Helga spent a good deal of time with Ken. They had dinner together several times a week and he took her home in his Daimler two-seater. He was always scrupulously correct in his behavior; he knew her attachment to Rolf.

"Why do you live in this part of town?" he asked her one evening as they said good-bye in front of the old apartment complex where she had rented a room from an elderly couple. His car was the only one on the street; Moabit residents traveled by bicycle or public transport. "It looks as if you're hiding."

She wondered whether Rolf had intimated something about her false identity.

"Well, in a way I am," she said. "Rolf thought that I should be low profile in my personal life. Working in the embassy is one thing, and the government knows about it. So my private space is as inconspicuous as possible."

In time he told her of his life. A career officer in the Marines, he served on detached duty at the Berlin embassy. He was in his mid-thirties and married, but the marriage had failed years ago and his wife had finally agreed to a divorce. They had two children, both in prep school in New England.

"Do you ever see your wife?" Helga asked as they stood in front of her apartment building. She found Driscoll an appealing human being and was intrigued by his story.

"Not anymore. I get all the news about the boys from my wife's father, Senator Browning. Good friend of President Roosevelt. We've remained close."

"You sound lonely," she said and wondered at once whether she had said too much.

"I am. I wish it were different."

He looked at her and found her blushing. She bade him a quick good night.

11

The man whom Schellenberg had selected to spy on Rolf, and thereby on Halder, was Heinrich Richter. The officer had already shown himself cruel enough for advancement in the SS. Richter had publicly punished a Jew for cavorting with an Aryan woman who was admittedly a whore but denied any involvement with this particular man. No matter, Richter's judgment was quick and stern. After humiliating the Jew by cutting off his beard, he had shaved off the woman's hair also, then had both of them collect horse excrement from the pavement and forced them to smear it in each other's faces.

"Eat it!" some gawking Hitler youth had yelled. "Make 'm eat shit!"

Richter had then forced the man's mouth open and the woman stuffed manure down his throat. When the man vomited all over him, Richter kicked him to death and had him carted away. The whore was decorated with a placard, which he had seen depicted in *Der Stürmer*:

> *I am a certified racial pig,*
> *I love to suck a Jewish prick.*

The sign was hung around her neck and Richter ordered her to stand at the street corner for twenty-four hours. Good show, Schellenberg thought. A tough man to keep in mind for future assignments.

He probed Richter for possible weaknesses. He learned that the young SS officer was a bit of a ladies' man; his exploits were recounted with some admiration. A minus point, in Schellenberg's view. Eagerness to lay a pretty prospect was apt to cloud one's judgment.

Did he have relatives?

"None that I know of, *Herr Sturmbannführer*. I was adopted as a baby from the Christian orphanage, and all attempts to find my natural family have failed."

"Yes, yes, I'm aware of that. What I mean is, who is around from the Jew family in which you were raised? Are you in contact with anyone?"

"No, sir. No contact at all. My adoptive mother had a cousin in England. I can't even recall her name. In London, somewhere. And as to my so-called sister, I did inquire about her, just to be sure she was out of my way. We never got on together. Good-looking bitch. Emphasis on bitch."

"And?"

"She left Germany shortly after her parents' suicide. The local police station has a record of stamping her passport for emigration and noted that she had a British visa. Her father transferred some money to England, and no doubt that's where she went. She would no more think of getting in touch with me than I with her."

Schellenberg noticed that Richter was agitated. Guilt feelings of some sort. *Her* parents, sure, but they had been *his* as well for some twenty years. Can't be rubbed out like a pencil mark. It'll be added impetus for doing a thorough job. He gave Richter the SS dossier on Baumgarten.

"Fill in the gaps, girl friends especially. I hear you're good at that. And don't forget that the boss doesn't like Baumgarten. First find out what facts there are to be dug up, and if they're sparse, we'll let our imagination roam a little. Go to it, and good luck. Heil Hitler!"

* * *

Consequences arising from the conquest of Denmark and Norway delayed Richter's activities. There were Jews to control in these countries and though they were relatively few, the general population, especially in Denmark, proved uncooperative. Obviously much work needed to be done to enlighten these benighted Nordics. A pity to see such splendid specimens of Aryan blood value their racial purity so little. But time was on the side of Germany, and the Danes too would soon produce their own Quisling. Thus spoke Himmler, and Heydrich agreed.

* * *

In early June General Halder called in his protégé.

"Baumgarten, I will detach you from your liaison duty. You've never liked it, and I can't blame you. Now I want you at headquarters. Big events are in the offing. Your talents will be better employed in the Army proper."

"I'm grateful, General," said Rolf. "Lately I've been made to feel increasingly unwelcome at Alexanderplatz. Heydrich's got a new toady called Schellenberg who stares at me all the time with a filthy smirk on his scarred face. I think I'm being shadowed, but can't be sure. I'll be happy to be away from them. It's a different world. For them there's no law except what they determine it is. If they suspect you of something, you're guilty until you prove yourself innocent, and for that you won't have time because you'll either be in a *KZ* or dead. Is this what tomorrow will look like?"

"I'm afraid so," Halder mused. "Meanwhile, there's *Barbarossa*."

"Sorry, sir, I don't understand."

"As a new member of my personal staff, you'll be fully briefed. In a few weeks Operation *Barbarossa* will get under way. We'll be taking on the Russians. I have advised against it. We'll stretch our lines and our capacity, though we'll do well in the beginning. We have the edge of surprise."

He paused and looked out of the window.

"But in the long run we'll get bogged down like Napoleon. Russia is immense and its manpower three times that of ours. We still haven't defeated the British and the Americans are making noises to join the fray. What does your friend Driscoll say?"

Obviously the general was in touch with Moltke and his circle.

"He says Roosevelt is ready. The isolationists are losing ground. He's only waiting for the right moment."

"Yes," said Halder. "Then we'll be back to 1914, and with the same bitter ending. Are the Kreisau people making progress?"

"It's slow, but they have recruited some excellent men."

"I've heard," said the general. "Men like Schlabrendorff and Stauffenberg. I wish we had thousands like them."

"I'm glad to be on your team, sir," Rolf burst out with warm admiration.

* * *

Richter had an interim report for Schellenberg.

"We've traced Baumgarten's background. Not much there that we can get at. Mother's side quite impeccable. She's the daughter of General von Friedrichsruh. Father is another matter. A Balt, apparently from Riga or environs. He died when Baumgarten was a baby. We haven't been able to get a line on him. The Russians have not cooperated. They don't trust us any more than we trust them."

Schellenberg seemed intrigued.

"You don't by any chance think that our precious major had a Jew father?"

"It's possible, but we can't get at it. The name is inconclusive. Same as with Rosenberg, a Jewish name if there ever was one. Yet there's Alfred Rosenberg, the Führer's chief philosopher. Right here in Berlin we have good Aryan Baumgartens, and we had Jews too, and no apparent relation between them. None had any Latvian connections we can trace."

"Well," said Schellenberg with some glee, "we may be able to clear up the Riga mystery in a little while."

"You mean?. . ."

"I mean nothing, Richter. Forget it. Perhaps the Russians will be more pliant in the future."

"Yes, sir," Richter said obediently.

"Anything more?"

"A little. Army career normal, no flaws. Stepfather a Bavarian count, skirt chaser and spendthrift. Von Bumm, what a name! Nothing there either, but in the guy's girlfriend department we're making a bit of progress. He's been seeing a Hilde Schmitt, translator. Funny that we can't trace her background either. She's registered as born in Königsberg, and the register for that year is lost. Strange coincidence. I've had someone look at the daily newspaper for the time of her birth. A few Schmitts in the birth announcements but no baby named Hilde."

"Interesting."

"Yes, sir, but now listen to this. She surfaces in Cologne. Nice blond, gets a job easily. Baumgarten visits her from time to time. They go on short trips together. Up the Rhine, Lorelei and all that. Very ordinary. Then suddenly she's transferred, changes the color of her hair, moves to Berlin and ends up working in the American embassy. We have a good contact there, an American who admires the way the Führer runs things. Their attaché, chap by the name of Driscoll, spends a bit of time with the Schmitt dame."

"Double-timing old Baumgarten, eh?"

"Maybe. Funny thing: he and Driscoll are quite chummy

and this Driscoll is anti-Nazi."

"Good work, Richter!" Schellenberg rose and offered him a cigarette. Richter declined.

"There's one other matter, sir. At present it's a bit fuzzy and I haven't got a handle on it. The people involved are important and well connected. I must be careful. Have you ever heard of Kreisau?"

"No," said Schellenberg, "can't say I have."

"Well, it's part of the Moltke estate – you know the famous family of the hero of 1870. In Silesia."

"So?"

"Baumgarten goes there once in a while. He meets with a group of young officers. They don't hunt or drink, they don't invite women. They're all nobility. Baumgarten fits in nicely. One of the old boys. Question: What the hell are they doing there? We've got a line into a couple of servants, but so far we've drawn a blank. I'm working on it, though. How much more time do I have?"

"Take all the time you want. I think the chief's instincts are right. There's a stink here somewhere. That embassy connection, the mysterious girl friend and the Kreisau gang. Keep it up. On second thought, maybe you'd better push for clear proofs of something pretty soon. I hear Baumgarten's being transferred to headquarters. Once he's there he'll be hard to touch."

* * *

On June 22 Operation *Barbarossa* began; German troops marched into Russia. Halder's headquarters moved eastward with the advancing German armies. Rolf and Helga spent the night together, her lovemaking almost desperate. She had a deep sense of foreboding. She had become accustomed to living an underground existence because Rolf was there; his presence was a protective shield. Now he would be gone, and he too would be exposed to untold dangers.

Yet Rolf appeared to be exhilarated at the prospect of going to the front. There at last he would be a soldier removed from political intrigue and the Nazi hierarchy. He assured her she would be all right – rather offhandedly, she thought, and chastised herself for feeling critical. In the morning they shared a last embrace.

* * *

As the *Panzer* divisions rolled toward Leningrad, Moscow and Kiev, it became clear that millions of Jews were caught by the Nazi juggernaut. *Einsatzkommandos* followed the troops like prostitutes did in earlier times. But while the whores distributed both pleasure and syphilis, the Nazi hordes had only death to dispense.

The mobile killing units assembled Jews under the ruse of "resettlement." The victims could not believe that they were to be herded together for merciless slaughter; they followed instructions, obeyed their elders. And when they discovered the bitter truth, they rarely found protectors among either the German Army or the local population, who returned escaping victims to their killers. Jews were loaded into trucks, taken to a ravine outside their town, made to dig their graves and then were shot. Every Jew was exterminated where the *Kommandos* operated. Smaller and midsize communities were thus cleared of Jews in the first few months of the war. A report delivered to Hitler in the fall stated that more than a hundred thousand had been dispatched.

Still, the Führer was displeased. The killings were haphazard, not organized with the kind of efficiency he expected. Ten thousand here, five hundred there; at that rate, the process would take forever. "And as fast as we get rid of them, they breed a new generation of parasites," he said at lunch at Wolfschanze, his headquarters in East Prussia.

On July 26 he handed Göring a note. It was headed: *Führer Order on the Final Solution.*

> *The solution of the Jewish question is as essential to our victory as is our success on the battle front. The head and body of the Jewish viper are to be smashed once and for all. I do not want to wait until the war is over. I want the Jews to disappear from the face of Europe. A single living Jew is a threat to the German people. I want Heydrich to submit a plan which will assure me that my objective is carried out systematically, expeditiously and as much as possible away from public scrutiny.*
>
> *There's no point upsetting soft-brained, weak-kneed people at home and abroad who still do not understand that my policy is aimed at the salvation of mankind. A separate plan is to be drawn up regarding the elimination of other sub-humans and undesirables, such as Gypsies, communists and certain elements of the Slavic population.*
>
> *(s) A. Hitler*

A few days later Göring transmitted the essence of the order to Heydrich:

> *You are hereby commissioned by me to proceed with preparations for the complete solution of the Jewish question in every part of Europe which we now control.*
>
> *You are also to submit to me at the earliest moment a draft setting forth what measures you have already taken for the final solution of the Jewish question.*
>
> *I expect to be fully apprised of your plans.*

Heydrich received his new extended charge with satisfaction. He had moved away from the Reichsführer SS and saw added reason for hoping that he might eventually replace him and even Hitler, should the occasion arise. With the total control of Czechoslovakia soon to be awarded to him, and now entrusted with the extermination of the Jews, he was advancing toward his first goal. He was wondering whether he should begin to shadow Himmler, but dismissed the idea as premature. For the time being Heydrich wanted to know whether it was the Führer and not just Göring who had singled him out for this supremely important task. Göring had not mentioned the Führer in his order and Heydrich wondered whether Hitler himself had issued the instructions in writing.

Heydrich was as bold as he was ruthless. He telephoned the Reich Marshal, as Göring was now titled.

"I understand that the Führer wants a report of my planning," he ventured. A stab in the dark.

Göring fell into the trap. His mind was on other things. A German art dealer was to assess his collection and suggest a proper place to house it.

"Quite so. The Führer says you should do it. So get on with it."

"With the greatest respect, Reich Marshal, the order involves millions of lives, maybe five, six or seven million. I think I should have the Führer's order in writing. I will be greatly obliged if you would send it over to me."

"All right, all right. You'll get it. Have someone from your staff pick it up. Heil Hitler!"

Heydrich's grin was stretched across his face as if it were a clothes line hung from his two ears. His ordinarily long nose seemed even longer, almost touching his lips with a joyous snort. He had bested the Fat One, no small feat. Possession of the Führer's order also meant that he had stolen a march on Himmler. Ah, precious letter or telegram or whatever! As long as it had the magic initials A.H.

affixed to it. I must get it at once while *der Dicke* is willing to surrender it, he thought. I can't go myself, that would be demeaning. I need a totally reliable messenger, senior enough to receive a top-secret message, yet not so senior that Göring will begin to wonder and reconsider.

A telephone call interrupted his deliberation. It was Schellenberg.

"Chief, very interesting news. *Sturmbannführer* Richter has struck oil. We can sink your buddy Baumgarten and tarnish his protector at the same time. Richter's come up with one witness who'll swear the bastard has committed miscegenation with a cute little Jew bitch, and another witness who can stick him with treasonable activities."

"Well, well!" The clothes line grin again. "This is my day. Why don't you have Richter come over and tell me his exploits personally. And while he's here I'll entrust him with a special task, to fetch me a letter from Old Fatso. Very important. I take it Richter can be trusted?"

"Absolutely. Hope the letter is good news for our department."

"Oh, it is, Schellenberg, it is. I'll let you in on it when I get it. So send Richter over after lunch, say three o'clock. I intend to celebrate a little."

* * *

Heinrich Richter appeared at Heydrich's office well before the appointed time. If one needed to do anything, it was to be punctual. Only ill-mannered people and superior officers might flout the laws of punctuality; anyone else did it at his peril.

It was Richter's first visit to Heydrich's lair. To meet the chief personally would be a feather in his cap, a lowly lieutenant meeting the lieutenant general, who was feared by his enemies like the Angel of Death. He wondered whether Heydrich knew that in certain circles he was referred to as the Hangman. Maybe he did and was proud of it.

The chief arrived in splendid spirits buoyed by some excellent wine he had shared with Gestapo leader Müller and Dr. Six, the new ideologue of the department. He greeted Richter with surprising cordiality.

"Well, Richter, let's have it. Your boss gives you good marks for your efforts. If we can trap our friend successfully, I won't forget your role in bringing him to heel. Give me the highlights only, the rest you'll put into a written report. Be sure to mark it 'Strictly Secret.' "

Richter related the main results of his investigation to date. Baumgarten was shacking up with a certain dame when in Berlin. Richter had been suspicious of her from the beginning, and now he had found a woman who knew that this girl was living under an assumed name. She had cleaned the wastepaper basket in some print shop and found pieces of old identity papers that showed Baumgarten's paramour to be Jewish. The print shop was no longer operative, the owner was killed in Norway. But we'll apply a little persuasive pressure to the moll, and unless she's made of iron she'll come across with the truth, Richter promised.

He then proceeded to tell Heydrich of Baumgarten's Kreisau connection and of his hobnobbing with Driscoll. A bit vague, but the contact man in the U.S. embassy was certain that Baumgarten was involved in some form of espionage.

Finally, now that the Germans had control of Riga, he had undertaken a search of marriages and birth registers in the city to ascertain the background of Baumgarten's father. Unfortunately, the city was in a mess at present, so the results were not yet conclusive. But there was an excellent chance that Baumgarten, Sr. was a rich Jew. No wonder the Friedrichsruh clan wanted no further contact with these unsavory relatives. "Of course," Richter concluded, "if Baumgarten is a half Jew we can't hang the crime of racial miscegenation on him. Instead, we can treat him as a Jew. So he loses both ways, unless General Halder protects him. But that's outside my assignment and competency."

The chief was pleased.

"Yes, go and have a talk with *Herr* Baumgarten's mysterious sleep mate. Test her resistance and maybe she'll remember all sorts of things about her lover and herself. But be careful, don't give her a tumble, not until you know it's okay. I hear you have quite a way with the fair sex. And while you go visiting the broad, make a quick trip to the Air Ministry. The Reich Marshal has an important letter for me direct from the Führer. Guard it carefully and deliver it to no one but myself. Okay? Now move your ass. Heil Hitler!"

12

A letter came from Rolf, who had received a front-line assignment. After describing the fighting, he shared his impressions of the Russian population, with particular emphasis on the fate that was in store for the Jews. He professed his love and became nostalgic.

> *Remember Leni from the olden days? I hear from friends that someone is showing her unwelcome attention, some guy that should be doing his patriotic duty here at the front but has managed to get himself a cushy job in Berlin and hangs around her.* C'est la guerre!
>
> *Don't forget, if you need something, don't hesitate to call on Ken. He's a good friend.*

When Rolf had written to her in England he had signed the note "Leni." She scanned the letter for hidden meaning. The reference to Ken: Rolf was obviously warning her that she might be in need of assistance. "Unwelcome attention": a hint that someone was after her? Now that she thought about it, she recalled that a man was always lingering across the street from her apartment house. She had surmised that he lived there and was out for a breath of air. And Rolf's description of Jews and their fate: a suggestion that her own Jewish origin was in danger of being discovered? The more she studied the letter, the more certain she became of the meanings.

She shared it with Driscoll. "You see," she told him, "you're an important key in the drama." She tried to make light of it but knew it was a forced exercise.

"It's clear," said Driscoll, "that someone is drawing a bead on you. Rolf has heard it because he's probably the real target and he's been tipped off. Now that he's away from Alexanderplatz, he's become fair game. We know he and Heydrich hate each other's guts, and the Hangman is becoming a very big cheese. Dangerous bastard who'd disembowel his own mother if it would help his ambition."

"Ken, what do you think I should do?"

"We may have to ship you out of here at short notice. There's a guy here who's very handy with documents."

He rang the bell and asked for Corcoran, who turned out to be a bald-headed little man with large horn-rimmed glasses and a rumpled suit, rather unprofessional looking for an employee of the embassy.

"You know Miss Schmitt," Driscoll said. "She's one of our translators. We may send her to England on a special assignment, or the States. Look through the photographs you have lying around and choose one that bears a general resemblance to her. Maybe a gal with glasses, we could hunt up a pair. American passport, new name, proper entry stamps, the works. Born in New York. What year shall we say?"

He looked at Helga.

"I was born in 1916," she said, "but I don't mind if you make it a little older."

"I suppose she needs a British visa," Corcoran suggested.

"No problem about that once she's out of the country. We'll give her diplomatic status."

"It sounds important and very serious," Helga said. "I

should be scared but somehow I'm not."

"Excuse me, folks." Corcoran was already at the door. "I'd better get going. When do you say you want this?"

"Yesterday, when else? The way I read it, this thing may pop anytime."

When Corcoran had left, Driscoll turned to Helga. "Very cool, despite your age. I think we could use you professionally, and I don't mean as a translator. I'll discuss it with the Chargé. Hang in there, and don't phone me from your place. It's bugged for sure if they're after you."

He kissed her good-bye, and she responded warmly.

* * *

Richter received a less-than-regal welcome at the Air Ministry. A man in SS uniform was an intruder in their territory, where Erhard Milch, though reputed to be racially a Jew, could function as a general of the *Jägerstab*. Richter went through half a dozen secretaries and adjutants and waited for several hours before he received a signal from the Marshal's office. He would see him within an hour.

Despite his lack of experience in the inner workings of the Nazi hierarchy, Richter understood that the discourtesy was directed at Heydrich, not him. He was a mere cog in the machinery of palace politics.

It was six o'clock when *der Dicke* received him. He sat behind a large desk in a vast room that was more like a hall. Göring had seen this arrangement in Rome and had been impressed; one of the few things that he cared to copy from the *Duce* whom he considered a windbag. Distinctly not in the Führer's class. Richter stood at attention, delivering Heydrich's request.

"Look here, young man," said the Fat One. "Your boss wants a certain document. I've agreed to show it to him. *Show* it to him, you hear? I want it back. Tomorrow, if possible. Guard it with your life. The letter is sealed, so restrain your curiosity. If that letter isn't back here within the week, there'll be hell to pay. Tell your boss I said it. And just to keep you interested, Lieutenant, or is it Captain? – I never can keep your screwy ranks straight – if this letter isn't returned to me within that time, I'll have your ass. Personally. I'll pretend you absconded with it and have you shot for treason. Tell that to your boss too. It's rough being a messenger boy in the big league. Could be dangerous." He handed him the envelope with the Führer's letter and dismissed him.

Richter put the letter in the inner pocket of his uniform and hurried from the building. Only when he was outside did he notice that he was wet with perspiration. He quickly made his way back to Heydrich's headquarters.

But the Hangman had suddenly left, and not just for the evening. He was being sent to Prague, in preparation for his special assignment as Protector of Bohemia and Moravia, a euphemism for overlord with unlimited powers. The realm had to be controlled more tightly, and Hitler considered Heydrich to be the ideal choice. He would know how to pacify the natives, and those who didn't like it would be dispatched quickly for eternal and irrevocable pacification. Heydrich would probably be back in a week, the adjutant said.

Heinrich Richter was more worried than he cared to admit. He hoped that Schellenberg would know how to proceed. Perhaps a trip to Prague was indicated; the Fat One did not like to be kept waiting. Schellenberg had gotten him into this trouble, and he would have to extricate him from it. Yes, he would see him first thing in the morning. Richter patted his pocket to make sure the letter was secure. Meanwhile, he might pursue his own prey. Hilde Schmitt, or whoever she really was, represented a nice diversion in his quest for information.

Schmitt could not very well be interviewed at her place of work. The Americans wouldn't let him past the front door. He could have her arrested as she left the embassy at night or at her home in the morning, but until he was sure of his facts he would avoid a public fuss. Relations with the Americans were not the best anyway, and the last thing he wanted was to stumble around in the quagmire of international politics.

He decided to see her at home. He drove to Moabit, using his personal car, a sporty convertible Adler.

It was dark now. The police shadow was not at his post, Richter did not know why. He certainly had not given orders to call him off. He parked the car in front of the building. As he got out and looked at the structure, he thought he saw a face behind a darkened window on the first floor, then the curtain was back in place. If one wanted to hide, this modest street in the workers' quarter was as good a place as any. Clever girl, little Miss Schmitt, but I'm on to you. Your boyfriend won't like what I'll do to you, and neither will you. . . . He had an erection as he contemplated what lay ahead, and was amused when he noticed it.

There was no concierge, not in this neighborhood. He lit a match to find a mailbox. No luck. He walked through to the first courtyard, then the second. He thought of ringing someone's doorbell to ask for information but decided against it. The sight of an SS officer on the prowl would be a minor sensation, mixed with fear and even hostility. This was former socialist and communist territory, and the old sentiments had not died out.

On impulse he decided to try the first-floor apartment where he thought he had seen a woman looking out. He rapped on the door.

"Yes?" A woman's voice, muffled.

"*Fräulein* Schmitt?"

"Who is it?" The voice again, a little nearer.

"Please open up, I'll identify myself." Vaguely familiar.

The door opened a crack. The apartment was dimly lit, hardly enough to make him discernible in the dark hallway. A young woman. Dark haired, good figure. It must be she. He thrust his identification card at her. She peered at it, trying to make it out. Then she looked at him but could not see his face hidden in the shadow of the cap's visor.

"Come in," she said at last. "The landlord is away, we can sit in the living room."

The room was sparsely furnished, an overstuffed sofa, two wooden straight-backed chairs, a side table with a faded cloth to cover its nakedness. Clean and unmistakably poor. The landlord will be poorer still, Richter thought, after I remove this dame from the premises. A single bulb hiding behind a reddish shade shone mournfully.

"Is this the best light you have?" Richter spoke with authority.

She knew that voice but at once dismissed the thought. It couldn't be. She knew but did not want to know.

"Sorry, yes. As I said, this is not my room. May I ask why you are here?"

Something stirred in him as she spoke. Her movement, her speech. He too was at the edge of recognition, but he blocked that unpleasant possibility from his mind.

"You are Hilde Schmitt?"

"I am."

"Let me see your papers."

She rose and went to her room. She looked around to see whether there was any incriminating evidence she should hide or cast out of the window. She occupied the back room which gave onto an air shaft, a narrow divide from the neighbors that had no access from the outside. Anything cast out was retrievable only if one could manage the two-meter drop.

"Where the hell are you?"

It occurred to him there might be a back door through which she could escape, but she returned before he had time to verify his suspicion. She could not think of anything that needed disposing. Besides, she had gone over the scenario a dozen times with Rolf.

Richter moved to the tired light bulb and looked at her identity papers. They told him nothing he did not already know.

He heard a stifled cry. The woman had slumped in her chair and covered her face. She was mumbling something that sounded like "Oh my God!"

Helga saw her brother's face in the full light. Changed somewhat, the features harder, the mustache thicker, eyes shielded by glasses, the voice a pitch deeper and more clipped. Of all the bastards in the SS, did it have to be he? I am sunk, she thought. I can fool him for another few minutes, my dark hair may throw him off, but he's bound to know me. I must make the best of it, throw myself on his mercy.

"Heinrich Raben!" Clear voice, no tremor.

He reeled back as if she had struck him.

"What? You really are?. . ."

"Yes, Heinrich. No point keeping up the pretense. I'm Helga. Changed my name just as you did. I too decided I had a right to live in Germany. So what will you do? Turn me in? Deliver me to your torture chambers?"

He looked at her as if she was an apparition in a bad dream. He tried to imagine her with blond hair but could not quite see the sister he had known. His simple plans had suddenly become complicated. The day had taken an unexpected turn.

Helga's eyes followed his appraisal of her figure. I'll turn her in all right, he thought. If the boss still wonders whether I've cut all my ties, this will do it. He remembered Himmler's speech at the SS induction. If you will be guided by mercy and pity, you fail in your highest duty. The new era demands supermen whose loyalty is to the Führer's vision and not to small sentiment. Killing and torture may be a greater service to humanity than the weak-kneed will ever be able to perform.

Richter peered at Helga, trying to scrape away the darkness.

The threat of using power is everything; power once used loses its potency. I wonder who said that? he thought. Keeping her in limbo will blackmail Baumgarten. Maybe he'll tell us something about his noble friends if we tell him that his precious girl's life is on the line. And what about her? If I let her off, she'll think me weak. If I turn her in, Baumgarten will claim that we extorted a false confession. Besides, she'll say we're brother and sister, it'll bring the past back. Lots of people don't know I was once Raben.

He was irresolute and started pacing the cramped room. Helga eyed him as a spectator follows a tennis ball on the court.

I know you, miserable brother. You're not really after me, you're after Rolf, you henchman of your long-nosed master. You can't stand a German who's decent and refuses to eat your shit. I'm no good to you dead, the dead don't testify. So you'll threaten me with Alexanderplatz, but you're not keen on having everyone know of your past. I know you, bastard. I didn't live in the same house with you without knowing you better than you know yourself.

She remembered how he had once sneaked into the bathroom when she was about ten. He'd come from behind as she was drying herself after a bath, put his arms around her and grabbed her nipples. She had screamed but her parents were out and the maids were in their quarters entertaining their boyfriends. "I gotcha," he had whispered. He had squeezed her and tried to explore her further. She finally wriggled loose, escaped into her bedroom and locked the door.

"Get up!" he now commanded with a high pitch she recognized. She did not move. Better an angry Heinrich than a calculating one.

"Damn you, get up!" Somehow he could not exercise his authority against a seated woman.

She rose slowly, pretending to be nonchalant. He stepped close to her, his breath falling on her with a sweetish odor. She looked at his boots, so well shined that even in the dim light they glimmered. He put his hand under her chin and jerked it up.

"Look at me while I talk."

She pushed him away. "Don't touch me! Whatever you do, stay away from me. You forget I'm a Jew and you're a certified Aryan. You wouldn't want to commit *Rassenschande*."

She regretted saying it. People like Heinrich want most what is forbidden to them.

"If that's the way you want it, that's your funeral," he hissed and slapped her face hard. She reeled back, fell over the chair and sprawled on the ground. He put a gleaming boot on her belly. She clawed at it but couldn't get away.

"Listen to me, Jew bitch. I'm going to be good to you instead of lighting candles for the dead or whatever Jews do. I'll report that I have interrogated you and found you *kosher*. You'll be Hilde Schmitt, Aryan, as your fake papers say."

"Then take that boot off, Heinrich. I can hardly breathe."

"Just a moment, princess. My generosity comes with two conditions."

His foot did not move.

"I want you to report on certain matters at the embassy. You hear things that could be useful to Germany. After all, if you pretend to be a German, act like one."

"All right," she said. "I'll do it."

"One more thing. I couldn't sleep with a Jewess, but there's no reason why I couldn't with a certified Aryan. Your man's far away. You think he's chaste in Russia?"

Her composure broke like a piece of china and she started to cry.

"I always wanted you, as long as I can remember."

"Please, Heinrich. No, I can't. For the sake of everything that's holy to you, respect me this once."

Her weakness fanned his amorous impulse into a burst of frenzied passion. He kicked her, then tore at her arm, forcing her to her feet and slapped her again, bringing blood to her face.

"Why fight it, Miss Schmitt? You are Miss Schmitt, aren't you? I'm going to have you one way or another."

"Just let me go, I'll do it," she blurted. Anything to stall him. "Let's do it civilized. I've got a bed, but first I need a drink."

"That's better," said Heinrich. "I've never forced a woman. Never had to."

Miserable scum, thought Helga. I'm being raped and I'll pay you back, God help me.

"So where's the stuff?" he bellowed as he removed his tunic. "I can use a couple of stiff ones myself. I'm in the mood for a long night."

"Some American bourbon right from the embassy." She brought the bottle. "Here, you open it."

A plan was taking shape. Heinrich would blackmail her into submission, threatening to expose her as a Jew and lover of Rolf. Meanwhile this misbegotten bastard would have it all his way, for as long as she was Schmitt she was allowed to him without reservation. Just another dame left behind and having some fun. Heinrich, a cornered woman fighting for her lover and her own self-respect is a dangerous enemy. You don't know what you've taken on.

She had become cold all over, perspiration clinging to her like a wet sheet. Rape is expensive, Heinrich, more expensive than you've bargained for.

She took a long drink. He finished his second and poured himself a third. One more, she thought, would do it. But he did not comply.

"So where's my lover's lair?" he said. "I'm ready." He took off his shirt. She filled both glasses and carried them into the bedroom.

"This way, *Herr Obersturmbannführer.*" Give him extra rank in that filthy hierarchy. Do anything to make him feel good.

He stepped behind and locked her in his arms, as if to replay the childhood scene. He tore off her clothes and threw her on the bed, falling on her like a hungry wolf.

She let it happen, tears covering her hatred and sharpening her resolve.

"Here, let's have another drink and take those damn pants and boots off," she coaxed. She felt ill with disgust.

He swallowed the whiskey as if it were a glass of water. He licked his lips and glared at Helga in the darkness. Then he was asleep.

She waited several minutes, then shook him. No response except his rasping snores. Her heart beat like a brass gong. Dear Father, dear Mother, forgive me for what I'm about to do. This is not your son. He has defiled me and become your enemy, allied with the devil.

In the dim light of a moonless night she looked at the man next to her. Slowly, as if to delay the fateful moment, she got up. Naked she was violated and naked she would take revenge. There was no going back now.

Her heart felt as if it were in an icy grip. She picked the pillow off the floor and gently placed it on his face.

"Now!" she said in a hoarse voice and pressed down with all her might. Heinrich stirred, thrashed violently for some moments while Helga held him down. Then he lay still. She looked at the hated figure. The man who was once her brother was dead.

For the next half hour she acted out a plan that seemed devised by someone else. She took Rolf's razor from the bathroom, placed newspaper under Heinrich's head and shaved off his hair. She gathered the hair and placed it in a bag. Then she took the suit Rolf kept in her room and dressed the corpse. She didn't bother with socks and shoes.

Faint with effort and rising terror, she pulled Heinrich out of the bed and to the window. There was no other window opposite hers, and therefore no fear of detection. It occurred to her that Rolf's suit might have an identifying mark. She cut out the label and made sure nothing was left in the pockets. She lifted Heinrich's upper torso onto the ledge. Then she took his feet, pushed up and heaved him over. He landed with a thud on the air shaft two meters below.

Helga threw Heinrich's clothes into her suitcase, carefully removing anything that might identify them. The car keys gleamed; she had not counted on a get-away car, for that's what it had become, courtesy of Herr Richter, erstwhile SS officer. She could not leave it outside in any case. To be sure, he would sooner or later be identified by the tattoo each member of the chosen horde received on initiation. But every delay counted.

Helga straightened out her room, washed the razor and the glasses, wiped the fingerprints from the bottle.

She dressed, taking her papers and money. The valise, the bag of assorted contents. One more glance in the living room. There lay Heinrich's shirt and tunic, forsaken by their owner. Quickly she put them into the suitcase, and as she did so, the letter with which he had been entrusted fell out. From the Reich Marshal's office, addressed to Reinhard

Heydrich. *Personal. Sent by hand. Top secret,* it was marked. She put it in her purse and scribbled a note: *Gone on a week's holiday. Hilde Schmitt.*

She put her baggage in the trunk of the Adler and drove off. Careful, I can't risk being picked up, she admonished herself. She parked on a side street near the American embassy and walked a block. She asked the night watchman to waken Ken Driscoll.

* * *

Ken became a rock of strength. He was at once understanding and decisive, a close and comforting friend as well as a cool analyst of their situation, ready to act on his conclusions. Helga felt drained of all emotion and her mind was shut against reality. Nothing had happened, yet everything had happened.

Very slowly, as he talked to her, she began once more to focus on her plight and heard what he was saying.

"The first thing we must do is go back and see whether we can move the body."

"I couldn't bear the idea of touching him again," she said.

"But you can't leave him there," Driscoll said. "First thing tomorrow someone will discover the body."

"No," she pleaded, breaking down in tears, "I'll do anything but go back there. And besides, the stake-out guy may be there again."

Driscoll weighed the possibilities. "Okay. Let's get the car out of the neighborhood. You drive it, I'll follow. Near the *Rundfunk* Tower."

By four o'clock they were back at the embassy. They had retrieved her empty valise and the uniform had been left in the trunk. They flushed the dead man's hair down the toilet along with his shredded identification papers.

"There's nothing we can do until Corcoran comes to work at eight," said Driscoll. "Doze a while, if you can, while I make plans."

He pulled up a footstool for the easy chair.

"I'm sorry, Hilli, more than I can say."

He kissed her on the forehead and closed the door to his office.

PART III

The Chase

WINTER 1941-42

13

Schellenberg had a habit of arriving at his office at an early hour. The night officer greeted him deferentially.

"Anything up, Kramer?"

"Yes, sir, five minutes ago. A call from Prague. From the chief himself. Call back as soon as possible."

When Heydrich came on the line, his voice had an edge of impatience.

"Why aren't your people on the job at seven o'clock? They're working for the SS, not the fuckin' Army. Has that *Wunderkind* of yours arrived yet?"

"You mean. . ."

"You know damn well. The guy you put on a certain party with odd parental background."

"Yes, sir," said Schellenberg. "I understand. One moment, please. I'll see whether he's arrived."

His adjutant checked. Negative. Heydrich was not pleased.

"I sent him on an important errand yesterday. Have him ring me the moment he gets in. Probably had a late night with some dame. Okay?"

"Yes, sir."

At ten o'clock Schellenberg rang Prague. Richter had not been seen, he reported. As he had feared, Heydrich exploded. The telephone seemed to tremble with obscenities.

"Find him instantly. Also call the Air Ministry, personal adjutant of the Marshal, and find out whether Richter saw the boss yesterday. Just yes or no. And don't talk to the Fat One or you'll get an earful worse than you got from me. I want a report within the hour."

* * *

Corcoran was in a good mood. The American passport he had produced for Helga had several American and English stamps, and showed a young woman with glasses that covered half her face and a hairdo that covered the rest. The document was for one Emily Byrne, born in New York. Diplomatic status. Assistant to the Attaché. He had also found glasses that had been left behind. Though they did not improve Helga's visual acuity, they could serve her long enough to cross the border.

The Chargé d'Affaires had been informed by Driscoll of the broad outlines of the case which had now been thrust in their laps. Go ahead, the Chargé had said, but be careful. He too had no use for Nazi machinations. He advanced them five hundred dollars from his emergency fund.

"We're leaving this afternoon for Switzerland," Driscoll announced to Helga. "By train, the least likely way to be detected. But I really think that you'll be safe, for a few days anyway."

She made no response. Since she arrived at the embassy, her body seemed to be increasingly separated from her mind. She complied with Driscoll's instructions like a programmed robot. Her voice had shrunk to a hoarse whisper as if afraid to utter sound.

"Rolf," she said several times.

Driscoll was not sure she was coherent.

"What about him?"

"Rolf will write and the letters will be returned. He won't

know what happened. Worse, if they connect me with the business, as they will, they'll land on Rolf and he gets it while I'm safe. I won't go until you answer."

She listened to herself speak and was astonished at her logic.

"Yes, I've thought about it," Driscoll said. "There isn't much you can do except warn him. Here, sit down and write him a note. He'll protect himself. Didn't you say he had tried to warn you?"

It suddenly came back to her. Rolf's mysterious letter.

"Do you have his address at the front?" Driscoll asked.

"I know it by heart."

Concern for Rolf had pulled her back into bitter reality, where inaction or error could spell death for a loved one.

She wrote to Rolf:

> *Dear Colonel Baumgarten:*
>
> *My brother came to Berlin. He was in your unit. He hopes you may remember him, blond and quite young. He lost his right arm and leg. He's all right and will make it, and he wanted to be sure that I would write you and let you know. He can't write anymore, not until he's learned how to do it with his left hand. He's off to a recuperation hospital now, I think, outside of the Reich.*
>
> *Heil Hitler!*
>
> *Leni Kostler*

She signed the last name in an illegible scrawl, hoping Rolf might decipher it. Leni, she knew, would provide the clue for recognizing the writer.

Helga showed it to Driscoll who complimented her. "One suggestion, though. Don't write recuperation hospital. He might wonder whether something happened to you. Why not just say, 'He's off recuperating.' That's positive and reassuring."

She readily agreed.

Driscoll put Helga's "Raben" passport in his pocket. She might want it once she was outside the country.

"The car keys," she reminded him.

"I'll dispose of them later. No point spending time on them now."

He rang for Corcoran.

"A marvelous job with the passport, old buddy. We're off now, Miss Byrne and I. If anyone asks for Miss Schmitt, the answer is: on vacation, left three days ago. And please mail this letter to Major Baumgarten for us, but not from the embassy box."

"Thanks for reminding me, sir," said Corcoran with a sarcastic smile. "Oh, and do bring me back some Swiss chocolate if you can remember. They say it'll make my hair grow back. And how will you get to the *Bahnhof*? Not by taxi, I suppose."

"Glad you asked," Driscoll said with affection and slapped him on the shoulder. "Why don't you drive us and take the rest of the day off. My responsibility. I'll square it with the boss."

"Splendid thought, sir. I'm happy to be of service."

His car was an old Benz two-door which would never pass a safety inspection. But it got them to the station on time to catch the express train to Leipzig, Munich, Basel and Milan.

* * *

"I'm sorry, sir," Schellenberg mumbled into the telephone. As it was, the Prague connection was poor, though the static had done nothing to meliorate the expletives with which Heydrich had showered him. "Most unusual situation, sir. Richter did not report in. In fact, he didn't return to his lodgings which he shares with two other officers. He got the letter from the Marshal. After that he apparently showed up here again asking for you, but you had already left for Prague. With your permission, I'd like the guys from *Kripo* to help us locate him."

Heydrich agreed readily. "Tell Müller to put as many men on the job as necessary. I don't give a shit about Richter, but I want the letter. It's from the Führer. Secret instructions. So move your butt and tell Müller's boys to do likewise. Ten to one Richter's been screwing some broad. Have the boys look at his girl friends."

"Yes, sir, and we'll also have a go at Baumgarten's sweetheart, the one said to be Jewish. Richter had all the facts in his head, but we'll be able to backtrack and find her."

"Very good," said the new Protector of Bohemia and Moravia. "Richter *was* going to look her up, he told me so, and I warned him not to lay her unless he knew she was Aryan. He promised, but in that regard we can't ever be sure our men will observe the rules, can we?"

Schellenberg kept quiet. For the moment the chief seemed pacified.

* * *

Kenneth Driscoll and Helga settled back in their second-class compartment. Driscoll had decided against first-class travel; too conspicuous, he reasoned. An elderly couple and an Army captain with an arm in a sling were sharing the travel.

Helga sat immobile, eyes closed, surveying an inner landscape passing by while the train clattered its way along its iron route. She dozed off. Rolf, Heinrich and Ken were all talking at once while her father looked into the compartment and opened the sliding door. She gave a start; the conductor was asking for the tickets. Her hands seemed unable to open her purse.

"Das Billet bitte, Fräulein." A second request, a little

more insistent this time. The Army captain looked at her.

"Of course. Excuse me." She fumbled, then stiffened. She had almost pulled the letter out instead of the ticket. Top secret, that's all she needed, and the game was over. Her hand shook as she finally produced the ticket.

The conductor punched it. "Thank you, Miss. You're not the first to lose a ticket in a big purse like that," he said, returning it to her.

Helga thrust the ticket back into the cavern of her purse, closing the snap. "I'd like to stretch my legs," she said to Driscoll and motioned for him to follow her into the corridor.

"I almost produced the letter instead of the ticket," she whispered when they were standing outside. "I'd completely forgotten about it. I think you'd better take it. They won't search you."

They walked toward the end of the car, by the washroom, and made the transfer.

"I'll have a look at it," he said. "Go back and stand near the compartment. I'll visit the toilet."

She was standing by the window when Driscoll returned. He seemed deeply disturbed and spoke so softly she could hardly hear him.

"It's a letter from Hitler ordering the extermination of every Jew in Europe. Addressed to Göring. Heydrich is supposed to be the chief executioner. It's beyond belief. The maniac really means to do it. Killing millions of people in cold blood because of his racial idiocy. Heydrich apparently asked your brother. . ."

He caught himself when he saw her expression.

"I didn't mean to put it that way. Richter must have been the messenger to obtain the letter."

"Now what?"

"This is news that needs communication on the highest level. I'm not a diplomat. Maybe we should discuss it with our ambassador in Bern. In fact, we have other business in Switzerland. Money, for instance. How much cash have you, if I may ask?"

"Not much," she said. "Something like fifty marks. But I have a good deal in England. I could wire for it, if that's possible in wartime and if it's safe to use my real name. That's the only way I'll have access to the funds."

"Once we're across the border, we'll inquire, though we'll still have to be careful. Even in Switzerland the walls may have ears. Meanwhile, the Chargé's five hundred dollars will go a long way, and you can repay it later. America won't go broke over it."

The train stopped laboriously. "Leipzig," the conductor called. A few people got off, among them the elderly couple and the captain from their compartment.

* * *

At five o'clock Schellenberg reached Heydrich again. He was making progress. Still no sign of Richter, but they had been to Miss Schmitt's room in Moabit. Found a note that she had gone on vacation for a week. A civilian was sent to the embassy and asked for her. Same story: on vacation for the last three days. So there didn't seem to be an observable link with Richter's disappearance. Unless, of course, they were lying.

"Keep checking," said Heydrich. "Americans have no character. Can't speak the truth. Infected by the Jew plague."

"Sir, there's one other development the *Kripo* came up with. They found Richter's car. By the Radio Tower."

"So?"

"There's a good chance Richter was involved in foul play. Door, steering wheel and clutch were wiped clean."

"Well, I'll be damned," Heydrich said softly. "I don't

like it, not one bit. I'd better call the Marshal. I'm glad I'm not in Berlin, he'd be tearing my balls off."

Schellenberg, perceiving his boss to be in an uncommonly vulnerable position, decided to confirm his own status as a confidant of the Hangman.

"If I may be permitted to ask, sir, what exactly are we looking for – the letter I mean? We could identify people who might have an interest in obtaining it. For blackmail, for instance. As it is, we're in the dark."

Heydrich was many things, but not a fool. He knew his subordinate's request made sense, yet the Führer's directive was so sensitive that it should not become public before it could be properly executed. And he himself could not go ahead full steam until he cleared up the mess in Bohemia which von Neurath had left behind.

"Sir? Are you still on the line?"

"I'll tell you this: it's a letter from the Führer himself. The content is classified. I don't think blackmail is involved or any profit motive. It's my judgment that the loss of the letter is an accidental by-product of Richter's disappearance. I'll go further and say that Richter is probably dead. Is there a chance Baumgarten got wind of our investigation? Be sure all his mail is intercepted. And go back to the dame's place. Maybe the clue is there. If the letter is lost or burned, it's not serious, we can live with that. But we don't want it in the wrong hands, especially Jews and foreign governments. One more thing: increase the reward for our contact inside the embassy. Schmitt worked there. Maybe she left some evidence."

"Yes, sir. And thanks for giving me new ideas."

"Don't spoil things with flattery. Call me in the morning. Heil Hitler!"

* * *

Driscoll and Helga reached Munich a few minutes behind schedule. There was enough time to buy a newspaper; no mention of any mysterious disappearance or murder in Berlin. When they returned to their car, the conductor greeted them with an apology. There would be an unforeseen delay. German trains had a reputation for punctuality, even in wartime, and it was bad form to arrive late in Switzerland where being on time was a religion.

"Be calm," Driscoll advised Helga. "Above all, don't show anxiety. I know it's tough but likely as not the delay has nothing to do with us. So let's not buy trouble."

"I'm worried about my accent. My German is too good and my English not good enough," Helga said.

"There's a trick. Speak German slowly as if searching for words. Pronounce the German 'ch' in *ich* as if it were a 'ch' in *kochen*. That may be enough to give credence to your papers. Remember, our tickets are to Milan, so there'll be less suspicion that we're escaping to Switzerland."

The conductor reappeared.

"The delay will be short," he told them. "There's a priority shipment for which the tracks must be cleared. Many rumors about it, but one doesn't ask questions. After all, there's a war on."

"Does this happen often?" Helga asked.

"Just lately, miss. Large shipments. Top secret, I hear. There, they're passing now. . ."

A long train rumbled by, hiding its cargo in cattle cars, forty of them, all identical, with nothing to give away the secrets stored within.

"For God's sake, Ken," said Helga as the conductor left, "are these shipments to the East? Jews and other undesirables?"

"I'm afraid so. That's what the letter is about, isn't it?" Driscoll patted his pocket. "So they've really started."

A car was moving alongside them. Two hands could be

seen clutching at the opening. Two hands begging for help. Helga stared as if transfixed, tears welling up in her eyes. Driscoll too was shaken.

A few moments later their train was on its way again, putting kilometers between them and the cars bound for hell.

* * *

In a fourth-floor apartment in Moabit a child opened the window of the rear bedroom to hear some pebbles he had collected hit the bottom of the air shaft. It was a game he and his sister played frequently. He listened for the expected *plop* but there was none. He peered into the gathering dusk below and screamed when he saw the dead man.

The homicide squad was interrogating the residents on the upper floors when the special unit charged with the Schmitt investigation arrived on the scene. A jurisdictional squabble broke out which finally resulted in a compromise. The two *Kripo* squads agreed that the earlier arrival would proceed in the accustomed way and establish the identity of the victim. The second team was charged with finding clues in the Schmitt habitat.

Night had fallen and flashlights had to supplement the poor illumination in the flat. The air shaft was darker still.

The body could not be identified, but in Schmitt's bedroom a number of hairs were found on the pillow, in sufficient quantity to suggest that they had been cut off in bed. Also the man wore no underwear, indicating a hasty exit from the room. The bed sheet revealed dried yellow spots which appeared to be semen.

The sergeant reread his instructions:

> *Scour the room for anything that connects occupant with Major Baumgarten or* Sturmbannführer *Richter.*

Gather all letters, note and address books. Report findings to central Kripo *headquarters. They'll direct you further.*

The sergeant decided that to move the dead man might disturb evidence. He would keep watch and examine the scene further, especially since at this midnight hour the corporal in charge of the other squad was happy to yield all investigatory prerogatives.

"I'm going back to headquarters. Anything I should tell them?"

"Yes," said the sergeant, a police officer of the old school, "report what we've found. If Schmitt or other occupants of this flat return, we'll detain them. Meanwhile, you might convey my preliminary conclusions that Schmitt was involved in foul play, possibly as an active agent or accessory, and that she ought to be found forthwith. She's left word that she's away on vacation, which increases my suspicion. I'll report first thing in the morning."

At two o'clock wires were going out to all national precincts as well as border points to locate a certain Hilde Schmitt, age twenty-four, medium height, dark hair. *If with companion, hold same as well.*

Shortly after two o'clock the train pulled into Lörrach and the police went on board. They came in teams of two, one to check passports, exit stamps and compliance with customs regulations; the other, from the Gestapo, to view those leaving the country. They knocked on Helga's door first. She, in turn, rapped at the dividing wall to warn Ken. By the time she had put an overcoat over her nightgown, Driscoll was engaging the attention of the officers.

"Ah, diplomatic status," said the customs man, handing Driscoll's papers to his Gestapo companion. "Bound for Milan, I see."

"Actually for Rome," Driscoll responded.

The Gestapo man leafed through the passport with exaggerated thoroughness, shone his flashlight on Driscoll's face and picture and went on to Helga.

"Emily Byrne," he read with a remarkably good English accent. "Also diplomatic status, I see. American. . ." There was an acerbic undertone in his voice. He looked at her picture, shone the torch in her face, then back onto the passport.

Looking at her once again, he gave the passport back. The customs man was already knocking at the door of the next compartment. There was no answer. They summoned the conductor and had him open the door, to make sure no one was hiding there. They did the same with the toilet, then left for the next car.

* * *

At the police precinct two blocks away from the station a supplemental telegram was delivered:

> *Schmitt may be in company of American diplomat K. Driscoll. Care must be taken not to interfere with him.*

The officer was alone at his post and wondered whether it was proper to leave and show the wire to the men on duty with the international *D-Zug*, now at the depot. He decided it was; he locked up and mounted his bicycle. As he reached the *Bahnhof*, he saw the tail lights of the caboose slowly disappearing into the night toward the Swiss border.

* * *

Driscoll was dozing when a tap at his door brought him to full alertness.

"Ken, it's me."

He jumped out of bed and opened the door slightly.

"May I come in?" Helga whispered.

"Of course. I should not have left you alone so soon after that ordeal."

"I'm all right, Ken. I've become pretty tough."

She closed the door behind her. The compartment was intermittently lighted by the street lamps of a town through which they were passing on their way from Basel to Bern. She watched the houses pass by, standing mute in the dark landscape.

"I owe you my life, Ken. Is it possible to love two men at the same time?"

She took Driscoll's face in her hands and kissed him slowly and gently. He disengaged himself and drew down the shade.

14

They arrived in Bern in the early-morning hours. There was no taxi in sight. Across the square from the station the gingerbread façade of a hotel proclaimed that Wilhelm Tell, if he had not actually lodged here, had at least given it his heroic name. They rang for the porter, who led them into a rather shabby lobby.

No, the clerk was not there yet, he would arrive at six. Sorry, there was no way he could rent them a room, but would they please make themselves comfortable. That was all he could suggest.

The clerk came in good time; his natty director's suit stood in pleasant contrast to the run-down appearance of the entrance hall. Yes, two adjoining rooms were available. He took their passports, seemed pleased they were Americans and led them to their chambers. He would return the papers in the afternoon when the police had gone through the formalities of registering them. Yes, even diplomats had to follow this routine. He agreed it was unnecessary, even demeaning – still, what could one do, law was law.

Driscoll had phoned the American embassy and made an appointment to see the ambassador. He turned out to be a pleasant man, not a career diplomat but rather one of Roosevelt's campaign supporters, a business executive with

Arab-American Petroleum Trust. At the Berlin embassy the scuttlebutt had it that Ambassador William C. Fairfax IV would be replaced if America went to war against Germany, and the Bern post, suddenly highly sensitive, would require a professional.

Fairfax listened to Driscoll's tale with detached amusement. The cops-and-robbers story appealed to him with his Texas background of daring and adventure. A bit irregular, but what the hell! The Nazis didn't play fair ball either. Driscoll depicted Helga as endangered because her Jewish background had been discovered and she had come into possession of a highly explosive document.

The ambassador read the letter and gave it back to Driscoll.

"How did you get hold of it, miss?"

"Through someone who wanted the document to reach U.S. public opinion. He knew I worked at the embassy."

She was astonished at the ease with which she had altered the truth.

"Don't you think, sir," Driscoll asked, "that the highest circles in Washington ought to see it?"

"Well," said Fairfax, "I don't know about that. We've taken the position that Hitler's anti-Semitism is basically an internal matter. We wouldn't want them to butt into our business and start stirring up the niggers, would we? And, after all, we did convene the Evian Conference and are generous with admitting refugees. I won't prevent you from showing the letter to the State Department, but I predict minor interest in another Hitler directive, although I'll say it might some day make a splendid collector's item. As for the young lady's cover, keep the U.S. passport until you get home, Major Driscoll. You were authorized to travel with her, were you not?"

"No, sir, not really. I was going to put her on a plane to Britain, with a letter to the embassy there, and let her go from London to America by herself. She has contacts in England where she's lived for a while. In the U.S. my father-in-law, Senator Browning, will take her in hand."

"I'll be damned," said Fairfax, "I know the Senator well. Sound man. My wife and I would be pleased to have you for dinner tonight, unless of course you're leaving right away."

They thanked him warmly and accepted. They would probably stay for a day or two.

* * *

The Berlin police had more than a mere suspicion that Driscoll had something to do with Heinrich Richter's demise. The pathologist had found that death had been due to suffocation; and Richter's identity was quickly established. Hilde Schmitt had been under investigation by Richter, and the confidential police report confirmed that he and the woman had had sexual relations. Whether Schmitt was Jewish, as an informant had suggested, remained unknown. She was working at the embassy and was seen socially with Driscoll.

Two days after Richter's death, a cleaning woman, attracted by the reward that the police had offered, had opened Driscoll's desk and found some car keys. They turned out to belong to Richter's Adler. The American was apparently an accessory after the fact and had spirited Schmitt out of the country. It was deemed likely that Driscoll had received the letter from Schmitt. From here on he would be on the Nazi hit list wherever he was, even in America.

The border police recollected his passage through Lörrach with a young woman who showed them a diplomatic passport. The suspects had remarked that they were bound for Milan and Rome. Meanwhile, there was a chance they might still be in Switzerland. Extradition would be requested for

Schmitt the moment she was found. Driscoll's movements would be monitored. The German envoy received the coded information and had his Swiss contacts stake out the American embassy, which was easy to do for the building was situated in a park-like setting with a limited access road.

* * *

There were rumors in Prague that Heydrich's increased cruelty in his treatment of the Czech population was partly due to the abuse he had to take from Göring. The Fat One had showered him with every vulgar epithet he could think of, and even some of which the Protector of Bohemia and Moravia had never heard, when he conveyed the news of the murder of the messenger and the disappearance of the letter. When Göring had finished his monologue, it was understood that Hitler would not be informed and that it would be doubly important to expedite the plan for the "Final Solution." This was the Führer's new cover word.

"I'll see to it myself, *Herr* Reich Marshal," Heydrich promised. "No messengers this time. Also, we'll spare no effort to apprehend the murderer or murderers. They probably have the letter and may already be abroad. But we shall track them down and see that justice is done."

"I hear you're suspecting someone from the American embassy. Don't let him get off easy just because he has a diplomatic passport. Even diplomats can have accidents."

* * *

Ken and Helga had spent the day arranging their finances and making plans. They had also secreted the letter. Driscoll thought that the original should be stowed away until it could be produced without endangering the carrier. Could Helga memorize the text?

The Berner Landbank and Savings Society was glad to

open an anonymous numbered account for her. Using the name Emily Byrne, she deposited two hundred francs and rented a safety box for the document; the two keys would remain at the embassy. She left written instructions that the rental fees for the box would be paid automatically from the interest accrued in her deposit or from the capital, if necessary. The manager was courteous and assured them that any inquiries would be turned away. It was not the habit of his bank, he asserted, to breach the confidentiality of their transactions. "And I mean for anyone," he added with self-righteous vigor.

The taxi deposited Helga and Ken at the embassy, where they found everyone in a state of shock and disarray. The Japanese had bombed Pearl Harbor; reports of the damage were incomplete; Roosevelt would be addressing Congress; and America was now at war. Germany would undoubtedly join the Japanese; Hitler was expected to make the announcement shortly.

"We're suddenly living on an island here," said Ambassador Fairfax. "We'll have to see what our instructions will be. If anything, we may be receiving additional personnel."

When Driscoll telephoned Berlin, the Chargé advised him not to come back. A declaration of war was expected momentarily; he would be one more person to be evacuated. "Let Washington decide where they want you to go next."

Dinner with Ambassador Fairfax and his wife was an informal occasion weighted down with the ever-worsening news. American warships had been devastated at Pearl Harbor. Only one other guest was present, Dr. Bertha Klaus, a dentist who practised in Bern. She was a handsome woman of about sixty, with jet-black hair combed straight back and an open face with sparkling eyes. She was a widow who had no children and came from a well-established family. Dr. Klaus had an estate on Lake Thun where she spent most summer days.

Helga liked her at once and her feelings were reciprocated. "If you need anything," Dr. Klaus said, "I'll be glad to help."

When Helga and Ken Driscoll returned to the hotel, the concierge was apologetic. He handed Driscoll his passport but did not have Helga's.

"I'm sorry, miss. The police have not returned it."

"Why not?" She was alarmed.

"I really couldn't say. They never tell us."

Early the next day a police constable arrived. Would Miss Byrne please come to headquarters? There were some questions to ask.

Driscoll went with her. They knew that Heydrich and company were after them and that Helga's part in Richter's death had been exposed.

The lieutenant in charge of Helga's papers was a short, stocky man with thick glasses and ash-blond hair. He spoke in crisp sentences and exuded authority. There was some doubt about Miss Byrne's identity. In the light of day the passport picture did not match her appearance as well as could be expected. He was led to his doubts by a request from the highest German authorities for the extradition of Miss Byrne who, they claimed, was Hilde Schmitt, probably an alias for someone else, who was wanted for murder.

"Wanted for murder?" said Driscoll. "You can't be serious."

"I'm afraid I am. We Swiss don't like to be involved in such matters, but we have little choice. We are in a precarious situation with Germany next door. We can't afford to provoke them."

"What will happen now?" Helga asked.

"Miss, we refer all extradition requests to the Minister of Justice. Meanwhile, I must ask you not to leave the city or change hotels."

They considered the alternatives. Sanctuary at the embassy was one option, but only as a last resort. The Swiss were afraid of the Germans and, in any case, accepting refugees was not their strong suit. The fact that Helga had some money in England was an advantage; new bank accounts were always welcome. If Helga were to return to her own identity, she would be marked as a Jew, and most Jewish refugees from Germany were either turned back at the border or deported.

Helga decided to see Dr. Klaus and tell her the whole story. The brave front she had maintained during the past days broke apart. She was once more the despised Jew who had lived underground, the child who had lost her parents, the violated woman and now the hunted fugitive.

Dr. Klaus was warm and sympathetic.

"I have some connections. There are people who owe me a favor. It will cost them nothing to leave you here. If they can accept you as a Jewish refugee, they can probably disregard the extradition charge. Frankly, I believe the Germans are after the document more than after you and they may reckon that Major Driscoll has it, if it has not already been sent to America. If I may offer a bystander's opinion, I would say that your friend is in some danger, even in our country. Tell him to be careful. And you stay put for a few days. Our bureaucracy does not work at top speed. Besides, I know the Minister, and he's away in Rome or Madrid."

She looked intently at Helga.

"Would you consider staying with me? I have lots of room here and even more at the lake. You said you had some training in dental hygiene when you were in England. Maybe you could work with me in my practice and have further training. I'll arrange a special permit with the Minister."

* * *

Driscoll agreed with Helga's decision. He would, in any case, be reassigned somewhere. Even in this shrinking world of great powers at war, there was still room for diplomacy. She could not come with him, unless she was ready to marry him.

She looked at him with deep affection.

"No, darling, not now anyway. I can't just leave Rolf stuck in the trenches in Russia. I don't even know whether he's alive."

"We could find out," Ken said. "The Swiss could act as our sleuths. They could make an inquiry of General Halder's headquarters."

* * *

Two days later Hitler declared war on the United States. The war, he stated, had been provoked by the Jews and American millionaires who had found their spokesman in the "real culprit," Franklin D. Roosevelt. He had brought his country to economic ruin and saw no other way to save his skin than to start a war, a resolution suggested to him by the Jews in his entourage. "We know that the aim of their struggle is to destroy one nation after another." The Reichstag members jumped to their feet and cheered. The American embassy was closed and its occupants left the capital.

That night Driscoll was returning from the embassy to the hotel when an automobile careened onto the sidewalk and knocked him down. The assailants drove off undetected. He was shaken but not seriously hurt. The car had tried to run him over, and there was a strong possibility that this would not be the only attempt on his life.

Ken and Helga knew they would be parting. One lover had gone east, the other would travel west. As she lay next to Ken, she wondered what would be in store for her.

Sooner or later she would be drawn back into the turmoil of a world where she could in some way avenge her parents.

The next day their hotel rooms were searched and vandalized. Swastikas were drawn with lipstick on the bathroom mirrors. Driscoll left for Portugal and America; and Helga, now officially Helga Raben and a natural blond once again, was permitted to stay in Switzerland as a Jewish refugee who had some funds and an influential protector. The war had now become worldwide, and Helga retreated into the residence of a generous woman. Emily Byrne had disappeared from the records of the Swiss police. "Left Switzerland" was the official entry.

15

"Be sure to order a good lunch," Heydrich said to his adjutant, a drab youth who would have served up his own mother if the chief had ordered it. "We have delectable business at hand which deserves proper reward. There'll be fifteen of us."

"Zu Befehl, Herr Obergruppenführer," acknowledged the young man, clicking his heels.

They were meeting at the R.S.H.A. offices on the shores of Berlin's most fashionable suburban lake. The city's wealthiest businessmen had their homes on the Wannsee. The presence of the SS served as a constant reminder to the financial elite that their power was mere window dressing; the real movers and shakers resided at No. 50-58.

On January 20, 1942, fifteen men assembled to lay final plans to exterminate every last Jew in Europe, including those who lived in as-yet-unconquered Britain.

Half of the technicians of death whom Heydrich brought together were academics with a doctor's degree. They had studied law and philosophy, knew the poetry of Schiller and the prose of Kleist; they could recite Latin passages from Vergil and Greek stanzas from the *Iliad*; and they had, in all likelihood, a fair acquaintance with the Bible. They had been raised in the days of the Weimar Republic and had risen to important positions in the bureaucracy. Their portfolios covered Justice, External Affairs, Eastern Territories, the Führer's chancellery and assorted SS departments. They brought to the operation a lethal combination of intellectual acuity, technical efficiency and moral corruption.

Heydrich opened the meeting.

"You all know why you are here. The notice you received made it clear to you, who understand the specially coded language of destruction we have introduced. This morning of course there is no need to hide behind coded terms. We are not as squeamish as some of our staid and stupid citizens who can't bring themselves to crush a mosquito even when it carries malaria. I'm glad to see Fritz Lange here. He has set an exemplary standard for action in Riga.

"The Führer has now asked me to carry out his long-standing policy directive and organize the Final Solution for the human mosquitoes of the world. We start with those presently in our reach. The others will come later."

He did not mention the missing document or Göring's part in the chain of command. He was also careful to omit any participation of Himmler, who was technically his superior.

"The general principle is simple. Ship all Jews to the East. We'll use them for labor until they die off. Then we'll use others until they too croak. Those unable to work will be given a final, unchangeable address. We're working on a particularly effective compound and have already tried it out successfully on a thousand or so Russians. The most dangerous of Jews are of course those who survive the rigors of forced labor and starvation, for they are the hardiest and might restart their bastard race. We'll therefore make sure that they too become part of our Final Solution. Am I making myself clear?"

"Sir," asked a young, bland-looking officer who had been taking the minutes, "where shall all this human cargo be shipped? Into existing ghettos or new special purpose camps?"

"Glad you asked, Eichmann," said Heydrich, "for I've decided to make you responsible for collecting every Jew you can lay your hands on and shipping him east, mostly to Poland. At first to existing ghettos and then to the new places we've developed. By the time we get through, we'll be proud of names like Auschwitz, Birkenau, Sobibor and some others I can't pronounce yet. Special cases – certain well-known figures and decorated veterans of the last war – will go to Theresienstadt. I'll take care of that myself. The Poles won't object to our work. Many of them will be only too happy to help. That also goes for the Baltic states, the Ukraine and of course the Slovaks and Roumanians. The Hlinka and Iron guards fully support our program and have already exhibited an exemplary enthusiasm for it. Use them wherever you can."

"Thank you, *Herr Obergruppenführer*. I shall do my best to merit your confidence," said Adolf Eichmann, an unremarkable German bureaucrat whose moral fibers had shriveled in a poisonous mix of power and perceived duty. He headed the Gestapo's section IV-B-4 and represented the new civil servant who considered himself a deputized agent of divine providence as represented on earth by the Führer.

"Just do it quickly in my jurisdiction," said Dr. Josef Bühler, who was Secretary of State for the occupied eastern territories and was representing the notorious Hans Frank.

"I'll try my best, but I'll need trains, many of them," answered Eichmann. "Remember, we're dealing with millions of people." His heart swelled with excitement over the prospect.

"Don't remind us of our duty, Eichmann." Heydrich never failed to put his subordinates in place. "Don't step out of line or you'll get shitted on." He fell back into the lingo in which he was most comfortable. "You'll have all the trains you need. This is the Führer's priority. You'll get transportation even if the Army has to walk. Don't quote me on this one, though," he cautioned *Ministerialdirektor* Kritzinger who was taking notes for Hitler's office.

"Sir!" Bühler again. "I'm anxious to get this problem out of the way because there are people who are raising some questions about our methods."

Heydrich jumped from his chair; his long nose assumed the threatening posture of a dagger.

"You mean there are lousy Polacks who don't like it? That's too damn bad. Shoot them along with the Jews. They're subhumans anyway, good only for slave labor or the lime pits. Don't tell me you've been pampering those unwashed cretins?"

"Excuse me, sir, but I didn't refer to Poles at all. I meant a few of our own, especially in the Army and the occupation service. Some were asked to supplement our special death squads and they begged off or got sick. We're not sure what to do with them."

Before Heydrich could answer, the representative of the Justice Ministry and head of the People's Court, Dr. Roland Freisler, spoke up. He was renowned throughout the country as the "hanging judge." It was his belief that anyone accused of disloyalty to the Führer deserved to be executed. He would allow him his defense afterwards, he once joked.

"Permit me, *Herr Doktor*, to point out that if someone refuses to obey a direct order, he's guilty of battlefield dereliction, which is akin to desertion. Your people must be out of their minds even asking such questions. Shoot the bastards. Period. Set an example."

"With the greatest respect, Dr. Freisler, it's not that easy. After all, if I may mention it here, there was the incident with Reichsführer Himmler."

Heydrich, who knew precisely what Bühler was referring to, played dumb. Let someone take a swipe at the boss. It could only weaken his position. Leaning forward, he said innocently, "The Reichsführer himself? What the hell are you talking about?"

Bühler knew he had made a mistake. He had to answer, but the answer would get back to Himmler in whatever garbled fashion the informer chose to transmit it.

"Come on, Bühler, you opened your big snoot, so spit it out." Heydrich relished the man's discomfort.

"Well, sir, we had the Reichsführer on an inspection trip and he asked about the death squads. So we lined up a hundred Jewish men, women and children for him and had them go through their routine: dig their graves, take off their clothes and stand at the edge of the pit awaiting their turn to be shot. There was a small delay, however. A child got away and had to be dragged back, and a pretty young woman turned around shamelessly – you know the bitch was stark naked – and shouted: 'Himmler, you bastard, you too will die a miserable death!' Then they all said something in Hebrew before we could shoot them. And that's when the Reichsführer got sick and had to be led away."

"So?" asked Heydrich, who had heard the story a dozen times. He himself had been present when Himmler had fainted at an execution in Prague.

Bühler continued. "It got around like wildfire. If it's too much for the Reichsführer, it may be too much for ordinary mortals too. Thereafter the practice has been to excuse those who don't want to be in the death squads. I only mention this to make sure *Herr* Eichmann or whoever handles this part sends us the right people."

Somehow the eager, almost joyous mood of the meeting had been darkened. It took a while to get back on track. The general outline having been approved and Eichmann chosen as the one to carry out the most difficult part, the discussions turned to related problems: what to do with Jews married to Gentiles and with half and quarter Jews.

They argued about them for a good hour and felt much the better for it.

Heydrich ordered a summary to be made – with the proper code words of course – to be distributed to the relevant departments. The secret was out and the push was on. Given enough time, the Jews of Europe, some ten million of them, would simply disappear.

The lunch was elaborate, the wine excellent and everyone was jolly again.

When the men were leaving, Heydrich detained Müller, who as the head of the Gestapo was Eichmann's immediate superior.

"Keep an eye on that little Adolf," he told him, "let him know from time to time he's not performing as well as he could. The trick is not to let him go stale. He's the German bureaucrat who'll strive for perfection in anything he does. If you'd ask him to collect nuts and bolts for us, he'd do it with the same zeal. So keep him smart. Let him understand he's never perfect. After he gets finished with that, maybe we'll let him round up all homosexuals or everyone with the name of Müller."

The Gestapo chief laughed dutifully and promised to irritate Eichmann sufficiently to improve his output.

"Oh, one more thing, Müller. Did you ever hear anything more in the Richter matter? You know, the missing letter from the Führer? Are your men still working on it?"

"Yes, sir. The woman who appears to have killed Richter and taken the document to the American embassy escaped to Switzerland with her American boyfriend. Diplomatic fake papers which weren't caught at the border. We got an extradition order for her, but before we could grab her she must have gotten wind of it and disappeared. We haven't a clue, but personally I don't think she has the letter. What would she do with it? We're concentrating on this fellow Driscoll, the American. We tried to nab him in Bern but our man bungled it. So we think Driscoll has the letter and is about to show it around. Our agents are trying to arrange an accident before he gets too far."

Heydrich was pensive. "All right then, do the best you can. The letter, as you may have guessed, has to do with what we discussed this morning. The Führer himself instructed me to carry out the project to the end. The death squads we have organized have done their job well. I calculate that so far they've dispatched a couple of hundred thousand Jews to meet Jehovah face to face. But that's peanuts with what's yet to come. And while I'd be proud and happy to do it on my own, I prefer to have the written order from the very top. I got instructions from the Fat One, but it's not the same. You understand, don't you?"

Müller nodded. Like his boss, he was well aware of the moral doubt that a lot of people, especially the older ones, had about the deportations, and they didn't even know what befell the deportees. A slaughter operation involving millions was a stupendous enterprise with incalculable consequences. Yes, he too would want Hitler's signature for it.

"Sir, I meant to tell you about an old associate of yours, Colonel Baumgarten, General Halder's protégé."

"Oh, yes, I'd forgotten all about him."

"Well, sir, you may continue to do so. He's been reported missing in action."

Heydrich's face brightened. He slapped his knee.

"*Gut weg*, that bastard!" he bellowed in glee. "An unreliable guy if I ever saw one. He shacked up with that dame who killed Richter, and I wondered all along whether maybe the letter got to him. Also, he had some fancy friends who were up to no good."

"Yes, sir, that circle is still alive. Now, with the Russian counter-offensive on and our troops temporarily stalled, some of the old Junker types are at it again. We hear rumors that there are Army officers who do not believe we can win this war."

"Well, crap on them! The Führer is in complete command

and he's committed to total victory."

"That's just what the rumor is all about," Müller said. "Apparently those officers want to replace Hitler himself."

Heydrich stared at him.

"Are you serious? Why aren't they being lined up and shot?"

"We're not really sure who they are and whether there's more to it than rumor. But indications are that if the Kreisau circle – around Moltke, you remember – if they had anything to do with such thinking, Baumgarten definitely belonged to them."

"Well, good. So there's one less. Keep it up, Müller. Good news about the letter will earn you a promotion. Now I've got to get back to Prague. My wife is pregnant. And, besides, it's time to teach those Czech rebels a few lessons. I'm thinking of using some of the torture instruments from the castle dungeon. You know, those policemen in the Middle Ages, they knew their business. Marvelous ingenuity! I'm learning from them. Good-bye for now, Müller. Heil Hitler!"

* * *

Driscoll's return to the States was uneventful at first. He had traveled to Portugal, via Vichy, France, had kept a low profile and after a while had caught a military plane to London. But when he reported to the embassy there, he was kept on special assignment to observe convoy activities. At last, in late April, he was ordered home. A liberty ship brought him to New York, after a German submarine had been chased away by an American destroyer.

He phoned his department in Washington and was told to take three weeks off before reporting for reassignment. The rather offhand way in which this welcome news was issued bothered him briefly, but he was soon involved in family affairs.

His wife Cathy was unpleasant when he called, his two

boys were in school and neither could come to see him. They sounded distant. Yes, Driscoll said, he would visit them in Boston, although the idea of a meeting with Cathy appalled him. Their divorce proceedings were dragging on. His lawyer had joined the Navy and had handed his file to a colleague who knew more about real estate than matrimonial law. It was not a happy homecoming. In New York, where he had taken a room at the Algonquin, he was very lonely. He missed Helga and discovered what in the swift currents of the last months had been submerged: he was in love with her. He was more than ten years older than she, yet her courage, her ability to face danger and her intelligence made her meet extraordinary challenges with maturity. And when the pressures were off, she was vivacious and outgoing, as he had discovered in better days at the embassy.

That she was also involved with Rolf Baumgarten did not worry him. He sensed that she was leaning away from the German, and who knew what the war had in store for him? If he could bring her to America, she would be his, he felt, and the conspiracy would be at an end.

He realized he could not communicate with her under his own name. This was one matter they had failed to arrange when they parted. The night had been long and the loving intense; intrigue had taken a holiday. Now the holiday was over, and in a strange way the tables were turned: she lived under her real name and he had to adopt a pseudonym in order not to jeopardize her.

Dear Helga,
You have probably wondered what happened to me since we saw each other last in England. I have been transferred to New York but will be here only temporarily. Even so, it might be better if you wrote to me at General Delivery in New York.

My firm wants me to take more German lessons so

I can better manage the Swiss trade, but I have real trouble with the pronunciation, as you know. I can never get the ch *right, when I try to say* ich *everyone laughs. And my* s *often acts like a chameleon and becomes a* th. *Why can't the whole world speak English? Everything would be so much easier.*

Do you think you could ever get time off from work and visit America? I'm sure a visa should not be hard to arrange. I'd show you a marvelous *time. Did you know that ever since we spent those few days together I have been dreaming about you?*

America is getting full steam into the war. Loads of stuff going to Britain. The tide will turn soon. We'll hold out, I hope the Russians will too.

Your Stephen Daimler

He posted the letter and took a leisurely walk through the theater district, now somewhat robbed of its peacetime elegance. His sons were on his mind and the rather abrupt telephone message from Washington jogged his memory. He decided to go to Boston and face his problems squarely. But when he returned to his room, he found it had been ransacked. His personal papers were gone, among them a summary of Hitler's letter. A swastika had been painted on the bathroom mirror with soap.

The letter – it was part of those things he meant to look after. Contact people, let them know, wake them up. He castigated himself for letting his personal concerns override the needs of millions. He decided he had come to a turning in the road and would take up the challenge.

On 42nd Street he bought a revolver, checked out of the hotel and, instead of traveling to Boston, took the train to Washington first thing next morning.

The Swiss embassy in Berlin did its job efficiently. Their inquiries, ostensibly made on behalf of a Bernese friend, received a terse reply: Colonel Baumgarten was reported missing.

Dr. Bertha Klaus broke the news to Helga as gently as it was possible. "I too once lost a lover," she added. "I have some idea of your pain, though that doesn't relieve the agony, does it?"

Helga looked blankly out the window. It was raining and from time to time large drops rolled down the pane. She watched them with an aimless, dull fascination, as if waiting for the last quick descent. The gray sky invaded the room, bathing it in a murky twilight. It was a mood hospitable to tears, yet Helga shed none.

"Missing," she repeated time and again. "Missing. . ."

Dr. Klaus shared Helga's desolation. "I wish I had something comforting to say. Yet 'missing' also spells hope, doesn't it?" Dr. Klaus held her hand. "I can ask our Foreign Service to inquire now and then whether there's news. . ."

They were silent.

"It's so unreal," Helga said at last. "Here I am safe and sound. Children play, people plan their future. And at the front, human beings are torn apart or disappear – missing – and I can't even cry!"

But cry she did, long and bitterly. Dr. Klaus embraced her like a mother consoling a child.

"You're not religious, are you, Helga? There's solace in relating to something greater than oneself."

"I think deep down I am a believer, though I'm a stranger to the synagogue. When I was in London back in '38, I sometimes went to prayer services on the Sabbath and didn't understand a word. But there was something there that spoke to me and made me feel good. Yes, maybe I am religious after all. And I think I would like to go to the synagogue here. There's a Jewish community in Bern, isn't there?"

"Oh, yes," Dr. Klaus reassured her quickly, "and they have a lovely building. I know the rabbi. I'm sure you'd like him. I'll be happy to go with you."

She kissed Dr. Klaus. "You've been so good to me. Like an angel from God."

Dr. Klaus, an occasional church-goer, and Helga, a Jew despite herself, attempted to make a largely incomprehensible synagogue service their ambience for seeking comfort. It was a Saturday morning; the attendance was sparse, older men predominated. The rabbi, a short, bespectacled man in a black robe, prayer scarf and four-cornered tiara, spoke about the special period of the Jewish calendar. "We are in the midst of counting time," he explained, "when we count each day between Passover and Pentecost, until the fifty days are full.

"The world too has its counting time, the world too is marking off each day. But while in our religious calendar we look toward a great and joyous festival which will climax this period, the world looks in growing anxiety toward Armageddon. Jews remember Pentecost when the law was proclaimed: today we fear that a German Pentecost may mean the proclamation of lawlessness as the greatest law of all."

He paused and fingered his prayer shawl.

"And here we seem to be living on an island of safety. We have our beautiful land and are, at least for now, a fortress of repose. Therefore, many of our countrymen don't want to get involved with the problems that surround us. They don't want refugees in Switzerland, they push them back into Nazi hands. Is this morality? Can there be physical security without an ethical foundation?"

The congregation stirred uneasily. The rabbi's critique of national policy, accurate though everyone knew it to be, was not a popular subject. The older generation were brought up to believe that Jews were best neither seen nor heard in public.

"Besides, it must be clear that Swiss neutrality will evaporate if the Germans should win this war. They leave us alone only because it is temporarily convenient for them. But let no Swiss citizen, and especially no Jew, delude himself and think that nothing can happen to us. Wrong! What happened in Czechoslovakia and Holland will befall us as well. And we Jews too will be loaded in cattle cars and shipped off to destinations unknown."

Several men rose from their seats and made a demonstrative exit. The rabbi waited until the protesters had left.

"Dear people, running away from reality will not save us. So what will? Faith of course, and prayer. But that won't suffice in the face of such overwhelming evil. Each one of us must do something. None is too insignificant. Each person has a realm of action, from giving charity to housing a refugee, from speaking to others about his convictions to opposing publicly the growing xenophobia in this country. And, finally, everyone must support the determination of those who will vow to make our free Helvetia strong and never surrender without a fight. Never!"

Helga felt as if the rabbi had addressed her directly, as if he had asked her: What are *you* doing? She was startled from her dark reverie when the service was over. Dr. Klaus introduced her to the rabbi.

"Helga Raben? A relative of the famous industrialist?"

She nodded.

"Ah, yes, of course, everyone knew his name. A tragic end. I'm afraid that your first visit here exposed you to some harsh words. I hope you'll come again."

"Thank you. Yes, I will. You spoke to me personally. I have not been doing enough. I must do more. Thank you for spurring me on."

Dr. Klaus put her arm around Helga. "Don't say that, dear. You've been doing at least one great thing: you have saved yourself. You're one Jew who has cheated the Nazis."

"Perhaps so. But I've promised myself that won't be the end. Look at you, Dr. Klaus, you've been a refuge to me and to others before me. I'm sure you don't ever say: enough. Well, I won't say it either. I made up my mind some time ago. This morning you, *Herr Rabbiner*, made sure I wouldn't forget. Thank you again."

The rabbi bade them good-bye with the traditional Sabbath wish. The May sun shone brightly on the gabled roofs of the capital.

When they returned home, the maid handed Helga a letter. She read Driscoll's coded message, paused a moment as if to assess the consequences, then passed it to Dr. Klaus. "If there is a God, He has given me a sign. I'll go to America. I have a mission to fulfill."

They spoke of Hitler's letter in the safety box.

"I must let the world know of it. You heard what the rabbi said, and he said it to me: everyone has a duty, everyone can do something. I don't want to kill, I want to save people. But if I have to kill to prevent greater evil, I will."

The dentist did not try to hold her back. She put her hand on Helga's.

"This house will always be open to you. If you need me, let me know. Your cause is my cause. Remember there are some good Swiss around who try to do the right thing. Our official policy is narrow and inhospitable and I'm ashamed of it. Some day we'll feel guilty. Today, I'm afraid, all we do is feel smug and self-righteous. Of course you know, Helga, I'm sad that you're leaving. I've become very attached to you. But my personal feelings don't count. There's a greater duty. Even a lapsed Christian like myself admits to that."

On Monday Helga went to the American embassy to inquire about a visa. She stood in line for an hour, and when her turn came the officer was cordial.

"Ken Driscoll has left a specific request to help you," he said. "He's also suggested the ambassador himself meet you in case you have a message for him. Let me see whether he's in."

The new ambassador, Leland Harrison, personified an American envoy, crisply clothed, erect bearing, yet with the informality of his countrymen. He greeted Helga with an outstretched hand.

"Glad you came. Driscoll asked us not to pester you but to wait until you're ready. Oh, and this is Howard Elting, our Vice-Consul in Geneva. He'll be interested in what you have to say."

Elting was of the same type as the ambassador, with quick motions and a concerned eye.

"Miss Raben," said Harrison, "Ken Driscoll told me the broad outline of your story and referred to an important letter you had chanced upon. Do you mind elaborating a bit?"

"No, sir, on the contrary. I was hoping to go to the States precisely to spread the news."

She told how an SS messenger whom she had known when she lived in Germany under an assumed name had "dropped the letter." She had read it and, without showing the contents to Driscoll, then her employer, had asked for help to escape the country because she was a marked woman. She had brought the letter to Switzerland and would be prepared to show it to the gentlemen. She had memorized its contents.

Helga recited the text. The two men sat still and did not speak for a long time.

"The letter is further confirmation of our suspicions," Elting finally said. "Rumor has it that large-scale measures against Jews are now being carried out in a manner far exceeding our worst fears. But we still lack proof and an exact picture of what is happening somewhere in the East."

The ambassador interrupted Elting.

"That Hitler document is damn important. If you don't mind, Miss Raben, let one of my men photograph it and I'll send it to Washington. You have the original stowed away safely?"

"Yes, sir, in a bank vault."

"Keep it there. We can have a copy made there and you put it back. Should the original be required, you can always produce it. A Swiss safety deposit box is safer than the lock on St. Peter's gate."

"I'll be glad to put it at your disposal, sir," Helga said, "but having lived underground I have come to suspect everybody. There was at least one spy in the Berlin embassy, and I'd like you to make sure that the person coming to the vault with me is someone you absolutely trust. If that's not too impertinent to suggest," she added.

The ambassador was impressed.

"I'll make sure. You're quite an operative for a young lady, you know. But let me add one caution: don't expect any miracles. Washington may have other priorities. Besides, they don't want to fall into some propaganda trap. So they'll be leery. Therefore, you go ahead and see what you can do to convince them. I'll make the arrangements. At such quick notice all I can manage is a visitor's visa. That means you're allowed a limited time in the States and you may not work."

"Thank you, sir, thank you very much."

"There's another reason why you'll run into some roadblocks," Elting spoke up. "If the ambassador won't mind my saying it: not everyone is crazy about Jews. They're not top-drawer interest, to put it mildly. The Evian Conference a few years ago was proof of that. I have some Jewish contacts in Geneva and they'll be worried about this document. Most worried."

Helga's visit to the bank turned out to be an obstacle course. She was suddenly unsure of the box number and, when asked for identification, could not establish herself as Emily Byrne. Her passport was with the Swiss police, or perhaps it had even been returned to Germany. Elting, who had accompanied her and the photographer, thought an inquiry too risky.

"Let it go for now, Miss Raben, and better leave for the States. After all, if the passport must be produced, we can manage a new one."

A week later Helga caught a plane to Madrid. By diplomatic pouch she advised Driscoll of her journey to the Iberian peninsula and her intent to reach the States by the first available ship out of Southampton. Her farewell from Dr. Klaus had been emotional. Both hoped it would not be too long before they would see each other again.

17

Heydrich and his pregnant wife attended a gala concert in Prague on a fine spring evening in May. A picture has been preserved showing them strutting down the aisle to their seats, the audience standing in respect for the bemedaled Protector of the erstwhile Czech realm. The Iron Cross, proudly displayed on his uniform, was earned for his valor in torturing prisoners and dispatching Jews, Gypsies and other unwanted creatures to premature deaths. In the photograph one sees the man: the hips a little too wide, the mouth smug with evident self-satisfaction. The wife is dumpy and not at all memorable. Nothing in this frozen moment in the midst of a devastating war reveals anything of the mind of the killer and the New Order he represented, or of the drama about to unfold.

According to rumors reaching the Nazi occupiers, the Czech underground was active. An informant had reported that several men had been parachuted from a British plane, but the story could not be verified. However, Heydrich was determined to ferret out the truth by doing what he knew best: applying terror and torture.

He was fond of employing curfew, announced irregularly and at short notice, as a means of keeping the population in a state of constant uncertainty. It also gave him a pretext for arresting violators in the hope that fear of torture might reveal some lead to the underground.

In April two men were found in the street after curfew hours. It so happened they were non-political and not connected to any resistance group. But on being questioned by the Gestapo in the dungeons of the castle, they admitted they had heard it said that "Czech nationalists," as one of them injudiciously phrased it, had sneaked into the country. That bit of information was enough for the inquisitors to apply torture to them, by methods that were invented long ago and had received a few modern refinements. Thumb screws and the pulling of fingernails were already popular methods of extracting confessions in the time of Grand Inquisitor Torquemada; now electric shock, called "truth therapy," was added to the catalogue of cruelties, as was the application of cigarette burns to selected parts of the anatomy.

Unfortunately, the two hapless victims had no real information, a fact the torturers would not concede. The result was that one of the men died and the second was mutilated. Interrogations of this type were soon known amongst the people and accomplished in a few months what Heydrich's ailing predecessor had failed to do: fan the Czechs' deep-rooted opposition to the occupiers into bitter hatred.

While the conductor intoned *Tannhäuser*, the real conspirators were finalizing Operation *Anthropoid*. Amongst their co-plotters, Jan Kubiš and Josef Gabčik were known as Ota and Zdenek. They had dropped from the sky equipped with weapons of destruction. They were soldiers in the Czech Free Army stationed in England and had volunteered for the dangerous task.

Both were young, bold and knew in their hearts that the chances of killing Heydrich were only fair and their own chances of survival very slim. Ota was twenty-seven years old, had gray, deep-set eyes and by his physique, speech and comportment gave the impression of outer and inner strength. In England he and his best friend Zdenek had been recruited for what they came to call "our suicide mission." He and Ota knew that a support group, safehouses and sufficient ammunition would be provided for them in Prague. They had landed undetected and ten weeks later had finalized their plans.

It was the last night before the appointed deed. This evening seven men had their last briefing. They met in the back room of a simple grocery store not far from the concert hall. Two of their women sat near the shop window, keeping watch. A German patrol passed by, looking for unknown enemies. The store did not attract their interest.

"Zdenek will shoot him, and I will throw the bomb for good measure," said Ota. "We'll do it when the bastard comes around the bend here." He pointed to the spot on a sketched-out map of the outskirts of the city. "Adolf Opálka will give the first sign when he sees the car. It has to be the Hangman's open touring Mercedes. If it's another car, we don't do it and wait for the next day. In that case, we meet here again tomorrow night. Is that clear?"

They had rehearsed the plot half a dozen times already. Josef Valčik, another parachutist, was to be stationed on the fourth floor of the apartment house at the corner to warn of troop patrols; Jan Hruby and Josef Bublik were to amble down the approach road and let the car pass by. They would signal to Jaraslav Švarc, the last lookout, who would give the go-ahead to Zdenek. The sun had to be bright – that was the final condition – for when Zdenek would flash a mirror to Ota, the attempt was to proceed.

"One final reminder," said Ota. It was warm in the small room, the windows were shut and the air was stifling. "When evil is not resisted, it will spread like the plague. Let the world know that the free spirit of our people can never be crushed."

"Amen," said the six, and two of them crossed themselves. Zdenek had the last word: "I have the smoke bombs. As soon as Heydrich's been hit, I'll let them go and create a screen. We all go to the Karel Borromaeus Church, as planned. The priests will help us from there."

They embraced each other and went one by one into the night. The women stayed behind.

* * *

It was Heydrich's habit to commute each day from his country home to Hradcany Castle, the old grand residence of the emperors of the Holy Roman Empire. On this day, the 27th of May, 1942, the sun was shining and he rode in his open Mercedes driven by his chauffeur, Klein.

The conspirators signaled each other, as arranged; Zdenek flashed his mirror. Klein, noting the man, accelerated the car. Too late. Zdenek's sten gun jammed, but Ota jumped forward and threw the bomb, fatally wounding the hated Hangman. His spine was shattered, but he was not yet dead. For the next few days he expiated some of the sins he had committed in his brief lifetime and died in agony.

Schellenberg was in Prague at the time of the assassination and helped to direct the SS in the hunt for the assailants. The details of what happened next have become part of Czech folklore: how the conspirators assembled at the church; how the Nazis were able to isolate them; how the defenders with limited weapons fought a heroic battle against their assailants in a struggle that was doomed from the outset. None made it to safety.

The Czechs were electrified by the news and so was the Nazi hierarchy. Hitler was furious over the lack of security for one of his brightest servants. Whether Himmler too shared these sentiments is not recorded. It was rumored that he did not. Blond Reinhard had become a serious competitor for the management of the vast security apparatus of the Reich and the control of the Palace guard. Himmler took charge of the state funeral and mounted a revenge that the world was bound to remember, one that would at the same time re-establish him as the ultimate master of savagery.

Jews, though not involved in the assassination, were nevertheless singled out for revenge. Three thousand were taken from Theresienstadt and shipped east for immediate extinction. Another death selection was made by Goebbels in Berlin who ordered 152 to be executed as a form of "just reprisal."

Then came the turn of the Czechs themselves. Himmler decided on the village of Lidice, near Prague.

Can a chronicler recreate the terror and the agony that befell its inhabitants? The walls of the old and modest houses in the village themselves must have shed tears before they too perished in the scorching flames.

First, the men. The order was given to assemble in the square, where the townhouse, with its faded pink and gray colors and weather-worn wooden beams and gables, became a silent witness to terror. The villagers were lined up ten at a time, turned to the wall and shot by an *Einsatzkommando* that Schellenberg kept in reserve, to serve him both as body guards and killers who would ask no questions and give no mercy.

The women and children of Lidice were made to watch the execution. One woman threw herself upon the rising pile of the dead and was shot along with the others. When the macabre ritual was over, trucks were rolled up to the square. The women and children were separated, the former sent to the concentration camp at Ravensbrück, the latter to Gneisenau. At Ravensbrück the women were to undergo medical experiments of the most gruesome sort: their level of pain was examined, teeth were extracted, toes and fingers amputated. They were submerged in ice water, and the time it took for them to die was carefully measured and recorded. Four women who were pregnant were first sent to a maternity ward in Prague where they were delivered. Thereupon, their newborn children were strangled before their eyes and they themselves then sent to Ravensbrück.

In Gneisenau the conditions were harsh beyond description. Teenage children were assigned to back-breaking work and died in short order. Those who were too young to work were killed at once and only those under one year were given a chance of life, if they passed Himmler's racial standards. They were presented to German families in the Reich and all traces of their identity were lost thereafter.

The end of Lidice came quickly. All homes were dynamited and blown up and what remained of the ruins was leveled, the ground scorched, the corpses consumed in a wave of fire. Lidice was meant as a warning to the Czechs; it became a lasting symbol of Nazism in action. To make sure the lesson was learned, a few other villages were exposed to a similar fate. Czechs would remember Ležáky, Bernatrice and Pardubice, along with Lidice; the world would remember only the latter.

Himmler made sure that Heydrich's replacement in the urgent task of exterminating the Jews was a more pliant and less ambitious man than the blond Protector had been. He thought of Heinrich Müller but rejected him as too closely tied to his dead chief. He settled on Dr. Ernst Kaltenbrunner, an efficient administrator who could be relied upon to dispatch Eichmann's shipments with a zeal totally bereft of human emotion.

PART IV

Voice in the Wilderness

SUMMER 1942

18

Ken Driscoll watched the landscape unraveling past his window. He remembered it well, for he had often taken the trip when he was stationed in Washington. He sat in the last row of the coach car to have a good view of the passengers. They seemed harmless enough: middle-aged businessmen looking for favors at the Big Trough; civil servants with their starched and strangely uniform look; a few women with children; and a group of noisy high school students off to see the Capitol and gain some insight into the history of the nation, a subject in which they were notoriously uninformed. A recent survey of Americans had shown that 12 percent of those asked could not name the President of the United States, despite the fact that Roosevelt was now in his third term. Driscoll wondered how many of these youngsters would fail the test.

He also wondered about the kind of person who might be after him. Was he a full-time agent for the *Abwehr*, Germany's intelligence apparatus headed by the controversial Wilhelm Canaris? Or was he a part-time associate, an American of German descent who had been active in the *Bund* and wanted to prevent the defeat of Nazism? Probably the former, he decided; the stakes were too high. Hitler must have personally given the order to recover the letter at any cost; he wanted to keep the West in ignorance of his true aims. He had even used one of his dinner monologues to inform his listeners that after the war he would settle all Jews in Africa; the hot climate, he averred, would render the cursed race indolent and unaggressive.

The *Abwehr* must assume I'm carrying the letter to Washington, Driscoll figured. Their people did not find it in my hotel room; therefore, it has to be on my person. Once I see a government official or my father-in-law, the Senator, the document will disappear into the bureaucratic maze and will be hard to locate, even by a good agent. Therefore, the critical time for them is now: here on the train, in the station, and then on the way to my contact person, whoever that will be. I should have called the Senator from New York, but I was in too much of a hurry to leave.

"Washington next stop!" boomed the conductor.

Driscoll's hand touched the gun, giving it a reassuring pat. I won't need you for long, he thought. After today, I'm useless to them, unless, of course, they want revenge for Richter. Unlikely. He was small fry, not worth risking an agent.

The train slowed down and familiar sights came into view. The conductor passed through again and issued his final instructions.

"Washington, D.C. Everyone out, please!"

Crowds swarmed on the station. Driscoll cast an eye at the news stand. *Nazi Hangman Heydrich shot in Prague* proclaimed a banner headline. He bought the paper and headed for a phone booth.

"Senator George Browning," he said when the secretary answered.

"I'm sorry, the Senator is at a hearing. May I tell him who called?"

Driscoll gave his last name but did not identify himself as a relative.

"The Senator should be in after four-thirty. Would you care to call again?"

The voice was solicitous and professional. Yes, Driscoll said, he would be in touch. He did not tell her he would drop by instead of telephoning again.

Three hours to kill, Driscoll thought. Better to see him first than go to the department. See what he suggests. He's a Democrat, a fan of F.D.R.'s; he knows the ropes. And he'll be glad to see me. He's fair and a good listener; rare in a politician. His wife, that's a different story. A social climber, a ruthless, self-important parasite for whom clothes and party invitations are the essence of life.

He stood irresolutely at the curb. A cab pulled up.

"Taxi?"

Why not, he thought, haven't been to the Smithsonian in a long time.

He opened the door and climbed in. He was about to pull the door shut when he felt a sharp blow on his arm. A vigorous shove thrust him against the other side of the car and a man climbed into the cab.

"What the hell are you doing?" Driscoll shouted. The cab had already driven off. It occurred to him that he had not even given the driver his destination.

"Easy, buddy," said the intruder, pressing a gun into his side. "One move and you're gone."

Driscoll detected a faint accent in the assailant, a light-haired muscular man his own age.

"Don't make a fuss, Driscoll, you haven't a chance. The cabbie is one of ours."

He reached in Driscoll's pocket and extracted the revolver.

"Prepared, weren't you! But not prepared enough. We want the letter. Where is it?"

Driscoll said nothing. The gun pressed painfully against his ribs. The man went through Driscoll's pockets.

"We get the letter and you're free. We don't get the letter and you're kaput."

The gun pressed harder. The cab was heading into Virginia.

"The letter is on its way to the State Department," Driscoll spoke at last. "The American embassy in Bern sent it by diplomatic pouch. Too dangerous for me to take, they said, and they were right."

"You're lying," the man hissed and hit him in the face. "You goddamn Jew lover, you're lying through your teeth. We know it wasn't in the last pouch."

"You're crazy. You can't know what's in our pouches."

"Can't we, though! That's how much you know about the *Abwehr*. We'll be driving a bit longer and you still have a chance to change your mind. A half hour, that's all, though. A half hour 'til *Götterdämmerung*. Where's the letter, Driscoll?"

He hit him again. The cab was picking up speed. Virginia was lovely on this day, but Driscoll did not notice it.

* * *

Senator Browning was late. A vigorous fifty-year-old, graying at the temples, given to a bit of portliness.

"Any calls, Dorothy?"

"Just the usual, sir. One fellow called who has the same name as your daughter. He said he'd call later."

"Driscoll?"

"Yes, sir. He didn't give his first name. I would have recognized it."

Dorothy Thomas had been the Senator's secretary for a dozen years and was privy to a good deal of his personal affairs.

"Ken is due back any day now," the Senator said. "He's been reassigned to the States, I'm told. It could have been him."

Senator Browning lingered in the office, waiting for the

call. It was not a reasonable thing to do. He had a dinner engagement and was ready to leave when on impulse he called his daughter in Boston. After formalities, he came to the point.

"Cathy, have you heard from Ken?"

"Yes, Dad. He's back in the States and has a thirty-day leave. He called yesterday and said he was coming today to see the boys. But neither one has heard from him. A bit strange. He's always been particular about appointments. Both boys phoned a while ago and asked whether he'd been in touch. That's all I know."

When there was no word next morning, he phoned Cathy again. The answer was negative. Neither the boys nor she had heard anything. For reasons he could not define, the Senator was upset and worried. He called Miss Thomas to his desk.

"Dorothy, find out who at State handles embassy assignments. Who's the guy that told Ken to take a leave, and if you can't locate him, let me talk to the Under-Secretary in charge of that department. Maybe Ken's reporting to the Marines, that's also a possibility."

Half an hour later Under-Secretary John Taylor was on the phone.

"Sorry, Senator, none of us here or at Marine headquarters knows anything. Driscoll's on leave and he hasn't contacted us since. No obligation, you know."

Browning felt frustrated. His anxiety increased.

"Well, thanks, Mr. Taylor. If you hear from him, let me know. But don't tell him I asked. Okay?"

"I'll pass the word down."

* * *

A week later Browning called Taylor back.

"I want your help, Mr. Under-Secretary. Driscoll is my

son-in-law and we want to find him. He's back in the States and no one has seen him. Totally out of character. I've taken the liberty of phoning Ambassador Harrison in Switzerland. He consulted a memo left by his predecessor and told me what you of course know: that Driscoll left and went to England, I think. But he told me something else as well. Ken has certain information, very sensitive, high level, that he'd come across in Berlin and that he intended to take the information to Washington. Also – and I don't like this a bit – that he was probably on the Nazi blacklist for having helped a certain German woman out of the country. She's apparently on her way to America. Harrison gave her a visa."

Taylor thought for a while.

"Aside from anything personal, Senator, there seem to be unusual circumstances. I hadn't heard about the high-level information. There are Nazi agents operating in this country and they'd probably know that your son-in-law has had access to it. I don't want to worry you, but would you mind if I called Mr. Hoover? Let the F.B.I. see what they can find. Of course, if they should establish that Driscoll has secreted himself for, shall we say, personal reasons, we close the file and forget it."

Another week went by. Taylor reported that the F.B.I. had turned up nothing. Major Driscoll, last seen in a New York hotel, had vanished without a trace.

When his month's leave was up, he did not report for work. The F.B.I. put additional men on the case. Driscoll was now officially listed as missing.

* * *

Dressed in a smart gray suit, Helga looked fresh and fetching, ready for the New World and Ken.

When the boat docked in New York, a man stood at the

foot of the gangplank waiting for her to disembark. He flashed his badge.

"I'm Jack Fuchs, Miss Raben, F.B.I. Please don't be alarmed. But there's a matter in which we need your assistance."

Helga was stunned.

"Perhaps you'd like to check in at your hotel and then we can talk. And please believe me, miss, you're not concerned personally." The agent was gentle and solicitous, not at all like the F.B.I. she had read about.

"Not concerned personally?" she said finally. "That's hard to believe. As for a hotel, I have no particular place in mind. Maybe you can suggest a place that's quiet and not too expensive. My funds are limited."

"I'm not a New Yorker," Fuchs said, "just came down from Washington for the day. I once stayed at the Gotham. I'll be glad to take care of the taxi."

"Thanks," she mumbled. Her composure was crumbling; she stumbled after Fuchs who had taken her two suitcases.

He took her quickly through Customs and Immigration, and loaded her sparse belongings into the cab. He did not mention his investigation again, and she didn't have the courage to ask.

The ride was interminable. The New York streets were crowded beyond belief. The air was drenched with the smell of refuse piled in narrow streets through which the taxi made no visible progress. The driver was cursing and nearly ran down pedestrians as he turned the corner onto Madison Avenue.

Helga's anxiety rose. This was a strange and threatening city, not like the New York she had dreamed about. The only excitement she felt came from the unceasing noise around her. The tall buildings made the streets look dark and shut out the sun. I'm in the wrong place, she thought, and could hardly breathe.

They arrived at the Gotham at last and she was given a room on the second floor. Fuchs carried her suitcases and she took the key which had a heavy metal ball at the end. She dropped it in the hallway, causing a sharp clang and a hollow, threatening echo. When she reached the room at last, she was trembling.

"Miss Raben, I might as well begin with some news about Major Driscoll. Your friend, I believe. We cannot find him. We hope you may be able to help us."

Helga listened but heard little. Her body was cold, her soul dried up like her tears. She barely grasped the tale that Fuchs unfolded, the Senator's interest, the State Department's involvement, and now the F.B.I.

"We can't rule out foul play," she heard him say.

Her lips had lost their last hint of color. She was shivering. Dear Ken, I was going to start a new life with you, and now you too are gone.

"I'm sorry. I wish the news were different," Fuchs said. "The reason we're contacting you has to do with the information that Major Driscoll apparently had. If it's injurious to the Germans, then their agents might have a stake in preventing it from reaching Washington. This is where you come in. What was the information? If we know, then maybe we have a better chance of pinpointing those who are after it."

Helga was muddled, though not too muddled to ask, "But Ambassador Harrison in Bern knows exactly what it's all about. Didn't he tell you?"

Fuchs was nonplussed. "Maybe he wasn't asked, although that's hard to believe. Are you sure he knows?"

"Mr. Fuchs, I was there. I recited the contents of the letter personally to Mr. Harrison."

"So there's a letter involved. Did Major Driscoll have it?"

"No, he didn't, and in case you're interested, I haven't either."

"Where is it?"

"In a bank vault in Switzerland."

The agent thought for a moment.

"It occurs to me, Miss Raben, that if the major was possibly – and I say possibly – targeted by the Nazis, you'll be too. I think you'll need some protection until this is cleared up. Do you mind if I phone my office?"

He also called Senator Browning. When he replaced the receiver, he said, "They believe you ought to go straight to Washington. Besides, the Senator wants to see you as soon as possible."

They took her suitcases and left the room. Fuchs checked her out of the hotel, telling the clerk that the lady's plans had changed.

Sitting in the lobby was a man who had not previously been there. Fuchs made a mental note of his appearance: light-brown hair, glasses, well built. He could not see his face distinctly. To Fuchs's professional eye, he appeared to be too ostensibly immersed in the reading of the *New York Post.*

The meeting was held in the Senator's office. Fuchs and Taylor were present; Dorothy Thomas took notes. Helga, pale, with eyes rimmed by dark shadows after a restless night during which an agent had been stationed outside her door, was relating her story. She quoted the letter from memory and concluded:

"I came to America to let people know the dreadful things that are going on. I've seen the train that takes them East, and can't forget it."

Her audience remained silent.

"Of course," she added, "Ken Driscoll was to help me. We were close friends."

She looked at the Senator who gazed out the window at the Capitol beyond.

"If necessary," Taylor asked, "you could produce the original?"

"Yes, sir. I would have to go to Bern personally. There would be certain complications with my identity, but I'm sure it could be managed."

"Well, we can leave that for now. I don't want to put cold water on your expectations, Miss Raben, but while the letter is interesting, it really doesn't tell us anything new. Hitler's been preaching this doctrine all along. But as far as we know, it hasn't been implemented. In isolated instances, yes, that's all we know. We'll need more solid proof than a Führer order."

"You mean testimony from the camps, maybe pictures? Come on, Mr. Taylor, you can't be serious," said Senator Browning.

"I am, sir, and so is the whole department. We were badly burned by exaggerated propaganda in the last war, dismembered babies in Belgium and stuff like that, and it all backfired. Yes, sir, I do mean to say that we need substantial, reliable proof that Hitler's order is being implemented on a large scale."

The Senator was not satisfied. "And meanwhile these poor people might be dying by the thousands."

"Thousands, Senator?" Helga was stung by the twin arrows of depression and exasperation. "Millions is more like it. Forgive me for being so forward. I'm pleading for others, not for myself."

"Come on, young lady," Taylor responded patronizingly. "That's so fantastic it's outside the realm of belief. The Nazis are cruel. Still, they are members of a civilized people. The majority of Germans wouldn't stand for it."

"Mr. Taylor, with respect. That's why they've put their machinery of death in the East, Poland mostly. In Germany proper their camps are inhuman. In the East they defy any adjective. That's what I've been told. Remember, I lived in Berlin as a Gentile, and I know what people talk about," Helga said.

"Exactly, they talk, that's all. Hitler too talks." Taylor remained unconvinced. "There's a big difference between a general policy and its execution. Don't forget, they are at war and it's going badly for them just now. They'll need all their railroad cars for transporting people and supplies."

The F.B.I. man spoke up. "If that's the case, sir, why is there a theory of foul play against Major Driscoll? Didn't we surmise that some German agents didn't want him to deliver the letter which they thought he had? If we don't believe it's so important, why do we think the Nazis might?"

"Damn if I know. Maybe it's because they're unpredictable and erratic. Maybe it's because Hitler is furious that an order of his has fallen into Allied hands. If you'll excuse me, I must run along. Glad to have met you."

Taylor shook hands all around and left. When he was gone and Miss Thomas too had returned to her desk, it was Fuchs's turn to go.

"Forgive me if I don't express an opinion, it's not my field of expertise. I'm personally inclined to take Hitler seriously, but then who am I to say? Just another layman mixing in. However, I do have an opinion about your safety, Miss Raben. I think you're out of danger. If they assume you possibly came to America with the letter, they'll also assume that after today you no longer have it and that in any case officials here are now privy to the contents. I'll check it out with my superiors. It will be my guess that after another day we'll call off your protection. But, please, if there's anything or anyone that arouses your suspicion in any way, let me know. Here's my card and number. My office will answer any time day or night."

Helga thanked him for his attention.

At the door he turned around. "Maybe I'd better tell you this: In New York yesterday there was a man in the Gotham lobby whose looks I didn't like."

He described him: light-brown hair, glasses, well built, face partially hidden by a newspaper.

"Something rang a bell. I can't say more. But should you notice him loitering anywhere in your vicinity, go to the next telephone and call me. That man might lead us to Driscoll."

When Helga was alone with Senator Browning, she spoke more intimately.

"I don't care anymore what happens to me. I want to find Ken, if he's still alive. And if he's not, I won't rest until justice is done. Or call it revenge. . . I'm very pessimistic, you see. If the Nazis were after him, they were people without mercy. A single human life means nothing to them. And neither do a million lives."

Browning said tenderly, "You like Ken a lot, don't you? I understand. Though he's still legally tied to my daughter, their marriage has been dead for years. I like him too. He's honest and courageous."

Helga avoided his eyes; she was embarrassed.

"I too am pessimistic," the Senator continued. "If there'd been a ransom demand, we'd have hope. There wasn't any. Ken just disappeared. We've learned that Nazis searched his hotel room in New York. Since they didn't find what they were looking for, they wanted to prevent him from talking or, of course, if the letter was in his possession, from delivering it to some authority in Washington. The F.B.I. thinks they kidnapped him after he made his telephone call."

They were silent for a while, each one remembering the man they cared about.

"I'm truly sorry, Miss Raben. Perhaps a miracle will occur. Could I be of any help to you? You're staying. . ."

"At the Raleigh. But I need to rent a more reasonable accommodation if I'm to be in this city for a while."

"Miss Thomas will be helpful. Meanwhile, have dinner with me tonight. I wasn't going home anyway, I have an evening appointment at the White House. I know you don't want to accept Mr. Taylor's assessment that nobody will believe you. He may be right and then again he may judge our establishment wrongly. Let's give it a shot. I'll try with you, for like you, I think that Hitler's letter means business, terrible business."

* * *

There was no sign of anyone tailing Helga and the F.B.I. called off her protection. The case of the missing Marine major was removed from the active file and listed as another of a thousand unsolved problems.

Helga rented a room on Massachusetts Avenue and began her rounds of law-makers, civil servants and Jewish leaders: anyone who was prepared to listen to her dire warnings.

Senator Browning gave her introductions to members of Congress, the State Department and the press. They were polite; some of them invited her for lunch and a young Congressman from Illinois dated her twice, but finding her resistant to his advances, dropped her abruptly. The issue she had originally presented to him was apparently of no interest. Neither was it to the majority of those she was able to reach. Some were cool, a few were openly hostile. An official in the State Department whose son had been drafted into the Army put his feet on his desk and lit a cigarette without offering one to Helga. "Look," he said, "while you're running around talking about the Jews, my son's getting ready to fight for them."

Helga was taken aback both by the discourtesy of the bureaucrat and by his view, which she was beginning to suspect was not his alone.

"But, sir, America isn't in the war to fight for the Jews, who are really quite incidental. Isn't America fighting to preserve democracy and decency in the world? I've come here to tell you how far Hitler is prepared to go. And, believe me, sir, from what I have seen with my own eyes, what he's doing to Jews he'll do to others as well."

The man was not impressed.

"Let's assume that you're right. The fact is that Mr. Hitler puts the Jewish problem up front so that when we fight him we fight him in part because of the Jews. And if I were you, I wouldn't press that point too much by singling out the Jewish problem."

Helga left, feeling deeply depressed, and did not find much consolation in other quarters. Congressmen who were used to distinguishing rhetoric from policy transferred their own proclivities to the issues she presented.

"So suppose he did write that letter," one said, "and I don't have any reason to believe that he didn't. He uses big words which he doesn't necessarily mean. He's a politician, you know."

The newspaper people were no more sympathetic.

"Hell, let's face it square on as it is. There's a war on and we've got to beat the bastards east and west. Your people will make it only if we teach the Huns a lesson. Without that, forget it."

Browning was one of the notable exceptions and on a few occasions went along with her. He even attempted to set up an appointment with President Roosevelt. But the two times he seemed to be successful there were last-minute cancellations. The President's speech-writer and adviser, Sam Rosenman, though himself a Jew, counseled his chief against giving the Jewish problem any prominence. He felt that calling attention to his people would increase anti-Semitism at home and weaken the President's popularity. He suggested that F.D.R. signal his qualified sympathy to the cause by ostensibly setting time aside, but at the same time leave no doubt in the Senator's mind or anybody else's that he assigned the Jewish problem low priority by failing to see the Senator and Helga.

One evening the Senator took Helga to a party given by the National Press Club. She found herself standing with some men to whom she had not been introduced.

"Come on, Joe," said a balding man in his forties, who wore expensive clothes with studied nonchalance. He was addressing a younger man. "I'm tired of hearing about these Jews. We've got a hell of a lot of them in the United States, which is too bad, but we can't do a damn thing about it.

They come here and take over everything. So the Nazis see the light and cut 'em down to size. I have no liking for Hitler and his methods, but when it comes to the Jews, I for one say he's doing the right thing."

"You don't really mean this," the younger man said. "Come on, that's prejudice of the worst sort."

"Well, maybe it is, but I'm not alone and you know it. Don't let them in here, I say. Then give the Nazis a chance to reduce the problem to a reasonable size. Let 'em do the dirty work for us. That's okay by me."

Helga hardly made it to the toilet, where she vomited. She begged the Senator to take her home, pleading illness. When she told him what had happened, he was silent for a moment, then said, "I'm afraid you have a lot to learn, my girl. I wouldn't say this attitude is widespread, but it does exist. I'd like to believe, however, that the majority of the American people don't think that way. I know the President doesn't."

Jews, of course, gave her a different reception. She was able to see the Secretary of the Treasury, Henry Morgenthau, Jr., scion of an old German-Jewish family. She had heard that the man was highly assimilated and would likely not give her much of a hearing, probably the same kind that she had received from Rosenman. But Morgenthau was different. He was warm, receptive, and the highest official she had met to take her message seriously. He would relay it to the President, he promised, and do his best to have the consequences of the Hitler order fully understood by America's policy-makers.

When Helga confided her despair over the reaction she had received from others, Morgenthau became pensive.

"Of course, Miss Raben, I thought I knew about it, but when I hear it from you, it all sounds so terribly cruel and real. I'm afraid we have a lot of difficulties to overcome. I'll do my best, that's all I can say."

While Jews listened attentively, they had a problem in

comprehension. Rabbi Kalman Sterner, a man in his sixties, with a shock of white hair and twinkling eyes, soft voice and manner, talked with her for hours. At the end of their conversation, he said: "Miss Raben, I wish we could talk forever, but it wouldn't change a thing. I believe you, and I don't believe you. Hitler is a monster, that's for sure, but will he really kill all the Jews in his domain? It's incredible. None of our enemies has ever attempted such a thing. Expelled, tortured, killed, but never systematically exterminated. So, you see, I have trouble believing that he means it, and you know that it's just like in the time of Moses in Egypt: the people didn't believe Moses, so how could he expect Pharaoh to believe him? You're a voice crying in the wilderness. I'm not sure we can hear you."

Tears came to Helga's eyes.

"Maybe the problem is too large for me," she said at last. "I don't know what else to do. The world is deaf."

* * *

The masters of the Final Solution were meeting again in Wannsee. After Heydrich's death, Kaltenbrunner, under Himmler's close supervision, had moved the operation forward with an astonishing degree of brutal efficiency. The machinery of death was beginning to reach full capacity. They were aiming at ten thousand gassings a day and were getting close. The chief was pleased and distributed kudos all around.

Eichmann was in his glory. Everywhere he was receiving splendid cooperation; the round-up of Jews had wide, popular support in the occupied countries, he said. Even in France, where he had expected delays and opposition, the bureaucracy supported Nazi measures against the Jews and showed a surprising eagerness to anticipate German plans in this respect.

"May I speak freely, sir?" asked Eichmann.

"Sure," said Kaltenbrunner. "What's the problem?"

"Not a problem, sir, just an observation. We're dealing with millions of Jews, but our own detachments of SS and *Wehrmacht* are small. Just a few hundred men here or there, that's all."

"So what's the big deal? We've known this all along," said Müller, who wanted to let Eichmann know that, though Kaltenbrunner was the boss, the disposition of the Jewish plan had to go through him.

Eichmann always sweated in Müller's presence. The man had been riding him lately.

"Of course, sir, you know all about it. Only sometimes I wonder what would happen to our operation if the Polacks or the Lithuanians and Ukrainians suddenly decided they wanted to protect their Jews, the kind of thing they did in Denmark. Without them rounding up the kikes and killing a few while they're doing it, without them ferreting them out from their rat holes and getting them to the trains, shoving them in and all that, our few German detachments would be unable to fulfill this glorious task."

"Eichmann's right, of course," said Kaltenbrunner, who in his turn liked to rein Müller in from time to time. "It only goes to show how widely understood the Führer's vision is. Even those half-humans in the East can understand it when it comes to the Jews."

Müller tried to regain the initiative. His usual method was snapping his leather whip, but in Kaltenbrunner's presence he did not dare to do it.

"Any transportation problems?" he asked.

"No, sir. Except that we don't always have enough carriages and are sometimes left with a couple hundred extra Jews at the collection point. So we stuff them in, as many as the traffic will carry. But there's a limit. You see, we maintain that we're 'resettling' these shipments, and as long as we can make this believable, there's little or no resistance. But if we pack 'em in too tight, we raise their suspicion and there might be trouble."

"Well, I don't know," said Müller. "Seems to me that's an excuse. Who'll give you trouble?"

Eichmann's self-satisfaction evaporated before his chief's implied reprimand which hurt him the more since it was delivered in Kaltenbrunner's presence. He explained hurriedly: "You see, sir, even Jews could give you trouble. They're cowardly, of course, and wouldn't fight. But press 'em too hard and they might offer passive resistance. Suppose everyone would simply lie down. We wouldn't have the personnel to carry them into the cars. And on top of that, some of the natives might get unhappy. There are some unreliable elements around, as you know. Just an observation, sir."

Müller relented. Eichmann was doing a first-rate job, he admitted to himself. Kaltenbrunner had watched the byplay and decided that Müller himself needed a little discomfort.

"The Reich Marshal asked me the other day whatever happened to the Führer's letter on the Final Solution. Anything to report?"

Müller cleared his throat. "Yes and no. We know who had it but we can't lay our hands on it."

"Why not?"

"Well, sir, it's like this." Müller extracted a file from his briefcase and leafed through it. "We established that just as the war with America broke out, a woman named Schmitt was involved in the killing of one of our men who acted as a messenger and was carrying the letter. This Schmitt, a somewhat shadowy figure, was rumored to be Jewish and working for the Kreisau people. We're watching them. They're rather inactive now."

"Come to the point, Müller, we haven't got all day. So Schmitt had the document. Then what?"

"She got out of the country before we could nab her, with the help of a Major Driscoll in the American embassy who accompanied her to Switzerland. False diplomatic passport. We asked for extradition. The Swiss were ready to help. Then the broad disappeared. Had everyone puzzled, clever little bitch, quite a looker too. Probably bought some favors spreadeagling."

He passed her picture around; it was the one from the passport, copy courtesy of the Swiss police.

"Our operative who's on the case in America thinks he's picked up the trail there, though he's got nothing definite yet. Excellent man, working under difficult circumstances."

"Who is he?"

"A German from Argentina whom we placed over there before the war. He's acquired American citizenship papers and lives under another name. His code moniker is 'Hummel.' He tracked Driscoll and got to him."

Everyone's interest was aroused. This was a better story than the dreary recital of how many Jews had gone up in smoke.

Müller continued. "This Driscoll arrives in America. Hummel searches his room in New York. A note about the letter but not the real thing. So he thinks maybe he's got it on his person, or even if he hasn't got it, Driscoll will spill the contents in Washington. After which the actual letter is no longer crucial."

"Agreed," said Kaltenbrunner.

"So when Driscoll arrives in Washington, Hummel, together with an assistant, grabs him in broad daylight and makes off with him into the country. He hasn't got the letter, claims it went by diplomatic pouch from Bern. He applies a little extra pressure, you know the usual procedure, but the guy holds to his story – and for all we know, it may be true. We have some contacts inside the State Department and are checking it out."

"And Driscoll?"

"He's now become a liability. The F.B.I. is trying to find him. His picture is posted in every precinct. Hummel decides that the American must permanently disappear. He drugs him and takes him down to the tip of Florida where he makes radio contact with one of our U-boats. They've been in touch with him all along. That's how we've received his regular reports."

Eichmann was all ears.

"Don't tell me he managed to get him on our boat!"

"You bet he did. How, I don't know for sure, because Hummel returned to America."

"Well, I'll be damned. He's got guts," Kaltenbrunner said. "That means you're holding Driscoll?"

"Yes. Of course we gave him a little treatment, but with no better result. Then Schellenberg, to whom I talked, had a brilliant idea. We change Driscoll into a Jewish name. He's already got his pecker shortened like most of these American Jew lovers, so who'll prove the difference?"

Müller consulted his folder.

"We now have Prisoner Number 457400, name of Abraham Silberberg, domiciled in the concentration camp of Theresienstadt. Schellenberg's keeping an eye on him. When the Red Cross idiots come around, he keeps Driscoll, excuse me, Silberberg, well out of sight. Later we make up our mind what to do with him."

There was general mirth all around, a proper framework for the dull reports on the oven capacities in Auschwitz.

Kaltenbrunner had the last word.

"Tell Hummel not to risk anything trying to trace this woman. The Americans know by now what our plans are, and they'll inform their Allies. It's the Reichsführer's guess, and I concur, that nothing will happen. No press campaign, no public outcry, no broadcast to the Reich. The truth is they don't give a damn about the Jews, they never did.

Hypocritical bastards, close their borders tight so the kikes can't enter, but weep crocodile tears. So I'll be damned if I risk an operative like Hummel on a whim that the Fat One has. I'm sure the boys in *Abwehr* would agree. So have Hummel lay off the dame even if he's spotted her. Maybe he can watch her from time to time so she doesn't do us any harm, and also so that we can deal with her after the war."

In Geneva a young German refugee received a mysterious visitor. Gerhart Riegner, graduate in law, had escaped from his native land and was now serving the Swiss Bureau of the World Jewish Congress. His visitor, a middle-aged German whose conservative suit matched his serious mien, spoke with evident hesitation. He was an industrialist, he said, and his conscience was troubled. He possessed incontrovertible evidence that a master plan existed to exterminate all Jews and that the plan was already being carried out.

For Riegner this was no ordinary revelation. To be sure, survivors who had reached London had told their horrid stories and a young Jew had committed suicide to call the world's attention to the mass murders. But the Nazis had always denied these reports and had characterized them as vicious propaganda, reminiscent of World War I. Now, for the first time, a German came forward to confirm the truth of the tales.

Riegner at once informed his friend, Howard Elting, the American Vice-Consul, who in turn communicated the report to Ambassador Harrison and with it transmitted the industrialist's name in a sealed envelope. The American, of course, knew of Hitler's letter. It was clear that what the

Führer had ordered was now indeed put into murderous practice.

That night Riegner, whose quiet manner belied his energy, sent identical telegrams to Washington and London:

> *Received alarming report that in Führer's headquarters plan discussed and under consideration according to which all Jews in countries occupied or controlled by Germany numbering 3½-4 millions should after deportation and concentration in East be exterminated at one blow to resolve once for all the Jewish Question in Europe stop the action reported planned for autumn methods under discussion including prussic acid stop we transmit information with all reservation as exactitude cannot be confirmed stop informant stated to have close connections with highest German authorities and his reports generally speaking reliable.*

Upper-level officials in both capitals decided that their bosses were not to be bothered with such trifling news. In Washington they did not even want Jewish leaders to learn about it, and when at last they shared Riegner's telegram with Rabbi Stephen S. Wise, they did so with the condition that he would not make it public until Foggy Bottom had checked it out. A million people had already died, and officials were wrinkling their brows wondering whether it might be true.

Helga knocked on a hundred doors. With every polite refusal or undisguised annoyance she met, her determination grew. She would not let up.

Through the Senator's contacts she was sent to Cuba where, after a few days' stay, she was to immigrate to the States.

The consul in Havana was courteous.

"You've been highly recommended to us and the affidavits are in order," he said. He asked her routine questions.

Had she ever committed or been convicted of a felony? No, she answered. To her, killing a rapist was self-defense. Had she ever broken the law? No, she said, withholding the information about her double life. Breaking Nazi law, especially when it was immoral, was akin to keeping a divine commandment. A Pan American plane took her back to the States, a potential citizen. At last she had found a home where she was accepted. She was immensely grateful and wished that Ken could share her happiness.

When she returned to Washington, there was a letter from Dr. Klaus.

> *Dear Hilli,*
> *I hope this finds you well and that you have made some progress with your mission. Going by the newspapers here, no startling revelations have been noted, although there are plenty of rumors. I am sorry to say that it is not a very interesting subject for my countrymen. They remain smug, feel secure and not inclined to be too charitable. Last week there was a bit of scandal: a few Jews slipped into Switzerland from Austria (or what was Austria) in order to escape the transports. They were caught by the police, and though I vouched for them and offered them my place in Oberhofen, the authorities would not agree to leave them here but took them back to the border and surrendered them to the Nazis. There were some protests against this shameful behavior. And these people call themselves Christians! Even our own Swiss Jews kept a pretty low profile in the matter. They wrote letters and petitioned the minister, but nothing more public than that.*
>
> *And now some news I've kept to the end. My contact in the Swiss legation in Berlin writes that further inquiries about your friend indicate that he is*

most likely a prisoner of war, caught with General Paulus' Army in Stalingrad. So there's a little hope!

Anything about the major? If so, I hope it's all good.

Affectionately yours,

B.K.

Helga read the letter again and again. She realized that in her heart she had given up Rolf for lost and now chided herself for her lack of faith. She felt in need of saying a prayer but did not have the courage to do so. A Hebrew sentence flashed into her mind, one that even she, the most recalcitrant of pupils, knew by heart: *Shema Yisrael*, "Hear O Israel, the Lord is our God, the Lord alone." It wasn't a prayer; still, it contained a mention of the God whose existence she had been taught to deny. Old Dr. Klappermann, her principal, had once addressed the student body, telling the story of the ancient sage who when being tortured to death had exclaimed these words. Was it appropriate to recite this formula for a Gentile friend whom she wanted to live, not to die?

She remembered how, on hearing of Rolf being listed as missing, she had sought the comfort of the synagogue in Bern. There was a temple not too far from her room in Washington and she went there on the Sabbath. Much of the service was in English, the phrases were sonorous and the music stately. She had no difficulty praying for Ken and Rolf.

Afterwards, when she shook hands with the rabbi, he recognized her.

"I'm much impressed with your remarkable efforts here. Rather slim pickings, I'm afraid."

Helga agreed.

"May I offer a suggestion?" he continued. "Go to New York. See Dr. Wise and other Jews. They've got the numbers, the cry must come from them. I'll be happy to give you whatever introductions you need."

The rabbi had suggested what she already knew she had to do.

* * *

Helga wrote a letter to Dr. Bertha Klaus:

> *Dearest friend,*
> *I have arrived in this city of cities, exhilarating, depressing, noisy, imposing – use any word and it fits. It's hard to think of New York and Bern existing in the same world, the difference is so great. Nothing here of Washington's serene landscape and broad avenues. Here everyone hurries as if the next hour is the last and the streets will become impassable.*
>
> *I don't know what lies ahead. The reason I'm here is that official responses to my mission have been bitterly disappointing. The American government feigns some interest in what is happening to my people in Poland and in Hitler's master plan. But underneath there is unconcern. Are they different from the Swiss? I'd like to think* the people *are, and that in this respect they're unlike their government. I'd love to know what the President knows and what he plans to do, if anything. The Jews see him as the great White Father who loves them. I wish I could be so sure. If he were, why not a simple, strong statement, speaking to everyone's conscience? I can't believe that he is unaware of what is going on. Too many people know.*
>
> *So I've come to the big city thinking (probably stupidly) that I can help to stir up people – I, a young inexperienced girl, who, incidentally, has acquired immigrant status under her own name.*

You are one of the few people who will understand what that means to me!

No word from my major, alas! But what you wrote about my other friend has given my hopes a great boost. Imagining he might actually be alive buoys me up enormously, and then I worry about what he must suffer in a Russian prison camp. Thanks so much for keeping up the inquiry, you are really a wonderful person.

I do love you and hope we will *see each other again. You have been a second mother to me and I trust this finds you well.*

Your admiring and adoring friend,

Hilli

* * *

"You're quite a young woman. I wish we had more like you."

Dr. Stephen Wise was warm and complimentary. Most of his battles were now behind him; still, his glittering eyes and stentorian voice let the visitor know that his spirit was as vigorous as ever. Confidant of presidents, spellbinding orator, defender of the exploited and champion of Zionist hopes, he shared his anxieties with Helga. No, he had not been aware of the Hitler order; he had by now, however, learned of the Wannsee conference, and the Riegner telegram had at last been communicated to him. Unfortunately, the State Department had put him under severe constraints. He could not rouse the Jewish masses until Washington had verified what Riegner's informant had revealed.

"My God," he agonized, "thousands are dying in ghastly fashion every day and the government handcuffs me. If I break our understanding, I'll never again have access to anybody that counts, and certainly not to the President."

"Do you think, sir, that the President knows?"

"I can't believe he does. I believe in his basic decency."

"Forgive me, Dr. Wise, if I don't share your trust. I can't believe he doesn't know. Everybody else does. Do you reckon there's any chance that he would receive me?" She did not tell him of Senator Browning's failed attempts.

Wise thought a while.

"Maybe he would. Let me see what I can do."

They talked for an hour, the man who had given his life to the saving of his people and the new immigrant who had just set out on that road. She told him of her background; Wise listened with rapt interest. When she had finished, he took a long look at her and said:

"Now that you have found your identity and a real purpose in life, why not learn who we Jews really are? Read about our history, our beliefs, our miseries, our glories. You're an intelligent woman, you owe it to yourself to get acquainted with yourself. Does that make sense?"

Helga was quick in her response. "I would love to do what you suggest. It took me a long time to get ready, but now I am. Can you tell me how to start?"

"I think I can," he replied. "Come to our home on Friday night."

21

For the fifth time Driscoll was beaten on his head and feet and put in solitary confinement. It was an unheated box in which he could only stand or crouch. He could not lie down, and an earlier attempt to sit on the slop pail had broken it and he had sat in his own excrement. He was coughing badly. The infirmary which he had visited was out of medicine. Dr. Biberstein was most regretful. A Jewish physician from Hamburg, he had lost a leg in World War I, and because of this he was sent to Theresienstadt rather than Auschwitz. Theresienstadt concentration camp was for the "privileged": decorated war veterans, highly visible public figures and others who were temporarily kept alive on minimum rations, hard labor and harsh treatment. Its purpose was not to kill its inmates outright, but to let them die of natural causes like malnutrition and untreated disease.

Dr. Biberstein knew some English and often talked with Driscoll, whose German was poor.

"You at least have a chance to survive this hell," he said to the American. "They know who you are and will be careful not to destroy you. They figure they may lose the war after all and the Americans will look for you. No one looks for us. They say one or two million have already disappeared and it makes no difference to anyone."

Driscoll told him the story of the Hitler letter. It caused no surprise to the doctor.

"That maniac is possessed with the urgency of doing away with us. When things go right, it's German genius which does it. When they go wrong, it's the Jew's fault. And to think that I gave one perfectly good leg to them!"

Driscoll crouched in his cell and for the thousandth time tried to analyze his possibilities for escape. He had made five attempts and failed. Twice they had caught him; on three occasions he had actually escaped from his labor gang and disappeared for the night. Dogs had found him, vicious beasts that emulated their masters.

Every request he made was denied.

"I want to see the camp commandant."

"I insist on my rights under the Geneva convention."

"I want to be transferred to a prisoner-of-war camp."

"I want to see the Red Cross representatives."

Their answers were always the same: "We know of no Kenneth Driscoll. Our records show that you are Abraham Silberberg from Berlin."

"But I don't even know German."

"That's your problem. Go see a rabbi, he'll teach you."

He had grasped that bit of advice, and as he thought about it, he decided he would.

On his release from solitary confinement he sought out Dr. Leo Baeck, whose reputation in the camp approached mythical proportions. White haired, slightly stooped, with a voice that had a charismatic touch, Baeck had been the head of German Jewry while it still had an organized existence. A famous scholar, he had received numerous offers from abroad but had refused to leave his community. He was their guardian and he would share their fate. In camp he remained the teacher. He had no books, only his memory. He gave lectures on Plato and Aristotle and ancient Jewish literature, and enthralled his listeners by transporting them into the world of the spirit. Some called him saintly; even the guards treated him with surprising respect.

Driscoll and Dr. Baeck spoke in English.

"I can't advise you on whether it is wise to try another escape," the rabbi said. "I can only suggest something to make your existence here more meaningful. Officially you are Silberberg, a Jew. Except for our persecutors, that isn't really so bad. In fact, if you make the most of it, it could be very good."

Driscoll was not sure he understood.

"As long as you are a Jew – one year, two years, maybe a lifetime? – *be* one. Find out who you are supposed to be, learn about your background, your faith. I'm sorry I have no book to give you, but I'd be glad to teach you. And please be assured that it is against our religious practice to seek converts. That's not the objective."

Driscoll – Abraham Silberberg – accepted with alacrity. The very thought of studying with this extraordinary man was exhilarating.

* * *

There was an illegal radio set at camp. The guards had unsuccessfully searched every nook and cranny; the commandant had threatened the inmates with the direst punishment. To no avail. Like religious Jews who assembled at daily prayer, the courageous few crouched around the receiver which brought them crackling noises, awful static and some glorious, if mutilated, bits of information from the BBC. As soon as the broadcast was over, the crystal set was disassembled and its small parts distributed to a dozen people for hiding. Silberberg-Driscoll was always present. He at least understood the English.

One night BBC transmitted a broadcast from New York, covering a mass rally in Madison Square Gardens to protest the slaughter of Jews and other innocent victims of the Nazi madness.

"At last!" the inmates proclaimed, and none exclaimed it more fervently than the American. The group was utterly silent, not a word was to be missed.

"Ladies and gentlemen, we will now hear from one who has lived in Hitler's kingdom of hell. She has escaped and now she's in America with a great mission: to let the world know of the master plan of murder and its execution. She's young, but in her years she has seen enough to last her a lifetime. . . ."

The transmission was fading. Driscoll's heart was beating so loudly he could hardly hear the words. *It must be Hilli, my Hilli. Oh God, don't let it fade out now.* A woman's voice was heard, far away, indistinct, yet there could be no doubt. Her voice, her accent – it was Hilli!

"I'm no orator. This is the first time I'm speaking in public. But you must hear my message. . ."

The sound faded again.

". . .a letter signed by Hitler himself. I know it by heart."

She was reciting the familiar text.

"I saw the trains. Traveling like cattle to their death. I saw the hands stretched out, begging for life, begging for freedom, begging for help. Can we look away? We can't, we must not. What can we do? We can cry, cry aloud. Let America hear, let the world hear! Protest, demand action! Demand that the President speak! Demand it now, tomorrow may be too late!. . ."

One could hear the deafening applause even over the crystal set. Driscoll cried like a child. When he collected himself, he told the listeners the tale of Helga Raben.

* * *

In New York a man who had taken notes during the speeches was slipping quietly out of Madison Square Gardens. The meeting had not ended yet, but he had heard enough.

When Helga returned to her room in Greenwich Village, she found it vandalized. She went to the bathroom, knowing what she would see: a swastika smeared in lipstick on the mirror.

* * *

Rabbi Wise at last obtained an interview with President Roosevelt. Wise came with Helga and Senator Browning. They found two State Department men in the Oval Office, Paul Culbertson and Elbridge Durbrow. The President looked tired; he was smoking incessantly.

"I happened to catch part of your speech at the Gardens," he said. "For one who professes to be no orator and for whom English is not her mother tongue, you did remarkably well."

She thanked him modestly.

"Mr. President, I'm aware how precious your time is, but every day thousands of people are being gassed and no one lifts a finger on their behalf. Forgive me for being so blunt. I speak for them who are about to die."

"Miss Raben, I know you have the support of my friends George Browning and Stephen Wise, but we have inconclusive reports. Mr. Culbertson tells me that he thinks the idea of exterminating millions of people to be fantastic, and Mr. Durbrow agrees. Hitler is anything but stupid. He would not waste a great labor resource like that. It is our opinion that he's using the Jews as forced labor at the front in Russia."

"Excuse me, Mr. President," said Browning, "Miss Raben has a letter written by Hitler himself which orders the extermination. She made a transcript. The original is in a safe in Switzerland, and if you would like to see it, she'll produce it."

Roosevelt glanced at the transcript.

"Yes, it's there all right. I don't have to see the original. But that order came before the war was global and before his Russian campaign turned sour. It's different now, circumstances have changed. I can't believe he's going through with it now. Besides, the salvation of your people depends on our winning the war, and that's our objective."

Wise had been silent so far. He stood up and addressed Roosevelt with a vigor that bordered on vehemence.

"Mr. President, the trouble with the argument is that Hitler is not rational when it comes to Jews. The letter which this young woman possesses shows his intention and every report we receive tells of unimaginable horrors. The Polish government-in-exile has confirmed them and has provided details. We know the names of the death camps, yet nothing happens to stop this unprecedented organized slaughter. We even have a public martyr in a Polish-Jewish witness. His name is Zygielbojm, and this spring he committed suicide in London to arouse the world's conscience. The result: nothing. Another precious life wasted."

Wise's intensity had affected Roosevelt as it inevitably touched his listeners. The President leaned forward.

"What is it, Dr. Wise, that you would have us do – I mean America and Britain? Assuming that the reports *are* true."

"Two things, Mr. President. One, a public declaration by you, and hopefully Mr. Churchill as well, that the Nazis are committing murder on a scale unprecedented in all of history and that the Allies will hold the perpetrators responsible for them as war criminals. Second, the Allies should bomb the rail terminal at Auschwitz where every day thousands of men, women and children are disgorged from the trains to be gassed with terrible efficiency. Think of it, sir, thousands every day! It adds up to more than a million and a half so far. Exterminated like vermin."

Wise could not control himself any longer and began to

cry. Roosevelt was visibly moved.

"I respect your deep feelings, doctor. I will discuss this with Churchill and see what measures we can undertake, always with the understanding that what you describe as fact is indeed so. Thank you for coming, thank you, George, and you too, Miss Raben. The Senator tells me you are on your way to becoming an American citizen. I think we are lucky to have you."

They thanked the President, the interview was over. Wise was optimistic, Browning was not.

"I know the old fox," he said. "He charms the life out of you and then says No. My instinct tells me that he'll do little, if anything, and certainly not what you suggested. But at least he knows that people will be watching, and that's something."

Before parting, Helga returned to questions about Ken which she had asked earlier of the Senator.

"Does the F.B.I. have any theory at all?"

"They now believe he's not dead."

"So where would he be?"

"Not in America, most likely. It would be too difficult to keep him hidden. Besides, what use would he be to them? He was abducted, so he couldn't show the letter around. The F.B.I. thinks they're holding him in Germany. They've asked the intelligence people to find out what they can."

"Thank you, Senator. You've given me new hope." She hugged him gratefully.

* * *

Hummel had decided on a way to keep track of Helga's activities. He learned that she was looking for permanent employment. For several weekends he placed an advertisement in the *Post*:

Intelligent woman needed for translating services. Knowledge of German required. Helpful if familiar with medical terminology.

One day Helga saw it. The job seemed tailor-made. When she called, a man with a faint accent answered.

"Dr. Cohn speaking."

"I'm calling with regard to your advertisement. I think I have the qualifications."

"Can you come and see me?"

The next day Helga visited Dr. Cohn. She found him in a simple, sparsely furnished office in the garment district.

Cohn was fairly tall with a strong face and light eyes that were framed by horn-rimmed glasses which gave him a scholarly appearance. Helga told him of her professional training in England and her experience in Switzerland.

"Yes, you might do," Cohn said in a professional voice. "You see, many German-Jewish doctors have emigrated to South and Central America and of course to Palestine. They want to keep up with their profession and the only material available to them is in English. They want the best of the current literature translated into German, and I supply this need. I myself don't practise presently. I give lectures all over the country, and occasionally I visit Army installations. I used to be a lecturer at Munich University until they threw me out."

It was a simple job, not exciting, he said, but he would offer her a good salary. He would mark the articles in magazines or the chapters in new books and she would do the work in the office and answer the phone in his absence. They reached an agreement and she began her work the next day.

Cohn was an attractive man who treated her fairly and courteously. He was about forty years old, a bachelor who told her he had come from a totally assimilated family in

Bavaria. His religious background was much like hers. He had never been to a synagogue, he said, and he had no desire to change his ways. He was a German and proud of it. The current aberration would pass, and when that happened he would go back. They argued on this point without either one giving ground. Beyond that, their relationship was correct, and as the months passed she found her work pleasant enough, though not overly challenging. She spoke at synagogue rallies and saw Dr. Wise from time to time.

One day she and Dr. Cohn had another of their discussions on Nazis and their Jewish policy. He insisted he could not believe that the Jews were being exterminated.

"How are you so sure, Miss Raben?" he asked.

"I've seen the trains, I've read the testimony. I know that Hitler wrote a letter ordering extermination. I've seen it, I know it by heart."

She recited it for him. He was thoughtful.

"Really! You have seen it? It must be a remarkable document. How come you saw it?"

Helga was about to tell him the truth but, in a mood of annoyance at the man's stubbornness, decided against it. Cohn was acting the German like her father, though in a brassy manner Manfred Raben would never have displayed.

"Dr. Cohn, I saw it once in Switzerland when refugees from Germany arrived. Some friends and I spent an afternoon with these people and the man who had this letter. One of my friends copied it down and I never saw it again. Later I learned it by heart because I thought the world should know. I don't know what became of the man who had it. I think he was shipped back to Germany."

The doctor seemed annoyed. "It's not a believable story, if you ask me," he said.

Her anger grew. "If you don't want to believe me, I can't do anything more to convince you."

Cohn was agitated. "Miss Raben, the letter doesn't mean that much to me. What is important is our relationship, which I thought was founded on trust. And now I find you're lying to me. Why? I asked a civil question and you're putting me on. I think I deserve better."

Cohn's displeasure caused Helga to have second thoughts. Why, indeed, should I lie?

"All right, doctor, you're right. I do know where the letter is. It did not go back to Germany. It stayed in Switzerland. The man put it in a bank vault."

"I understand the delicacy of the matter, Miss Raben, and I forgive you for treating me with such mistrust. But I believe 'the man' who put it in a safe was a woman, and maybe that woman was you."

This time Helga remained unmoved.

"No, it wasn't me. And I don't think I have to stand cross-examination from you or anyone else."

Her anger was mounting. She fairly shouted: "If you think our trustworthy relationship has been injured, I'm prepared to leave."

"Please, my dear, I didn't mean it that way. Forgive me for appearing overly inquisitive."

At five Helga caught the subway home. The crowds were thicker, the shoving at the doors more brutal, the dour smell of the sweating multitude more intense than usual. She was glad to get back to the street and to her room. Two men were coming down the stairs brushing by her, strangers whom she had never seen in the house. She took out her key but the door was open. A sickening premonition came over her.

There it was again, the bathroom mirror smeared with lipstick. Only no swastika this time. Instead, a single name scrawled diagonally across the glass: *SCHMITT*.

She sat down heavily and thought what she must do next. The last time they had left a "message" for her was after her speech at the Gardens. That was for Helga, the Jewish agitator. This was different. They were on to her, and aside from whatever thugs the Nazis used in New York, they could make trouble for her with immigration authorities. Technically she was an "enemy alien," always subject to scrutiny. Her past as Schmitt might throw suspicion on her for having given wrong answers to the consul in Havana. She felt she had to act at once. She had to disappear – again.

Helga found herself praying for inspiration, for some way out of the jungle of her life. The prayer calmed her, and with her eyes still closed she suddenly saw clearly what she had to do.

She called Senator Browning.

"I'm in trouble, sir."

"Not with the law?"

"The Nazis are after me again and I must lose them quickly. I have a simple plan and will write you about it as soon as I have an address. Could I use you as a temporary mail drop? I don't want to be traced through the Post Office. May I leave your office as my forwarding address? I'll know in a few days how you can reach me, and maybe you'd permit me to phone you from time to time."

"Of course, Hilli. And if you can manage it, visit me in Washington. Meanwhile I won't ask any questions. I trust you. I wish you good luck from my heart!"

At eight o'clock the next morning Helga, her few belongings packed in a suitcase, said good-bye to her landlady. She gave her the Senator's address and asked her not to reveal it to anyone. She left her five dollars for postage and her trouble. She was heading out of town, she said. An urgent call from a sick aunt.

She took a cab to the nearest recruiting station of the Women's Army Corps and enlisted. Her papers were in order, her health was good, her age just right. They were glad to have her.

By noon she had sworn the oath and was issued her uniform. Private Helga Raben, WAC, was on her way to Ft. Ord, New York. From there she was in due time transferred to Camp McCoy in Wisconsin.

PART V

Master Agent

WINTER 1943

22

Military operations were going badly for Germany. More and more of its leaders realized that the tide had turned and the war was being lost.

In Berlin, at Gestapo headquarters, Heinrich Himmler was meeting with Martin Bormann, the Führer's new intimate. He had taken the place of Rudolf Hess, now incarcerated in Britain after his peace initiative had failed. Bormann, who faced the world with squinting eyes, square jaws and compressed lips, had managed to obtain the chief's complete confidence. He and Himmler were the same age and, in effect, the unchallenged masters of much of Europe's civilian population. Himmler, in addition, controlled the ongoing extermination of the Jews.

Now, in the waning days of 1943, Auschwitz was at the height of its operation. Two and a half million had already been gassed, another two would be dispatched in the months to come.

"Look, Heinrich," Bormann said, "let's be clear about our views and our long-range goals. As long as the Führer believes we can win, the war goes on and we support him loyally."

"Absolutely," Himmler agreed. He adjusted his pince-nez.

"But we make long-range contingency plans for what happens afterwards."

"Precisely," Himmler agreed in his schoolmasterly, condescending voice.

"You and I and a lot of others know the war will be lost. The Führer has aged terribly and is not well. He goes to that insufferable quack Morell who treats him with leeches, gives him pills and more pills. I think he'll die or go out of his mind. Then what?"

Himmler was quick to answer.

"If we play it right, we can keep our machinery going. Together we control the party apparatus and I can rely on the SS. I'll checkmate the generals. I have a whole gang of conspirators under surveillance. I'm giving them some rope so I can get a full list of all of them. You'd be surprised who's in with them."

"And the Führer?"

"We canonize him. When he can no longer function, we lift him onto the pedestal of eternal sainthood: Germany's greatest hero, fearless, flawless, forever guarding the soul of our nation. Meanwhile, we make peace with the British, then with the Communists, and the Nazi party continues to dominate the future. Do we see it the same way?"

"We do," said Bormann, though with less fervor than Himmler had hoped. Perhaps he suspected that the SS man who controlled his own Army and Praetorian guard had distinct ambitions that left little room at the top for anyone else. "There are some conditions, however," Bormann added. He ran his fingers through his dark hair.

"Naturally," replied Himmler.

"One is that neither Göring nor Goebbels has a role to play. Both are to be retired. The Fat One can hunt foxes and contemplate his art collection – that greedy thief! – and the Club Foot can hunt women and write his memoirs."

"Agreed. And second?"

Bormann opened his collar. He suddenly felt warm.

"The second is a matter close to you, Heinrich. The

Final Solution. You know as well as I, it will *not* be final. You can kill another few million Jews but you won't exterminate them. They'll exist in England, in Russia, in Palestine, in South America, and of course the U.S. You may succeed in cleaning them up in our realm, but they'll come back. And they'll haunt us."

"Bullshit," Himmler said hotly. "The world doesn't care what we're doing to the Jews. In fact, they secretly welcome it. I'll get rid of as many as I can, and as quickly as possible. We're running at full capacity now in our Auschwitz installations. Jews are expendable, and we're doing the job. Who will come to haunt us – their Jehovah?"

"You don't get my point, Heinrich. The fact that no one outside really cares about what you're doing doesn't mean they won't *pretend* otherwise. The Final Solution will raise one hell of a stink after the war, even in Germany. And there'll be enough Jews around to see to it that everyone will smell it."

"So?"

"This means that if we are to preserve the Führer's image, we must separate him from your operation."

Himmler was nonplussed, his face flushed.

"Separate him? You must be kidding. It was his idea in the first place and we carried it out on his specific instructions."

"Written?" Bormann asked.

"Yes, addressed to Göring who transmitted them to Heydrich."

Bormann responded in clipped tones that bore the unmistakable stamp of a man used to authority.

"That becomes part of my second condition for cooperating with you: I want those instructions back, and I want the record revised. The Führer did not give the order."

Himmler fell silent. Then he asked, rather tentatively:

"You mean the record is to show that we acted on our own initiative?"

"Not necessarily. You did what you *thought* the Führer wanted, though he did not himself specifically order the extermination. If I'd ask him today, he would probably agree. That's one reason why he's never visited one of your famous camps. So give me the letter and I'm with you."

The SS chief cleared his throat.

"Martin, there's a problem."

"A problem?"

"The letter's gone. We can't lay our hands on it."

It was Bormann's turn to be stung with angry surprise.

"Why not? Where *is* the damn thing?"

Himmler proceeded to outline the story of the letter and of the repeated attempts to recover it.

"Maybe you want some update. Müller will know."

He asked his adjutant to find the head of the Gestapo. Müller was available and brought the latest information with him.

The American major, accessory to the theft, was in Theresienstadt and harmless for the time being. He did not have the letter, which – according to Hummel, an ace agent in America – was in a bank vault in Switzerland.

He, Müller, had received orders from Kaltenbrunner to let the matter rest there until further notice. Hummel was invaluable and could not be exposed unless it was absolutely essential.

"Well, it's become essential now," said Himmler. "Tell your chief I said so."

Bormann added, "The Führer wants the letter back." Strictly speaking, Bormann wanted it to burnish Hitler's image, but Müller did not need to know. "So what are the chances?"

Müller consulted his files. "The latest information we have adds a bit of mystery. Hummel is confident he's identified the thief as a pretty Jew bitch who lived in the Reich as an Aryan and was the lover of General Halder's protégé who's since been listed as a POW in Paulus' debacle at Stalingrad. This woman now lives in America and Hummel had her pegged under the closest surveillance. She's recited the text of the letter at public meetings, but she's never shown it because it's in Switzerland."

Himmler licked his lips and tugged at his mustache.

"Tell Hummel then to snag the bitch and take her on a free ride to Germany. We'll give her the kind of treatment that will make her happy to produce the letter."

Müller was not enthusiastic.

"Reichsführer, unfortunately there are two problems. The Navy's hesitant to commit a submarine that far away. Our fleet is decimated as it is. There'll be resistance on the Admiral's part. And if that could be overcome, there's the mystery I talked about. The woman has disappeared. She knew Hummel was on her tail and *abracadabra*, first you saw her, then you didn't."

"I'll be damned," Bormann said. "Jewish or not, she must be quite a number to give your ace agent the slip."

"She is that," Müller agreed. He came as close to admitting a form of grudging admiration for a Jew as he ever had. "Also, she has protection in high places. She has seen Roosevelt and is friendly with a Senator who is or was the father-in-law of the American we're holding in Theresienstadt. Incidentally, that's one reason we have to be a bit cautious with this guy, although officially he doesn't exist for us. We're having him in custody as a Jew with a phony name, and when the Red Cross inquires after Major Driscoll, we say, 'Sorry, we don't know him.' "

"Driscoll?" Bormann asked.

"Yes, sir, he was screwing this slut and they stole the letter together."

"You mean he was another lover she had? She must have

hot pants for Aryan men. Typical."

"And very clever. The classic Jew type. I'd like to get my hands on her."

"I bet you would, you lecher. Don't you know the penalties for race pollution?" Himmler was laughing now. The idea of Müller consorting with a Jewish woman appeared comical to him. Then again, there had been increasing numbers of SS men who were reported to have raped Jewish women before disemboweling them.

Müller was not amused. "I didn't mean it that way. I. . ."

"All right, enough of this. Just get the letter, I don't care how." Bormann stood up. His stocky figure and stern mien bespoke authority. "I don't care how," he repeated, and the conference ended on that note.

23

Being a spy, conspirator and occasional hit man had become second nature to Hummel. He thoroughly enjoyed his work; he was good and he had even come to relish his repeated brushes with danger. It was a game, and he played for the team in whose cause he believed. He had contempt for the American chase after material goods which had not been slowed perceptibly by the war. Democracy, he believed, was a system by which weak people kept strong leadership from taking hold, so that even a Roosevelt had to maneuver constantly to keep divergent factions in line, which was a sure way of corrupting his goals, if he had any besides keeping himself in power. Hitler was different, Hummel knew. His sight was set on the conquest of the world, and though the fortunes of war seemed to have turned against him, the strength of his will and the persistence of the German people would win in the end.

Born Hermann Gradewohl in Buenos Aires, he had attended university in Argentina and would have majored in biology, possibly with a view to entering medical school, when intelligence work for the Nazis became a full-time occupation. He was an avid reader, admired the manly styles of Hemingway and Steinbeck without sharing their political sympathy for Commies and Oakies. To be a spy, especially in wartime, required imagination, flexibility and a good deal of daring, something the Jews called *chutzpah*. When it came to Jews, he had no strong feelings; he considered Nazi enmity for them politically useful and morally neutral. In any case, what the Christians called morality had no substance; it was at best something to talk about and at worst an obstacle to doing what one's objectives required. Nietzsche was right.

In 1934 he and his boyhood friend George Snyder had been transferred to the United States where both men became citizens just as Hitler's troops marched into Poland and unleashed World War II. "I swear allegiance. . ." they had recited and neither one had the slightest intention of observing the oath.

Snyder, who was the head of the American operation, had called Hummel for a briefing in Chicago. Their procedure for meeting was always the same: a woman would be at Midway Airport holding up a sign saying "Miss Garfield" or "Miss Jackson" – which would mean that their meeting would be in Jackson or Garfield Park or wherever. The time never varied: sixty-nine minutes after sunset, on the second day after arrival; the place: a park bench. If the Jew Bernard Baruch could conduct his business from that kind of location, so could they.

The plane rolled to a stop; the terminal was crowded. Chicago was becoming the busiest airport in the nation. A young woman stood near the gate. "Miss Jackson" her sign proclaimed. Hummel checked into Palmer House. The bigger the hotel, the less likely that anyone would remember him. Then he went to a movie, a Broadway musical which he did not appreciate.

They exchanged brief news about their families in Argentina, then Snyder came to the point.

"The orders came from Himmler through our drop in São Paulo. Apparently there's been a change in thinking regarding the Führer's famous letter that you were dealing with quite some time ago. You remember the case?"

"Of course," Hummel replied. "But I laid off the chase some time ago. Orders. The American government had seen the letter, or a copy. In fact, almost certainly the latter."

"Why?" asked Snyder. "Fill me in. I haven't followed the case since they blew the whistle. But tell me while we walk a little. The park is pretty much deserted."

Hummel spoke with the precision of one who knows exactly what the facts are.

"Have you heard of a little Jewish girl, a rabble-rouser, who's gotten all the way to the President?"

"Yes, I remember her. Talked on the radio about the Final Solution."

"That's the one. Our people in the *Abwehr* suspected early on that she was the woman they were after."

"Yeah, I remember."

"So I shadowed her after she arrived on the boat and then kept tabs on her by employing her for a time in my fake medical office in New York. I'm sure she's our long-lost Hilde Schmitt. And she too has said the letter is in Switzerland. But tell me, why the sudden interest?"

"Damn if I know," said Snyder. "They didn't tell me and I didn't ask. The order was explicit: The original was to be recovered 'at all costs.' I have a feeling. . .but never mind, it doesn't matter. We'll follow the command. I suppose it means that they'll put another submarine at our disposal, even though it's a great risk. We've lost a hell of a lot of them lately. So I'm asking you, since you know the Jew dame, to send her the way of the American major. Let them do the questioning over there. You just see she gets on the boat. Okay?"

Hummel cleared his throat.

"I'd love to do that, George, but I can't. Not now, anyway."

"What's keeping you?"

"She's disappeared once more. That's the final proof that Schmitt is Helga Raben, the magician who can make herself vanish. If she weren't a Jew, I wouldn't mind having her on my team. Clever little item. And quite a looker too."

"And a lay as well, no doubt. So we find her. She must have left tracks somewhere."

"Probably," Hummel said. "Let me think about it, and maybe we can brainstorm together. Shall we say two days from now? I need a little time."

Their new venue was Garfield Park, once a pretty neighborhood with solid middle-class apartments. Now it stood at the edge of neglect; the Graemere Hotel surveyed a rapidly changing scene. They met at the park's north end, where the rattle of elevated trains guarded them from being overheard.

"I checked at the woman's room in New York some time ago," Hummel related. "No dice. The landlady has no forwarding address. But Schmitt must receive mail. She's got a relative in England and a dentist friend in Switzerland. She used to stay there, working as a hygienist. So if they write, Raben has a mail drop somewhere."

"General Delivery?" Snyder wondered.

"Possibly. I can check that out, at least in New York where most likely she'd have it. If she has it in another city, we're stuck. Unless, of course, my other hunch pays off."

"Namely?"

"Senator Browning who shepherded her through Washington. He's more likely than the rabbi with the big mouth."

"Wise?"

"Yes. I'd tackle the Senator, though I'm not sure how. But give me the word and I'll get on with it."

"You've got it," Snyder said. "Report in a month."

Hummel went back to New York and, as Dr. Cohn, posted a letter to Helga, care of Senator George Browning. He wrote that strong personal reasons must have moved her to leave so suddenly. But he owed her a half-month's wages and he felt unjustified in holding onto money that did not belong to him. He had taken a chance on sending it via the Senator, for he knew that they were friends, and he hoped that the letter would reach her. Good luck to her in whatever she was doing now.

Helga wondered briefly how Cohn knew her mail drop, but then forgot about it. She was pleased he bore her no ill will. She had had some guilt feelings about leaving her employer so precipitously and without explanation, and had buried them under the protective cover of self-preservation. She thanked Dr. Cohn and wrote how much she appreciated his thoughtfulness and apologized for her sudden departure which, she said, was due to personal circumstances beyond her control. She was now well established in her old career as a dental hygienist and was happy with her work. She sent him her regards, but added that presently she did not wish to reveal her whereabouts. She gave the letter to a fellow soldier who was on a three-day pass to Chicago and asked him to mail the letter from there. But the soldier forgot, and not until he returned and got off the train in Tomah, near the camp, did he remember and put the letter in a box.

24

Major Cross in the dentistry unit at Camp McCoy received a message from the camp commander's office: to send Private Raben to the adjutant; it might be necessary to detach her for special duty.

"Your record shows," the adjutant told Helga, "that you've been doing public speaking on Nazism."

"Yes, sir, before I joined the service. I had a particular subject: the extermination of the Jews. I wanted to call people's attention to the plight of my people. Hitler has murdered over two million already and he plans to kill them all."

"Rather improbable," said the adjutant, who in civilian life was a shoe salesman in Rockford, Illinois.

"Probable enough, sir, for President Roosevelt to set aside time to speak with me."

"You're kidding. *You* spoke with the President?"

"Yes, sir. Senator Browning took me to see him. I had some personal knowledge that I shared with the President."

The adjutant was impressed, and puzzled as to why no one seemed aware of this young woman's connection in high places.

"I must tell General Cox about you," he said. "I'm wondering, though, why you're tucked away at our camp as a dental technician."

"I had personal reasons for joining the Army, and I wanted to do my share in the fight against the enemy."

A large phrase, she thought, to describe the importance of cleaning dental drills for filling cavities in the mouths of American soldiers, many of whom would never come near a battlefield either in the West or the East.

"Well," the adjutant continued, "you'll have a chance to do some things a little more attuned to your experience. We'll detach you temporarily from the hospital for work with two other branches, Information and Intelligence. Both have requested that we look for qualified personnel for part-time assignments. I think you can fill them both."

Helga's interest was piqued. Without admitting it to herself, she had felt shunted aside from her real purpose. Her quest for safety had made her anonymity both acceptable and advisable. It was time to step forward again.

"Sir," she responded eagerly, "I'm most willing to do whatever I can. May I inquire what these assignments would entail?"

"Of course, though I can give you only a general description. Information wants you to give some orientation lectures about the Germans. And Intelligence needs an interpreter at the German prisoner-of-war camp. There is one just outside of McCoy."

Helga had heard of it, though the knowledge had meant little.

The next day she was asked to see Major Albert Krinsky. He was forty-two and had a speech peculiarity: he mixed his s and sh sounds, often comically. "Smash" might come out as "shmash" and "shoes" as "shoosh" or "soosh." He was intelligent, the managing editor of a weekly newspaper in Indiana. He had a hearty laugh which came readily and frequently. He welcomed Helga as if he had known her for a long time.

"We have orientation lectures for our soldiers, both the new ones in camp and those about to be shipped out. The former we tell about V.D. and the latter about the Huns and the Japs – wherever they'll be going. I remember you from a rally I heard over the radio some time ago. You were very good."

"Thank you, sir."

"Now, Private Raben, we'd like you to work up a talk that tells the fellows what Germans are really like and why it's important to fight them. Half of them don't know why they're here or whom they'll meet once they get there. Do you think you could do that?"

"I think so, sir."

"Good. But soft-pedal the Jewish issue. I say this though I'm one myself. I don't want these guys to think they're fighting this bloody war for the Jews."

"Soft-pedal? I'm not sure I understand. It's part of the picture, isn't it? Our people are being slaughtered wholesale, and you're suggesting that I should go easy on it? With respect, sir, I don't think I can do a good job that way. Shouldn't they see the Nazis as they really are, in their horrible brutality?"

Inferior ranks were not supposed to speak with such vehemence. Krinsky took note of it, though in a kindly fashion.

"You're upset, and I understand why. What Hitler is doing should be talked about. But there's a time and place for everything. Biblical advice, you know."

"Yes, sir."

"Look," said the major, "motivation and information go hand in hand. Your task is to give our G.I.s a good reason to fight. Make them understand that they're on the right side. Picture the police state for them as you have known it. Speak of the society they'd impose on us if they're successful. Yes, tell them what they're doing to non-Germans or those they define as non-Germans, what they've done to subjugated nations – Norway, Denmark, Italy, Poland, the

Czechs, the French. There are a lot of Scandinavians coming in here, from Minnesota and Wisconsin, and a lot of Bohemians, Poles and Italians from Chicago and vicinity. By all means tell them that they've concentrated on Jews as the weakest element, that they chased you out simply because of your parentage. Just don't make it the centerpiece. Enough of the guys you'll talk to aren't exactly our friends. They think we killed Christ, so what else is there to know about us?"

Helga waited for Krinsky to continue. When he did not, she indicated she'd do the best she could. When would she start? Next week, he said, and maybe there would be occasions when she would travel to some other camps. They too needed the kind of orientation she could provide. Meanwhile, he would send her over to G-2, who wanted her right away in another capacity.

"You see, Private Raben, you've become a most desirable person. I'll be in touch."

Over at Intelligence a young lieutenant greeted her. Carl Keller, he introduced himself, charged with interrogating German prisoners at the compound.

"Most are from the *Afrika Korps* of Rommel," he explained, "but now we also have a good many from the Italian campaign. It's these guys we want to question: about morale, how indoctrinated are they, is there an anti-Nazi underground, and so on. We have a list of topics we're supposed to cover. My grandparents came from Germany, but I'm a cripple when it comes to languages, and our chief interpreter was transferred out. So you're it. The way I get it is that you'll work regularly for us but are released for special assignments with Information."

"And the hospital?" Helga asked.

"They'll have to do without you for a while. Let's see how things work out. This is priority stuff."

He looked at her appraisingly, a young woman with a

fresh face and quizzical gaze who looked dashing in her WAC uniform.

"You're obviously someone who can do more than clean teeth," he added.

Major Krinsky was at least subtle in his double entendre, she thought. This guy has already undressed me with his eyes.

* * *

Hummel, alias Cohn, received Helga's letter. Suspicious wench, he cursed. Have you found out who Dr. Cohn really is? No, he concluded, you're not suspicious enough, my little pigeon. You probably mailed it yourself, didn't you? You took the bait but didn't swallow it. Yet you're hooked and don't know it yet.

At the 42nd Street library he consulted an atlas. Tomah, central-western Wisconsin. Small town, probably only one dentist. He was tempted to explore the possibilities via long-distance telephone, then decided against it. If I hit it right, she'll know from the dentist that someone asked for her and may take it on the lam again. I'll ride the train from Chicago after I talk to Snyder.

They met near the zoo in Lincoln Park. Hummel reported his findings. Once he found her, he said, he would manage to abduct her to Florida. Was this still the best place for a rendezvous with a U-boat?

No, it wasn't, Snyder informed him. In fact, the submarine caper was temporarily out. He did not know why, though he could venture a guess.

"Namely?" Hummel asked, much intrigued.

"Large funds are being transferred to South America. The sums are being shipped in a number of boats to lessen the risks. That's what I hear from São Paulo."

Hummel was aghast.

"Is it that bad? Are some cowards making sure of their future? Or is this an official action? Six ships is one helluva lot. Only the top brass could order that many. George, I don't like it one bit."

"Believe me, neither do I."

"So what am I supposed to do with this dame? Lay her and good-bye? Or build my own Zeppelin and fly her across? I suppose I have to take her to Mexico and southward from there. And then what? Send her back on an empty U-boat from La Plata?"

Snyder tried to encourage his friend.

"Look here, Hermann, why don't you locate her first, keep track of her and we ask them what they want us to do next. Leave the responsibility where it belongs. We're action people, we don't make policy."

"I'll do what you say, but I don't like the whole thing. It's taken the wind out of me, and the fun. Duty alone is dull. Fun and duty are powerful motivations. Maybe a good lay is all I'll get out of it. I'll let you know what I find."

* * *

The first POW interviews were routine. Helga found Carl Keller at Intelligence reasonably competent, though not imaginative. After she established that his knowledge of German was minimal, she decided to supplement his questions with her own, based on her intimate knowledge of the country. She became discursive at times and when Keller registered impatience she told him that the German did not understand the question or that she needed to gain his confidence.

The Germans from the African campaign were generally Nazis who were still convinced that Germany would win the war and that the British who had captured them would get their come-uppance. Their officers were arrogant and demanded that Helga salute them, as the Geneva conventions suggested. She did not translate the request for Keller, fearing he might agree and force her to comply.

She was particularly upset by a youngish *Hauptmann* who greeted her with a Hitler salute and insisted that she render him proper respect. Her patience snapped when he addressed her with the familiar *du*, reserved for children, subordinates and Jews. She warned Keller that the man had insulted her and had made improper advances. She would repay him in kind, she said, and the lieutenant agreed.

"You little tin soldier," she said icily, using the same *du* he had used in addressing her, "I want you to know that you have the misfortune of having me as your interrogator. Stand at attention while I talk to you!" she bellowed, hardly recognizing her own voice.

He looked at her in surprise, then abandoned his slouch and clicked his heels.

"That's better," she said. "Now behave yourself or I'll put you in isolation." She had no idea whether such punishment existed for prisoners. Her new role grew on her.

"You may wonder who I am. I'll tell you this: you bastards drove my parents to suicide. One wrong move and I'll give you a taste of your own medicine."

* * *

One day she was interviewing a German who had been captured at Anzio. He was a captain and had originally fought the Russians, was taken prisoner and had escaped to the West, rejoining the *Wehrmacht* after some harrowing encounters with partisans and starvation.

"Ask the name of his unit and the name of his commanding officer," said Keller. "Not that it matters, and he really doesn't have to answer. But he seems a bit more interesting than the others. Maybe we'll come across some worthwhile things."

Helga automatically translated the query; her mind was unfocused.

"Sixth Army," the captain said, "215th regiment, commanded by Colonel Baumgarten."

Helga jumped as though struck by lightning.

Keller was puzzled at her reaction. "What was it he said?" he asked. The German too was startled.

"Say it again," Helga commanded.

"General Paulus' Sixth Army, 215th Regiment."

"Commanded by?"

"Colonel Rolf Baumgarten, as courageous a soldier as you'll ever meet."

Helga sat down. She had broken out in a cold sweat.

"Captain, what I'm about to ask is purely personal. I lived in Germany once and I knew your commanding officer. Is he alive? And, if so, where is he?"

She feared the answer. Quickly she explained the question to Keller.

The captain answered slowly. "I'll tell you what I know. Colonel Baumgarten and I were captured together. Conditions in the Russian compound were terrible. A large number of our soldiers froze to death. The colonel decided he would try for a break. Better to be shot escaping than die a lingering death, he told us. And I remember something else he said: 'Maybe what's happening to us is retribution for what we're doing to the Jews.' He was no Nazi, and neither was I – but please don't tell this to my fellow officers."

"Go on," Helga urged, yet afraid of what she would hear.

"He told us of official plans to kill all Jews of Europe. They were being gassed systematically by the millions. If it hadn't been the colonel saying it, I wouldn't have believed it."

"What happened to him?" Her voice had shrunk to a whisper.

"We escaped together. It was winter, our footwear gave out, our uniforms were in rags. Besides the colonel and me, there were three others. One was shot by partisans, two died of exposure. For three weeks we crawled through the snow, dug for roots and tried to keep each other warm. I had lost three toes from frostbite when we were picked up by one of our patrols. I was in better shape than the colonel. He had a terrible cough, was spitting blood and one leg was almost frozen. But he too made it, I don't know how. On guts, I guess."

Helga was fighting her tears.

"Colonel Baumgarten was shipped off to a military hospital. I heard they decorated him. I lost track."

* * *

The train ride from Chicago to Tomah was slow, the stops were many. Hummel entertained himself by studying the faces of his fellow passengers. Lots of good Aryans around here, he thought. This was German and Scandinavian country. Would these people accept Nazi philosophy? For reasons he could not fathom, he was suddenly unsure. Better not to know. A quotation from Schiller came to mind: "Knowledge is death."

As they wended their way toward Tomah, more and more soldiers boarded the train. Obviously there was an Army camp nearby. Could the woman be there?

An enlisted man was happy to provide the information. Yes, he had seen a few women there; they were in offices mostly, some in the Special Services section. There weren't enough of them around to make things livelier at McCoy.

McCoy. . . The possibility had to be kept in mind.

"Tomah next stop!" called the conductor.

Rich soil, ample forests, lots of room in this rich country, Hummel thought. Misused by its people, in need of strong leadership.

The town was small and gave a satisfied, sleepy appearance. The telephone book showed one dentist. In the station's washroom Hummel put on a wig with brown hair, steel-rimmed glasses and a small mustache, checked his suitcase and walked into town.

He climbed the flight to Dr. Lakoonen's office; the waiting room was crowded. A young woman in a white uniform that fit too tightly over her large breasts approached him. A quick scan convinced him she was the only employee.

"When will the doctor be free?" he asked.

"Is it an emergency?"

"No, but I have to leave in a couple of hours."

"I'm terribly sorry," she said, "the doctor couldn't take you until late today. Maybe Dr. Honig in Sparta is free."

"I'll go only if he has a hygienist as good-looking as you."

She smiled warmly. "Thanks, mister. Nice of you to say that, but Dr. Honig doesn't have an assistant. If you're chasing skirts, go to McCoy. There's someone there who's worth your trouble."

He called the camp and asked to be connected with the dental office. With luck she might answer the phone.

"Dentistry, Private Bencovski speaking." A male voice.

"Excuse me," Hummel said, "could I speak with Miss Raben?"

"Call Special Services. Private Raben is temporarily assigned there."

Hummel took the next train back to Chicago. Having located his prey, he needed to discuss strategy with Snyder.

* * *

Helga was convinced it had been her fault that she could not put her message across. She had followed Krinsky's instructions, underplayed the Jewish aspect and stressed the dangers of tyranny. The soldiers had paid more attention to her figure than to her speech. Germany was far away;

politics held little interest for most of her listeners. Helga's lecture was not much different from the one that had preceded hers, which had dealt with the prevention of venereal disease. The soldiers agreed that Hitler and V.D. were dangerous to their health and then forgot about both.

"Are you Jewish?" a soldier asked Helga.

"Why?"

"I've never met a Hebe in my life, that's why. If they all look like you, I like Jews."

Raucous laughter.

"Isn't it true that Hitler made the trains run on time?" another G.I. asked.

"That was Mussolini and that's not the issue. What good is it if trains run on time only to carry innocent people to their deaths? We're fighting an inhuman enemy, that's what it's all about."

"Do you go out on dates?"

Loud applause.

Major Krinsky decided to end it there.

"Don't feel so discouraged," he consoled her later. "We have a tough task ahead before we can begin to match the Germans' devotion to their cause."

"I just didn't get to them," she said disconsolately.

"Maybe you did better than you think. Suppose there were a few in that crowd who had their eyes opened. That alone would make it worthwhile."

A saying from her school days flashed through her mind and it comforted her. "He who saves one soul, it is reckoned unto him as if he had saved the whole world."

25

Rolf Baumgarten was lying in a hospital bed in a Berlin suburb when the radio crackled the news: Allied units had launched their long-expected assault on Western Europe; but the Führer's troops had been prepared and had inflicted enormous losses on the enemy at the Normandy beaches. A few pockets of resistance still remained, but it was expected that they would soon be pushed back into the sea. It was Dunkirk all over again, said the announcer.

Rolf felt no joy. Besides, one had to take these battle reports with more than a grain of salt. He knew that Germany was being beaten in the East, yet newspapers and the radio had spoken of "strategic retreats" as if they were resounding successes. The longer the war lasted, the more profoundly he wished for an end to the Nazi regime. It had corrupted every aspect of national life. Truth was composed of what suited the Propaganda Ministry. Human life meant nothing. He feared the coming invasion of Germany and hoped that somehow the futile sacrifice of millions could be brought to an end before Europe and his own country lay in total ruin.

For a year now he had been hospitalized. He had become more inward; he read a lot and rarely spoke. He had made up his mind that he would not recover. The severe pneumonia he had contracted had resisted all attempts at full control, and no amount of medical expertise could save his gangrenous leg, which was amputated above the knee. But the gangrene, like the pneumonia, had persisted; further operations were indicated. He weighed a mere 120 pounds and was as emotionally flat as he was physically weak. The sterile atmosphere of the hospital did nothing to buoy his spirits. Also, he was alone most of the time. His mother, with her set face and starched manners, came occasionally and depressed him further.

The authorities were concerned about him. The other men who shared the officers' ward had wives or girl friends who came to see them and were afforded some privacy for intimacies. Rolf had no one.

"You need a woman," the chief surgeon suggested. "You've been a celibate for too long. I'll get you one, and not a real pro either. No fear of disease. She'll be thoroughly examined."

"All right," Rolf said wearily, without anticipation. He wondered how they would find a woman who was not a prostitute. Maybe she too was in need of sex. After all, most eligible men were at the front.

"Tomorrow then," the doctor said. "We'll move you to one of the private rooms."

"Thanks," Rolf answered, although he was not sure he could perform as expected.

In mid-afternoon the next day an orderly led a young woman into his room.

"Please ring the bell, Colonel, when you wish me to return," he said and closed the door.

She was in her twenties, had black hair that was combed back severely and dark eyes that conveyed sadness. Silently, unceremoniously, she undressed and stood by the bed, facing him in her nakedness. To his relief, Rolf felt his manly urge returning with full and demanding force. Yet her eyes held him back, an indefinable quality that spoke of resignation.

"Please, miss," he said, "we are strangers to each other, at least for now. Put your chemise back on for a moment and sit by my bed. I need to talk to you."

Puzzled, she did as bidden. Rolf wiped his forehead; he was strangely embarrassed.

"I don't know whether they told you of my condition. I've lost one leg and still wear bandages. I have pneumonia, though they assure me it's not contagious. I would not like you to be disgusted with me. Frankly, miss, I don't know how much manhood I have left, and I have no idea why you'd agree to sleep with me. I hope it isn't charity."

She looked at him, then began to cry. Between sobs, she told him her story.

No, it wasn't charity, far from it. She was here under duress. She was a Jew; they had experimented with her at Ravensbrück, and had performed ovarian surgery without anesthetics. She had almost died. On recovery, they had assigned her to an officers' brothel. She had come to know her masters in every way. Her arm bore the telling numbers of the concentration camp.

Rolf was appalled. He had heard about experiments and other atrocities but had never inquired further. The Army was an insulating place where Himmler's minions penetrated only on occasion. He had never connected brothels with forced labor. Now, in the person of this young woman, the ugly truth stood revealed.

He asked gently for her name.

She cried again. "My name? You're the first one to ask in a long, long time. I'm a number, temporarily useful, until they'll dispatch me to Auschwitz. I've almost forgotten my name. It is. . .it was. . .Naomi."

"May I ask how old you are?"

"I'm twenty-five, and feel I've lived for fifty years or

maybe I've hardly lived at all."

Twenty-five, he thought. That would be Hilli's age.

His desire for this woman was gone. For a while they did not speak.

"I would like to sleep with you," she said finally. "You're the first person in years who's treated me as a human being and not an object. And I don't care whether you have bandages. They're not disgusting. Believe me, I've been exposed to real disgust."

Her warmth and affection stimulated him, but that was all. The experience left him deeply depressed. Would she come back tomorrow? She would gladly, she responded.

He rang the bell for the orderly, who took Naomi away.

Hilli, he thought bitterly, have you fared like this? No, you wrote me that you were leaving the country. Where are you now? In England, most likely. Or did Driscoll take you to the States? This damn war, look what it has done to us. Would you still love me in my condition?

That night he had terrible dreams of Helga being dragged to a brothel while he lay helpless.

* * *

"So you found her! Good for you." Snyder complimented Hummel. "Your hunch paid off. From here on, it shouldn't be too difficult. Do you need some help?"

"Yes, I've thought about it on the way down. I think you ought to go along. Abducting someone from an Army post is likely to be noticed. It's tricky."

Snyder had his doubts. Risking two operatives on one venture was against the rules, to be done only under extraordinary circumstances. Was this such a case? Probably. But how would Hummel reach his prey?

"I've already made a plan," Hummel said. "I have composed a letter to Raben which may do the trick." He read his note to Snyder:

Dear Miss Raben,
I'm sure you will be surprised to get a letter direct from me. I got your address by pure accident. I have a nephew who is at Camp McCoy and he wrote me about a lecture you gave. He was much impressed and mentioned you by name, "Raben." It must be you. So you have joined the WACs, doing your patriotic duty. Good for you.

I'm writing to tell you that in the next few days I expect to visit my nephew before he goes overseas. I have a lecture to give in St. Paul and it's not too far from there to the camp. So I may have a chance to say hello to you too.

Sincerely,
Dr. A. Cohn

"What do you think?" Hummel asked.

"Good," was Snyder's judgment. "Go ahead and send it."

* * *

Dr. Klaus received one of Helga's rare letters. She was still running from the enemy, she wrote, though perhaps now, with the war going so badly for the Germans, they might have lost interest in her.

Still, she was not at peace. She was struggling with herself, her background, and with God. And there were the others with their prejudices who thought her lectures to be a lark and didn't take Hitler seriously.

She wrote of the prisoner who knew Rolf and who told how the two had escaped. *So he's still alive after all!*

Dr. Klaus read the paragraph again. Hilli's no longer in love with Rolf, she thought. A year ago the news would have dominated her letter; now it was only incidental, though Hilli made it the subject of a request.

Would Dr. Klaus's contact approach General Franz

Halder, now retired? Perhaps he had Rolf's address.

She concluded by telling her benefactor that she was hoping for an overseas transfer, and maybe there was a chance of seeing her again.

Dr. Klaus replied that she was not well at all. Arthritis had crippled her and she had to give up her practice. She had retired to Oberhofen where she continued to house refugees. She was familiar enough with the degenerative effects of her disease to know that sooner or later she would have to surrender her independence. She informed Helga that efforts were being made to contact the person she had suggested.

It was her unshakable belief that with the victory of the Allies Helga's troubles would diminish. She hoped that Army service gave her the satisfaction of contributing her share. How did she know that there was not one soldier who had his eyes opened by her lectures?

* * *

General Halder had retired to his villa in the country. Being unceremoniously relieved of his post as Chief of the General Staff had been a terrible blow at first, yet in retrospect he was glad. He had always been against the ill-conceived Russian campaign and despite the early successes had known that sooner or later Germany's extended supply lines, its two-front war and Russia's enormous manpower would become insuperable obstacles. The Führer was impervious to any advice; as supreme warlord, he listened only to those advisers like Keitel and Jodl who, lackeys that they were, always agreed with him. In retirement Halder was distancing himself from the inevitable coming defeat and was working on notes for his diary which he hoped to publish after the war, circumstances permitting. He was convinced that Hitler had to be removed forcibly to save

Germany before the Allied troops would invade it and while a respectable German Army was still in existence.

Now that the invasion in the West had succeeded, time was running short, and he had once again made contact with his old friends of the Army underground. They were glad to have him on their side, even though he would play only the role of elder statesman. Their latest plot to assassinate the Führer had jelled; it was set for July 20, 1944. The leader of the group, Count von Stauffenberg, would himself kill Hitler at his headquarters on the Eastern front, and co-conspirators in Berlin and across the country would assume pivotal positions of power once the word was given that the Führer was dead.

Franz Halder was careful not to have the plotters visit him at his estate; he made his contacts while in Berlin from time to time. The big city still afforded the best cover, and Halder, in his civilian clothes, could fade into the anonymity of the crowds.

In a small cafe on Pestalozzistrasse he met with his old friend Werner Krinzli, a Swiss banker who had occasionally been his intermediary in sensitive matters. They discussed the war and its irreversible course. They agreed that Germany's new weapons, the V-1 and V-2 bombs, would make no difference. All they could do was to stiffen the Allied will to exact the severest terms of surrender.

Krinzli turned to another subject.

"Franz, do you know the rate at which the Final Solution is proceeding? The figures I hear are staggering. Three thousand or more a day – is that possible?"

Halder looked around to make sure they were not overheard.

"It's not a matter to be talked about. The bastards shroud everything in secrecy and give it code names to cover their tracks. They say 'worked through' when they mean killed. They say 'relocation' when they mean transport to an extermination camp. They have an orchestra play at Auschwitz while they march their victims to the gas ovens. Anything to hide from the world – and the Jews, of course – what they're doing. I fear they've already succeeded past their wildest dreams."

"And the German Army stands by and lets it happen?"

"Look, Werner, it's not that simple. The Army is fighting a losing war and isn't standing around. It's the SS who're in charge of the operation. They organize it and carry it out. Still, the Army has its share of guilt. I have, everyone has. We know about it and do nothing. And even those who don't know the details are carefully looking away to salve their brittle consciences. This thing will haunt us for generations to come, long after the physical ravages of the war have been repaired. But, Werner, are we alone to blame? Isn't the silent bystander also an accomplice?"

"You mean us, the Swiss? Come now, don't load your guilt on us, old boy."

"I don't mean you alone. I was speaking of the Poles, Lithuanians, Russians, Ukrainians and God knows who that watched and let it happen or even helped it along. I was speaking of the Allies too. They knew about it and didn't even raise their voices, let alone bomb the rail lines at Auschwitz and Birkenau, which they could have easily done. I remember how they bombed the factories in the city of Auschwitz and I expected that they'd spare a few hits for the death installation. Nothing."

Krinzli was visibly relieved, and Halder noticed it.

"Don't look so smug, Werner, I don't exempt the Swiss either. You could have shown a bigger heart toward the trickle of refugees who made it across your sacred borders. I heard Himmler once say that he considered your nation an ally in the fight against the Jews."

"That's a dastardly lie. We were never like that!"

"Of course not," Halder said soothingly. "I only mention it to show how our chief Jew hunter viewed the Swiss. That was the impression you gave. I really didn't agree with Himmler. In fact, I don't remember when I ever agreed with him on anything."

Krinzli made no further comment. He was aware of the bad record which the Swiss bureaucrats had helped to create.

"Let's drop the subject, Franz," he said. "Anyway, while we may not have a noble record, we do have our moral nobility too. I want to speak to you in behalf of one of them. She's a splendid woman who uses her estate to house refugees, and she constantly remonstrates with authorities about this case and that. Everyone listens to her. Moral force still has standing with us. She's asked me to inquire after a friend of yours. Someone she knows wants to find out without going through official channels."

"Really! And who's this friend of mine?"

"Someone formerly on your staff, a Colonel Baumgarten."

"Rolf Baumgarten? First-rate man. Insisted on being detached from headquarters and put in a field command. I'm sorry to say he was reported missing in action. There is of course a chance he was taken prisoner."

"Well, he was and we know he escaped."

"He did?" Halder was delighted. "I've been away from the service and haven't heard. Where is he? Back at the front?"

"No, he's apparently not well and had to be hospitalized. That's what a fellow officer reported who escaped with him. My friend wants to ask whether someone like you could find Baumgarten so that an old chum of his can write him."

"Of course, no problem at all. I can't tell you how happy I am to hear the news. I only hope he's not too sick. Thanks a lot, Werner, your friend in Switzerland has given me great joy. You'll hear from me very soon."

Halder was whistling when he left the cafe, something he hadn't done in quite a while.

In Theresienstadt the unusual happened. A small group of inmates were to be released and shipped to Switzerland, in transit to Palestine. No one knew precisely why it happened and why particular people were selected for the unheard-of, unbelievable return to freedom. It ran counter to everything the Nazis stood for: once a Jew was caught in the dragnet, he was caught for life or, more likely, for death.

Rumors abounded: The lucky ones were to be exchanged for prisoners in Allied hands; no, the Germans were getting a hundred trucks for every freed Jew; those released had special Nazi protectors; they were very rich and had dollar deposits in neutral countries which they were turning over. The Germans knew they were losing the war and wanted to show themselves to be humane. The last of these rumors was the most popular.

Driscoll-Silberberg, who had let his beard grow and now looked the part of a traditional Jew, saw his opportunity. He approached Moritz Pelz, the leader of the "lucky dozen," as they were called, and asked him to deliver a message to some authority, the Americans if at all possible: Major Kenneth Driscoll had been abducted and was being held under the name of Abraham Silberberg. If he could not contact any official, would he write a note to that effect to Dr. Bertha Klaus, dentist in Bern.

Moritz Pelz agreed, though he, like many others in the camp, was not thoroughly convinced that Silberberg's story was true. To be sure, the man's German was imperfect and bore a strong foreign accent, but the camp commandant had publicly ridiculed Silberberg's claim as a ploy to win special attention and had put him in solitary confinement on several occasions. It was safer to accept the official version; and after a year of it, inmates believed the Nazis – even as growing numbers were beginning to consider themselves inferior because their masters expounded on that theme day after day by word and deed.

Pelz promised to deliver the message, if possible. A thousand others also wanted to communicate with the free world. He did not know, he warned, how and when he could do what they asked.

A prisoner deathly ill with malnutrition and typhoid fever had a Hebrew Bible with German translation which he gave to Silberberg before he died. The American was attending study sessions with Rabbi Leo Baeck, held at night when the lights were out. Baeck, as always, lectured from memory on Christian theology and its relation to Pharisaic thought and, of course, Jewish literature. He traversed vast stretches of homiletical material which he knew by heart, and quoted so often in the original that Silberberg decided he had to learn Hebrew. Rabbi Baeck agreed and snatched a few moments after his chores were done, which consisted of dragging human excrement to a dumping ground. He and another prisoner were yoked together like dray horses for the haul. He was asked once how he could manage to get through a day while doing his disgusting labor.

"I never think about it," the rabbi said. "The other horse is so intelligent, we have a marvelous time talking."

Using the Bible, Baeck had no trouble teaching the ancient language to the American. By the time of Shavuot-

Pentecost, a few days after the Normandy invasion, they were reading the *Book of Ruth*, and for the first time Silberberg vocalized to the rabbi the decision that had been slowly ripening within him: forcibly made into a Jew by the Nazis, he wanted to be one voluntarily.

Rabbi Baeck did not encourage him and neither did he turn him back. "These are not circumstances amid which one could be said to act freely," Baeck told him. Once they were liberated – and everyone now spoke of that day with growing certainty – he would have enough time to make his decision.

"I'm not sure I want to wait that long," said Silberberg. "I might die before the Americans get here, and I do want to die a Jew. I want you to convert me."

Baeck put him off.

"Wait a little longer. Study some more. We'll both know when you're ready. Read your Bible, such a rare treasure. Read it over and over again and learn as much of it as possible by heart. It'll keep your mind nimble and off your predicament." Baeck smiled. "And don't forget to read my favorite book, the *Song of Songs*. It'll focus your heart on the ones you love, and that will give you the will to endure what you must."

"I'll commit it to memory," the American said, and thought of Helga.

* * *

The warm air of a summer's night enveloped the two men sitting on a bench near the Garfield Park conservatory.

"The plan is ready," Hummel said. "Here it is. We drive two cars to St. Paul, leave one at the station where it won't be noticed, drive one car to wherever she'll meet me, exchange cars in St. Paul and leave the other one there, minus plates. We'll etch out the engine number in advance.

The rest shouldn't be too hard. Karl Heinrich in Houston will help us across the border to Mexico. From there we'll take her to Argentina, if necessary."

Snyder grunted. The project did not appeal to him. Besides, he had recently acquired a new girl friend who was proving to be a real find, in the bedroom and out of it. Her husband was with the F.B.I. and currently overseas on special assignment, and the straw widow turned out to be highly indiscreet in every way. Snyder feared that by the time he would return from Mexico or worse, South America, his chance for romance and for exploiting this rather remarkable source of information would likely have dried up. The husband was due back in two weeks.

"Damn you, Hermann," he said at last, hissing his imprecation. "You've messed me up but good. I'm in the middle of a once-in-a-lifetime opportunity." He did not explain. "But I suppose I have no choice. So let's go, and the sooner the better. But I'd like to leave you in Galveston. I shouldn't be out of the country. Things are getting tight in France and bad in Russia. When they want something from us, they want it yesterday. I'll fly back from Houston and you go on with Karl Heinrich."

He figured he'd lose four to five days this way. In any case, no more than a week. He felt better about it.

"Yes," said Hummel. "Today's Tuesday. We can leave Thursday and should be at McCoy by Friday. Saturday or Sunday we make our move. Three days later we'll be in Texas. I'll report tomorrow night."

"Lincoln Park," said Snyder.

* * *

The small hospital, formerly a private clinic operated by a Jewish doctor, was located at the edge of Dahlem, a fashionable suburb of Berlin. It stood on lovely grounds with stately trees and a broad lawn. Wounded officers who required long-term care were quartered here.

Colonel Rolf Baumgarten was happy when his old protector, General Franz Halder, came to call. The five other patients applauded when they recognized the general. He thanked them and sat at Rolf's bedside.

"I wish I had known you were here. I would have come much earlier," he said. "You look well enough. Are you making good progress?"

Rolf looked at Halder with clouded eyes.

"The doctors tell me 'yes,' but I don't see it. The wound doesn't heal, so they can't fit me with a prosthesis. And the pneumonia has been as stubborn as you know who."

"I hope it isn't that bad," Halder said, looking around the ward. The other men seemed to pay no attention; some had visitors of their own. In a whisper he continued: "I wish you were well, the boys could use you. Big moves are in the offing. I'm not familiar with the details and only know the plans in general. If they succeed, we'll all breathe easier."

"Your ideals are mine," Rolf said with fervor. "God, how I would work for the cause! Having been a soldier at the front, then a prisoner and now ill for a long stretch, I've lost touch with the real world. I've come to know a little about it recently, and in the strangest way. Through a Jewish girl who visits me three times a week."

"A Jewish girl? Here?"

Rolf told him the story of Naomi, whom he was seeing regularly and with whom he had formed close personal bonds. She was a gentle and even fervent lover, whose veil of infinite sadness was lifted occasionally when they were together.

Naomi Landsmann, he learned, had been born in north Berlin, in Pankow, where her parents ran a small notions store. She was good looking enough to be popular in school and was a fine athlete. In Berlin's school tournament she had surprised everyone by winning the high jump and had entered the German-Jewish championships, participation in the larger competition no longer being permitted. She did well, though she did not win, and found congenial friends in these endeavors. She was vivacious and a fair student. Her first affair, with a long-distance runner at the national Maccabi Games, left her disappointed. She experimented briefly with one of her teachers in a thoroughly unsatisfactory lesbian relationship.

Relatives of her mother lived in Holland and urged the family to leave before it was too late. But her father, a gentle and pious man, did not feel that they could go penniless and live on the charity of their relatives. So the Landsmanns stayed, lost the store in the aftermath of Crystal Night, and when at last they decided that leave they must, the war broke out and their escape hatch closed tightly and irrevocably. Naomi, her younger sister and her parents lived for a while in Berlin and eventually were shipped east.

After three terrible days of being shunted from one cattle car to another, being given no food, no water and no means of decently relieving herself, bathed in the stench of excrement and the horror of death in the darkness of a car, she arrived in a place she later learned was called Treblinka. She saw her mother briefly and thereafter never again.

Another train ride six days later and this time to Auschwitz, where a nattily attired officer holding a riding crop waved her to one side. The Angel of Death had separated her out for life, but she would often wonder whether her mother, who hopefully had died quickly, was not better off.

For Naomi had caught the Angel's eyes, the Angel being the notorious Dr. Josef Mengele, who picked her out as a likely candidate for his special experiments. His latest investigation aimed at establishing the physiological reaction of a woman when she was sexually assaulted. Naomi was gang raped and between each assailant her pulse and her blood pressure were carefully measured and recorded. And when Mengele was finished, he had his assistant perform a hysterectomy on her to study the effect of rape upon her reproductive system. For weeks she hung to the slender threads of life and eventually was assigned to the brothel service. She tried suicide twice and then gave up, lapsing into a near catatonic state of detachment. Then came her visits to Rolf, and her life force began to flicker again.

Rolf lowered his voice.

"You know, General, it's strange: I seem to have an affinity for Jewish women. I can confess it now. When I was your deputy to the Gestapo and was sitting there among Long Nose Reinhard's gallery of rogues, I was seeing a young Jewess with whom I was head over heels in love. Maybe I still am, although it's just one heel now," he added ruefully. "I don't know where she is and whether she still remembers me. It's six years now."

"Well," Halder said gently, "maybe that 'Swiss chum' who wants to get in touch with you has a line on her. It could be the girl herself, couldn't it? Ah, it's really cruel of me to raise your hopes. But soon, if all goes well, you'll be able to make open inquiries and write letters everywhere in the world, and that racial crap will all be considered a bad dream."

"I hope so, sir. Except that too many people had to die to feed our dreams."

27

"The Day" was July 20. Count von Stauffenberg himself carried the bomb that was to kill Hitler to Rastenburg in East Prussia, where the Führer's headquarters were now located.

In the anteroom Stauffenberg pulled the pin, which allowed for a ten-minute lapse before explosion. He placed the bomb near the Führer and left the room, confident the assassination would succeed in another minute or two. But in that interval a Colonel Brandt innocently moved Stauffenberg's lethal briefcase a few inches. It was now separated from Hitler by a heavy oaken table support. When the bomb went off, Brandt was killed, while Hitler received only minor injuries. The attempt had failed, and in short order the conspirators were identified by Himmler's apparatus.

Hitler's revenge knew no bounds and unleashed a wave of terror not only against the plotters but any suspects and their families. An orgy of blood covered the Reich. Those who were not shot on sight or tortured to death or strangled by suspension from meat hooks were sent to concentration camps where death often became a preferable alternative to life.

The executions were filmed, showing the men in mortal

agony, beltless trousers slipping from their bodies, leaving them dangling naked as they struggled for their last breath. Hitler viewed the films time and again. Goebbels looked at them briefly and could not continue. He, like Himmler, had no trouble disposing of thousands of people, yet could not face the stark reality of seeing human beings of flesh and blood going to their death. Five thousand perished in the days and months that followed, among them some of Germany's best generals and brightest spirits.

The dragnet caught General Halder as well. He was imprisoned and kept at Niederdorf in the Tyrolian mountains. For months on end he sat in solitary confinement in a dark cell. Grilled and tortured, he was forced to trace his movements for the last six months in great detail and account for every person he had seen.

Was it true that he had contacted Colonel Baumgarten? It was true, Halder admitted, that he had visited the hospital to see the badly wounded soldier who had been a former member of his staff. The visit was one of mercy, nothing more. However, the mere fact that Rolf had been seen by Halder the week before the Rastenburg attempt was reason enough for the Gestapo to call on him.

Sturmbannführer Witzleben, who came with an SS driver-and-secretary, was a distant relation of his famous namesake, the general who had been implicated in the plot. He displayed the zeal of one who feels he must constantly show his loyalty. Big, bald, a heavy beer drinker with a large belly to show for it, he was crude in language and deportment. Kaltenbrunner valued him as a subordinate who did not shrink from cruelty. Witzleben brought with him a file that dated back to the days when Rolf first represented the Army as a liaison officer at Alexanderplatz.

Rolf had followed events with avid interest and was worried about Halder whom he had not seen again. He was surprised to find the inquisitor at his bedside. It had not occurred to him that he too would be suspected. The interview took place in the private room in which Rolf met Naomi.

"Let's get down to business," Witzleben said curtly. "I guess you know why we're here."

"Frankly, I don't. I've been removed from the outer world for a long time and have lost touch."

"Sure, but not so much that you didn't have a meeting with General Halder."

How stupid of me not to have made the connection right away, thought Rolf. A coughing spell seized him.

"A meeting?" he said at last. "We had no meeting. He came to visit me. Didn't know I had lost a leg."

Rolf threw back the covers and showed his stump. The bandages were soaked with discharge. The wound was suppurating again. Witzleben looked away; this was not in his plan. He suddenly felt on the defensive and resented it. He resumed his prosecutor's tone.

"How often did you see the general? Name dates and times exactly."

"He came once, a short visit in the ward. I can't remember when, some weeks ago. When you lie in bed as I do, time loses its meaning."

"And before that? Any contact? By letter or any other means?"

"Not since I said good-bye to him two years ago at Headquarters East. He was still Chief of the General Staff at that time. I requested service at the front and commanded a regiment in the Sixth Army."

Witzleben spat on the floor and spread the spittle with his boot.

"Sixth Army, *pfui*!" he exclaimed with contempt. "That's the outfit which brought us all the trouble at Stalingrad. That traitor Paulus! Ran away and gave up."

Rolf reddened with anger. He would have hit this hulking

beer bully if he had been healthy, but he also knew that Witzleben would not have talked to him in this fashion had Rolf been on his feet.

The Nazi plodded ahead. He opened the file.

"I have a report here that states you had contact with the so-called Kreisau circle. Traitors all, mostly dead by now. True?"

"That they're dead? I don't know." Rolf could not help puncturing the bloated hunk of Gestapo blubber with a bit of innocence.

"Clever jokes yet! Wait until I'm finished. You won't feel like making jokes. Were you a member of that circle?"

"I attended a few of their discussion groups. Quite apolitical. We spoke of such topics as: 'Morality in international relations,' 'Politics and the ethical impulse.' Themes like that. I assure you that had it been more, I would not have attended."

The investigator smirked.

"Wouldn't you, though! Your file testifies to the contrary. For instance, you were shacking up with a certain Hilde Schmitt?"

"Yes, I knew her for a while before I left for the front."

"Were you in touch with her later?"

"No, not that I recall."

"Think hard now, Colonel. Did you know what she did after you left?"

"No, what would she do? Get married, I suppose."

"Please spare me your clever remarks. Did you know she committed murder?"

"Murder? Not she, never!"

"Well, the little fucky-ducky did. Killed an SS officer, Heinrich Richter."

Rolf had enough self-control not to show his amazement. He sank back on his pillow with a groan of pain. Richter was Helga's brother. She killed him! It must have been revenge. For her parents maybe.

"You have a bad record, Colonel," the inquisitor was saying. "Gave yourself up to the enemy, contact with General Halder, being hotsy-totsy with a woman who ups and kills an officer. Nice work, but that isn't all. The little dame who wiggled her ass for you was, or is, a kike. Didn't you know that? You committed *Rassenschande*, pollution of the Aryan race."

"Nonsense," said Rolf with as much force as he could muster. He was still in a state of shock. "Schmitt was an Aryan like you."

"Maybe yes and maybe no. Likely the latter. She's alive and kicking and a sworn enemy of the Reich. Does Jew propaganda in America and will come to a bad end if we can help it."

"Schmitt in America?" Rolf could hardly believe the good news. "How would she get there?"

"Damned if I know." It was Witzleben's first admission of ignorance. Interrogators usually put up a front of omniscience. "Of course she parades under her original kiky name, Helga Raben. Or maybe that's old hat to you?"

Rolf did not respond. He wanted most of all to be left alone and relish the wonderful news. Hilli alive! He opened his eyes. The despicable Witzleben was still there.

"*Herr Sturmbannführer*, I'm tired. I'm not well. Can we bring this to an end?"

"All right, but I don't think we're finished. You didn't tell me half of what you know."

He rose, gave the Hitler salute and threaded his fleshy mass through the door.

* * *

Helga was attracted to the simple services at the camp's chapel and to the young chaplain who conducted them.

Lieutenant Morris Goldberg had become a good friend. Helga performed various chores around the chapel and studied with Goldberg when he held Bible and history classes on Wednesday nights. Laura, his pregnant young wife, would also attend and the two women established a warm and easy relationship. Helga would visit the Goldbergs in their rented rooms off the post. An enlisted person might not be permitted to socialize with ordinary commissioned officers; a chaplain and his wife were different.

One evening in August Goldberg was late for his class. When he arrived, he apologized, waving a piece of paper.

"It's going to be our last session. I've received my overseas orders. I'm sorry and I'm glad. Glad to go and be part of the action, and sorry because I have to leave my wife. She's packing tonight."

Lieutenant Goldberg would be present for services on Friday night and leave on Sunday.

"How about a good-bye party after services?" Helga suggested.

The chaplain observed the tradition of not traveling on the Sabbath; he and his wife would stay at the post and go home after sundown.

It was agreed. Volunteers would spread the word among the personnel and advise the representative of the Jewish Welfare Board who would take care of the social aspect. The top brass of the post would be invited too. There was enough time.

A group of civilians from Sparta and Tomah attended on Friday evening. The chaplain had become a friend to many. Catholic and Protestant clergy crowded the chapel.

Helga was sitting in the last row. Halfway through the service someone slipped into the seat next to her. At first she paid no attention to the latecomer; she was praying with particular concentration this night. When she finally looked, she saw Dr. Cohn.

"I visited my nephew this morning. He'll be transferred

out on Sunday," he said when the service was over and the farewell for the chaplain was under way. "I thought I might find you here. Do you have a little time tomorrow to go off the post?"

"No," she said, "not tomorrow. I no longer ride on *Shabbat*."

"Maybe Sunday then? I'll still be here."

The idea of socializing with her former employer held no particular attraction for her. He had always been distant and she still remembered his reaction to the news of the Final Solution. Still, she did not want to be ungracious.

"Maybe Sunday afternoon would be okay."

"That'll be fine. I'll go off to St. Paul later that day. What time shall we make it?"

"Come by about three o'clock in front of Special Services. Ask at the gate."

"Splendid," said Cohn, and they drank wine, she to celebrate the Sabbath and toast the chaplain and his wife, and he to savor the impending success of his mission.

The next morning Major Krinsky called her into his office.

"We're going to lose you too, Sergeant Raben."

"Sergeant?"

"Yep – *mazel tov*, it's about time. A double promotion. Frankly, I wanted you to go to Officers' School and had put in an application for you. Hope you don't mind. And now this!"

He held up a piece of paper.

"European Theater, you're on your way."

There it was: *Report in three days to Camp Reynolds, Pennsylvania, for European staging.* Orders were like earthquakes: one couldn't do a thing about them.

An idea struck Helga. She walked over to see the Goldbergs. The two were also going to Reynolds. Could she drive with them?

They left early in the day. Not until they reached Madison did Helga remember her date with Cohn. Maybe it's just as well, she thought, he'll think I stood him up.

* * *

Hummel-Cohn was pleased with himself. It would be much easier than he had feared. She'd be in his car voluntarily. They'd pick up Snyder on the road. He'd administer a quick sedative injection and the rest would be routine. Their other car was in St. Paul. In three days at the most they'd be in Houston.

They were having coffee in Sparta. Snyder looked at his watch.

"We'd better go, you want to be on time."

"Don't be so jumpy, George," Hummel said in an expansive mood. "You'll be with your girl friend before her husband returns."

"How in hell did you know, you son-of-a-bitch? You're supposed to spy on Americans, not me."

"Dear George, a good agent knows everything that touches on his work. You touch my work, so you're part of my professional interest. Nothing personal, just careful."

Snyder understood only too well. He would have done the same in Hummel's place. Besides, he himself had investigated his own agent from time to time, although Hummel was elusive and his private life almost inaccessible.

Hummel reveled in his successful ploy.

"The girl's clever, but of course an amateur. She never knew my real work when she was in my office. She swallowed the Cohn story holus-bolus. Well, won't she have a surprise!"

He let Snyder off near the prison camp, then drove to McCoy. At three o'clock he parked in front of Special Services. When at four o'clock she had not appeared, he went inside.

"Sergeant Raben's no longer with us," said the clerk. "She's left for the war in Europe. Drove off with the chaplain this morning."

When Hummel, bitterly disappointed, imparted the news to Snyder, his boss was rather pleased. Hummel had been humiliated, and his own girl friend was waiting. All's working out for the best, he thought, and couldn't remember where he had heard this comforting philosophy.

PART VI

A Piece of Glass

WINTER 1944

28

Much to their delight, Helga and Chaplain Goldberg found themselves on the same plane bound for England. It was a refitted DC-3 which sat down in Gander, Newfoundland, and then made its way through the clear October night to the Azores and then to Prestwick in Scotland. There were some seats around the side and a soldier had courteously offered to surrender his space to Helga. She declined with thanks. She wanted no special privileges as a woman. Like most of the passengers, she spread out the bedroll and slept on the floor. She dreamt of Rolf. He had come back from prison camp and could speak only Russian. She tried to tell him that she now cared for Ken but Rolf did not understand and reached for her to make love in public. She drew back violently and awoke with a start. A soldier next to her had turned and touched her. He was snoring loudly, competing with the roar of the four engines.

The sun had made its slow ascent and sent its morning promise slanting through the little windows. We are flying into the arms of a new day, Helga thought, and wiped away the sour aftertaste of the dream. Am I returning to the past? I was in England six years ago, a willful, spoiled girl, madly in love with Rolf. What a world it was then. Father and Mother still alive; Jettie Kostler in Hampstead – such a warm companion. Where is Jettie now? she wondered. Their correspondence had been spotty. She could not recall whether the dear woman still lived at the old address. In her hurry to pack, she had left the information behind. With a few other belongings, it was on its way to Senator Browning.

Suddenly Heinrich intruded in her thoughts. She had repressed that darkest portion of her past. Now on her way to a bloody Europe that could hardly recall its peaceful yesterdays, she was able to think about her brother: full of mischief as a boy, cruel in his adolescent victories, good looking, arrogant, hard to know and to love. When did he first decide to forsake our family, to become a certified Aryan and a Nazi? In her mind she saw him standing across the street after her parents' funeral, the SS man who was her brother and who wasn't. She perceived him dispassionately and clearly. No guilt or regret clouded her recollection of the man and the night she made a violent end of his rapacious desire.

A deep calm descended on her and she gratefully said her morning prayers.

Helga was quartered in a small WAC compound outside London and assigned to Intelligence. She translated German broadcasts and found her tasks dull and unchallenging. The women whom she saw after work were preoccupied with their social needs. She shared little with them and tried not to appear distant and cold. She read a great deal and became steeped in Jewish history and saw Jettie on the Sabbath.

Jettie had given up her job and lived on a modest retirement pension. She was renting the spare room to an American serviceman and his English wife. The war had been hard on Londoners. Even now the new V-2 bombs rained sudden destruction from the skies.

* * *

A letter came from Dr. Klaus, forwarded from McCoy:

My very dear Hilli,
I have good news for you. I learned through a good friend that R. is safe and currently recuperating in a hospital. Apparently he had some rather harrowing experiences. That's all I know at this point. By the time you write I will probably have his address. So you see, things are turning out better than anticipated, and the way the war is going it won't be too long before the world returns to sanity.

Like you, I wonder of course whether you might be assigned overseas, and if it would chance to be Europe, who knows? You might find yourself in liberated France and get a pass to visit Bern. I'm dreaming, you see.

I wish my health were better. This terrible arthritis is really crippling me. If I have to go to a nursing home I would have to give up Oberhofen. That would be a terrible wrench, and where would my guests go?

Any news about Major Driscoll? If so, I hope it's good.

Faithfully and fondly yours,
Bertha

Late into the night Helga read the letter and tried to come to terms with her feelings. Rolf had become a distant memory, part of her rebellious youth. After he went to the Russian front, there had been letters from him, notes of affection and loneliness. When they had ceased coming, she was on the run. Ken became the focus of her life. America and Driscoll were her future; and then this too had become a chimera. Bertha Klaus was her only constant link with the past. And now there was Rolf again. She would write him, but what would she say – that she still loved him, or that their erstwhile relationship belonged to irretrievable yesterdays?

* * *

George Snyder heard from Bormann through the Argentinian contact:

> *The issue of the letter of credit is becoming more and more urgent every day. If it has been destroyed, inform me personally forthwith; that will end the matter. If it is extant, it must, repeat must, be repossessed. Spare no effort or expense. You may have to have recourse to some new and untried approach. Unorthodox methods, especially when they involve surprise, sometimes work wonders. The chief of our bank insists that his wishes be followed.*
>
> *Sincerely,*
> *Ignacio Bornstein*

The dispatching officer evidently thought that a Jewish name added a special ironic dimension to the underlying message. This time Snyder took a plane to New York and met Hummel in Central Park. He let him read the message. Hummel studied it and handed the letter back irresolutely.

"I don't know what he means by 'unorthodox methods.' I haven't exactly gone by Roberts' Rules of Order. Personally, I thought the Dr. Cohn ploy was rather ingenious. After all, I had her under close supervision for quite a while. She slipped through our net by the sheerest unforeseeable accident."

"Well," Snyder said, "think of something else."

Hummel loosened his collar. He felt warm, though a cool wind played on his back.

"It so happens that ever since she got away I have wondered how I could catch the bird. I do in fact have an idea but I have to tell you it's far out, and in any case you'll be minus my services for a time."

Snyder was intrigued. Anything that might work to please Bormann, who would mention his effort to the Führer himself.

"Let's have it, Hermann. The more extreme the plan, the better it will likely be."

"Well, George, wait till you hear it. Here's the way I see it. Our bird is now in Europe. Sooner or later she'll be in France. If I can get to her there, a Swiss side trip is a real possibility."

"And how will you get there?"

"That's where my idea is far out. I would join the Army and hope for the best."

"You're crazy, Hermann, that's gambling with very poor odds."

"Not quite as poor as you might think. I have some contacts in Washington. I think I can get an officer's commission with the objective of working for military intelligence. My knowledge of German will make me a likely candidate for a European assignment. After all, as Hermann Gradewohl, I am an American citizen, Uncle Sam's most loyal servant."

Snyder was bemused. "You would be gone from here just when things are popping all over. I'd miss you badly. But then at least the new one would spy on the American Army and not on my private life."

Hummel smiled. "Don't be so sure. The next man, if there will be one, will do what I did. If he doesn't, he's not fit for the job. So what do you say?"

"What choice have I got?" said Snyder sourly. "The boss wants it. We are to spare no costs. I suppose that includes people like you and me. Go to it, Hermann, and good luck. I'll let them know and ask to be sent another operative. I hope he's half as good as you. No crap. I mean it."

"I'll lay the groundwork right away. You'll hear from me. Just be sure when I see you next you salute me properly."

* * *

Rolf was not improving. He was spitting blood when he coughed and wondered whether he had contracted something worse than pneumonia. The wound continued to fester, he sustained a constant fever level and the doctors were now planning a further amputation. For a while he was thought to have an atypical case of diabetes, but that was eventually ruled out. His illness caused him to oscillate wildly between silent resignation and high irritability. He chided himself for both, believing that depression and mental anguish would hinder his recovery, and then found himself unable to control his emotions. Except for Naomi and occasional visits from his mother, who lived in Bavaria, he rarely saw anyone.

He had a confused dream of Russians chasing him for his life and then, inexplicably, inviting him for a toast with vodka and offering him the services of a beautiful blond. Someone looking like Naomi was standing nearby and declared that sex was sinful and she would enter a nunnery. He protested and tried to convince her that Jews were not acceptable in such places, but when she insisted he broke out into tears.

"My, my," said Witzleben, standing by the bed, "look at him crying even before he hears the bad news."

The SS man appeared to Rolf like an evil apparition; he was not sure whether he was still dreaming. Rolf said nothing and laboriously turned away. The effort produced a prolonged coughing spasm. If the maneuver was designed to put his fleshy inquisitor off, it proved useless. The man moved to the other side of the bed, wheezing audibly. He grinned contemptuously.

"Well, Colonel, I let you go last time, despite all the mysteries and coincidences you failed to clear up. You see, we have your girl friend on our mind, but even more, your contact with proven traitors like Moltke and Halder. Just to let you know what's ahead: most of your buddies are dead or awaiting judgment from the People's Court."

Rolf kept his eyes closed and tried to conjure up the image of his friend and erstwhile protector. He did not dare to ask whether General Halder was still alive.

"I'm afraid your silence is not going to help you one single fart," said Witzleben.

A new expression, thought Rolf. There's always something to learn, even from the devil.

The devil extracted a piece of paper from his pocket and waved it at the sick man.

"Here, explain that," he ordered, "and it better be good." He stuffed the paper under Rolf's chin.

Rolf had no choice but to take it. Easy, he said to himself, whatever it is, take it easy, betray no surprise, no emotion. When he looked again he saw he was holding a letter. Typed, the signature was Leni Kostler.

He shut his eyes again. Leni – at first it merely rang a distant bell, then the sound became louder and louder until it threatened to burst his ears. Hilli, he rejoiced, God be thanked! We are in contact again. Outwardly he gave no sign of his feelings. Then he began to read:

Dear Colonel,
You do not know me, but I am merely the intermediary for a friend. This lady used to know a certain Captain Bading who was in your regiment in the Sixth Army. We heard that you and he made a daring escape from a dreadful Russian prison camp. My friend wonders whether you have any idea where he is. Did he survive the ordeal with you? If so, could you let me know the details? Write to me, please. My friend is traveling a great deal and uses my address for correspondence.

I note that you are in a hospital. I hope your illness is temporary and that you will recuperate quickly and completely. Please forgive this intrusion into your time from a person unknown to you. I am sure, however, you will understand.

Faithfully yours,
Leni Kostler

The return address read: *Care of Dr. Klaus, Am Berg 15, Oberhofen, Switzerland.*

Was she in Switzerland, he wondered, or did she merely use the address of a friend? My God, I'd lost track of her so completely, and now she is suddenly here again.

"We've taken the liberty of reading your mail," the Gestapo man broke into his rumination, "and we want an explanation."

Rolf looked at the face hovering over him and found it repulsive. He glanced at the letter again.

"What explanation do you want? Bading? Yes, I knew him. Do *you* know where he is?"

"Don't be so cute, Colonel. You're in deep trouble and you know it. Our Swiss contacts have a line on this Dr. Klaus. Has a great reputation as a Jew lover who once housed a certain Helga Raben, now in America, who makes vicious anti-German propaganda. You wouldn't know this Raben, would you?"

Rolf made no response. How did they find out, these bastards? he wondered. What else do they know?

"Well, did you or didn't you? Mind you, Colonel, you don't really have to answer. We have the facts. You had a lover who's a Jew. We have you on a charge of miscegenation. You had contacts with the conspirators who planned to kill the Führer, from Moltke to Halder. You're a swine wallowing in the filth with Jews and other swine. You should be glad you're sick or we'd have you strung up in no time, and we may do it anyway. Meanwhile we're moving you to a compound reserved for rats like you, away from the decent Germans in this ward."

He had raised his voice so he would be heard. Soldiers in the other beds had followed the interrogation in silence.

"Heil Hitler!" shouted Witzleben and left.

* * *

In the afternoon Rolf saw Naomi again, in the privacy which the hospital now regularly afforded him. He shared his experience with her and related the story of his early love. He and Naomi had established a warm and open relationship that was punctuated by their occasional sexual encounters. She gave of herself willingly and, as the weeks had passed, looked forward to her visits to the hospital as the highlight of her week, when she became a human being again, treated with respect and affection. To her this strange and very ill German officer represented what little light and reassurance there was in her bleak existence. He was kind and generous, solicitous of her feelings, full of contempt for the men who held her hostage to every craven sexual fantasy, a man who made no secret to her of his hatred for the system that had dehumanized her.

Eventually, she told Rolf tearfully that her visits would soon have to end.

"We're being moved. Of course we don't know where, just rumors galore. Some say it's east again. But then we hear the Russians are coming. Oh God, will it never end?"

She cried bitterly.

"And I won't see you again, the only human being who's treated me like a person. I do want to thank you. I remember you in my prayers every day. May I be bold and tell you what's in my heart?"

"Of course, I won't mind whatever it is, and I won't tell."

"Colonel, if I weren't a Jew who's good only for dirt and extinction, and you not someone who belongs to a nation that has done this to us, then I. . ." She could not continue.

Rolf tried to comfort her. "I understand," he said. "If we were just two normal people. . ."

"Yes, I could fall in love with you, like the girl friend you once had. I have no trouble identifying with her feelings for you."

"Thank you, Naomi, you're as generous as you are beautiful. Going for a sick cripple like me!"

"You're no cripple to me. You're whole in a world that's in pieces."

Rolf looked intently at her.

"We may share the same fate, Naomi. They're going to put me away too – somewhere. I'll learn what you learned long ago."

She held his hand tenderly. It was her turn to reassure him. He looked at her with clouded eyes, then lapsed into sleep.

Naomi kissed him softly and rang the bell. The orderly hustled her back to the waiting truck and the reality of bondage.

The next morning Witzleben and two men came to take Rolf away.

The hospital's medical director objected vigorously. "This officer is too sick to be moved. I'm in charge here and cannot allow you to proceed. The Colonel might die if he does not receive proper care."

"No kidding," Witzleben shot back, "you don't say! Well, don't worry, doctor, I'll take the responsibility for this traitor and *Rassenschänder*. And if he croaks, he'll merely be cheating the hangman. So kindly get out of my way or I'll have to report you for obstructing justice."

He signaled his men to grab Rolf.

"On your feet, buster!"

There was an aura of disquiet in the ward.

"Shame on you!" someone cried.

"The Colonel is ill and has lost a leg at the front."

"At least treat him with decency," shouted another.

"And why aren't you fighting?" a third.

Witzleben was taken aback. No one talked like that to the SS and got away with it.

"Take a stretcher at least," said the doctor.

Witzleben was anxious to get away. He felt that he was at a disadvantage. "All right," he conceded.

Rolf remained silent and passive.

When at last they were leaving with their victim, the men in the ward spontaneously applauded him and sang the national anthem.

Moritz Pelz had been in Palestine for a number of months when, like the chief cup-bearer in the Joseph story, he remembered his promise to the American in Theresienstadt. He had been too briefly in Switzerland to carry it out then. Besides, the heady taste of freedom had thrown him, like all the other ex-prisoners, into a state of confusing euphoria. After they landed in Haifa, the demands of a new life were so overpowering that the past receded quickly.

But when he found himself in Jerusalem to have his papers put in order at the office of the British administration, the Jew Silberberg who claimed to be a major in the U.S. Army came to mind. He spoke to officials of various ranks, none of whom found the information exciting or urgent.

"There are lots of prisoners around these days," the last one told him. "We can't look after every one of them. We'll get to your man when the war is over."

"He may not be alive then. A concentration camp is not a POW compound. The inmates are expected to decay and die, and many are shipped to Auschwitz for burning. Haven't you heard?"

"Personally I don't lay much stock by it. Your people have a habit of being too tragic."

Pelz restrained his urge to respond. He was not here to

teach this man a lesson.

"Sir, I came only to ask a simple thing: tell the American authorities that the Nazis have abducted an American Army major and are holding him in the camp under a Jewish name. They've treated him badly and he's tried to escape. The Germans gave him the name of Silberberg, while his real name is Bristol or Driscoll. He's sure they're looking for him in Washington. Someone in his family is a senator, I've heard."

"Well, that's a bit different, I admit," the Britisher said. He was a giant of a man whose nose ran constantly. "I'll pass the word up."

* * *

The news of an impending "resettlement" had spread throughout the camp. Germany was lying in ruins. The fate of the Third Reich and its masters was all but sealed. Only in their battle against the Jews would they record victories. Nearly six million had already been "worked over" and though the death factories were closing down one by one, thousands could still be sacrificed to the Moloch of Auschwitz before the war would end. Theresienstadt had been the place for the more privileged; now this privilege too would cease. The German armies were short on rolling stock, but there was an ample supply of cattle cars for delivering Jews to the chimneys.

Driscoll-Silberberg had heard the warning over the BBC, and when the trains pulled up, the fate of the ghetto was not in doubt. With luck – if the Americans or the Russians came soon enough – some might be saved; but for the majority, the road would lead to Auschwitz.

Silberberg was among those who were to join the first transport. "Tomorrow at 7 A.M." was the order. He went to see Rabbi Baeck, who had been his mentor and friend and who was among those still spared the final journey.

"I've come to say good-bye," said the American. "Remember our discussion about conversion and your reply some time ago?"

"Of course, how could I forget!"

"Well, sir, the time has come. I will die in the next week or two and join the millions already sacrificed. I want to die as a Jew. In their eyes I am one, and in my eyes too. I want you to say yes to me too on behalf of the Jewish people. I was forced to be a Jew when I came. I want to leave here as one who willingly identifies himself as a Jew and does so with all his heart. Will you do this for me, doctor?"

Baeck looked at him with affection. Tears came to his eyes.

"Yes," he answered. "I'll ask two other men to join me as witnesses. You've been surgically circumcised? I understand it's customary in America."

"Yes, sir."

"All we need then is to draw a drop of blood as a symbolic ritual circumcision, to bring you formally into the Covenant of Abraham."

"What about immersion?" Silberberg asked.

"Well, of course, that's out of the question here. We haven't any collection of water, let alone a ritually fit *mikveh*. We'll have to improvise. A shower will do. Our rabbis always met special conditions with special adjustments. Tonight then, and God bless you."

* * *

The orders were to take Colonel Baumgarten to Niederdorf in the Tyrolian mountains where the SS kept a compound for its favorite internal enemies.

The truck onto which Rolf was loaded rumbled unsteadily along the *Autobahn*. Several times the SS driver and single guard had abandoned the vehicle and Rolf to dive into the ditch by the road when Allied bombers flew low overhead and bombed the convoy. Shrapnel had hit the cab and torn the door away, but the truck remained serviceable.

The guard, Fritz Buntze, was a sixty-year-old carpenter who had been wounded in World War I and had spent a year recuperating. He understood that his ward was a prisoner of the SS, and he suspected the reason. A socialist from his youth, he had fought the Nazis at first, but later on, after they had gained power, he joined the compliant, silent masses. The colonel elicited his sympathy; he could see himself in his position. The SS had not taken his decorations away, and there were enough of them to testify to a man of courage.

Some hours out of Berlin, Buntze noticed that the colonel, who had submitted to his transfer without complaint, was in agony. The guard tried to make him more comfortable and realized that his prisoner-patient was burning with a high fever. They had little water and no medicine. Buntze signaled the driver to pull off the road.

"The colonel is very ill," he told him. "If we go on without getting him medical aid, he'll die before we get him to the south. He won't survive, not in the shape he's in."

The driver, whose brawn exceeded his intelligence, was irresolute. He consulted his orders:

> *This important prisoner must be delivered to authorities at Niederdorf camp without undue delay.*

"Well, that's quite clear then," Buntze declared firmly. "It says 'delivered,' which means alive, and certainly 'undue delay' would make no sense if the man were dead. So the way I see it, we've got to find a doctor or a hospital."

"We're in the soup either way," said the driver. "If the bastard dies, it'll be my fault. If we stop, they'll get me for not obeying orders."

In Sangershausen they were told that a German soldiers'

hospital was nearby. "At Nordhausen, not far from the factories, and right next to the place where they keep the Jews, just a few kilometers down the road."

"Thanks," said the driver. "If we can't get this bird to Niederdorf, maybe he'll end up with the Jews. Serves him right."

They found the hospital, which accommodated short-term patients, men who were expected to rejoin the service after recovery.

The doctor in charge was a Major Bernhard Toller. He complimented Buntze and the driver on their alertness. "You would have had a corpse on your hands," he said. "We'll do what we can."

When he learned of Baumgarten's identity, he bent low and whispered, "I've heard your name, Colonel. You're in the right place. I'll keep you here come hell or high water. And maybe the way it goes now, the Americans will be here first anyway."

He suggested to Baumgarten's driver that he and the guard find some accommodation in town. "It'll be a while before your man's fit to travel."

"One day," said the driver with rising anxiety. "One day, that's all. Positively. Fix him up somehow, and when we get him where he's supposed to go, he can croak for all I care."

"Lovely, my good man. Spoken with true soldierly spirit! Now listen carefully: this is an Army installation and I'm in command."

He held the order up to the light as if to see it better.

"I'll have to hold this paper until I release the colonel. And if you obstruct me any further, I'll put you under lock and key in our psychiatric ward. Here, take this pill and off with you."

Buntze smiled at the doctor and, when the driver turned his back, saluted him warmly.

Silberberg was not sent on the morning transport after his conversion. For reasons he did not know, his name had been scratched off the list and several weeks passed so that he began to think that perhaps he would be spared. Rumors had it that the Russians were at the gates of Auschwitz. But then, on a dreary morning in November, with a cold rain presaging the inevitable snows to come, his name was called, though a guard had predicted that no more shipments would be made.

Solitary confinement and repeated beatings had hardened Silberberg yet found him unprepared for the train ride to Auschwitz, the destination now no longer a secret. So many people were pressed into the cattle cars that those who stood could not sit, and the few who sat along the wall had to draw their knees close to their bodies lest others be forced to stand on their legs. They received neither food nor containers for disposing of their body wastes; the Nazis had abandoned such offerings as useless luxuries. Tomorrow they'd all be dead anyway.

He was one of the first to be loaded and crouched in a corner. During the week he had saved some crusts of bread which he secreted in his pockets along with a make-do knife which was a piece of glass with sharp edges. He wrapped it in a rag to protect himself. Perhaps, he thought, I'm going to dispatch one of them before they offer me up to their gods. Yes, he would try that. The resolution made him feel strangely confident, even though the ride proved to be appalling beyond his worst imagination.

Many of the men and women were elderly. Some died on the first day from lack of oxygen, fear, cold, the inability to shift position which caused excruciating pain, and the stench of urine and excrement. People had to relieve themselves where they stood or sat, and a rush of vomiting spread through the car like a plague. Silberberg fainted when a man standing over him died and slumped across his head, burying him with a cold cover of death which he could neither lift nor move. He revived after a while and used the dead man as a shield when he ate his bread.

He slept, prayed and fainted again. His knees felt as if they were on fire. He shivered uncontrollably, but reminded himself that he had experienced similar pains in his isolation cell and that there too he had persisted. Plans for revenge against someone – anyone – lessened his agony. Then he lost consciousness again while more of his fellow prisoners died.

* * *

The International Red Cross in Geneva received an urgent telegram from the F.B.I. in Washington:

> *Reliably informed Major Kenneth Driscoll, U.S. Marine Corps, was abducted from America and is now held in Theresienstadt (Terezin) concentration camp under Jewish name Silberberg. If so, he should be transferred to POW camp to join other Americans. Will appreciate early visit and report on his well-being.*

The telegram was dated January 3, 1945. Two weeks elapsed before Claude Mérou, a Red Cross representative, was able to visit the camp. The commandant was courteous, considerably more so than he had been in the past. With the end of hostilities and Germany's inevitable defeat in sight, it was prudent to appear compliant and humane.

Mérou asked to see an inmate called Silberberg. The commandant consulted his file.

"The last Silberberg we had was shipped out ten days ago. We emptied most of the camp. Food shortages and deteriorating hygienic conditions, lack of medicine. It was better for the inmates to be moved."

"Moved?" asked Mérou, fearing the worst. The commandant shrugged his shoulders.

"That's out of my hands. I merely follow orders, direct from Berlin. They came here and didn't like what they saw. At any rate, Abraham Silberberg is no longer in our ghetto. Is there anything else I can do for you?"

His main purpose thwarted, Mérou thought he might as well go on a brief inspection of the camp, although he knew he would see only what they wanted to show him.

He left a few hours later. The commandant had spoken the truth in at least one respect: the camp stood partially empty, in stark contrast to the crowded condition Mérou had seen on previous visits. Had they all been shipped to Auschwitz, of which his friend Dr. Riegner of the World Jewish Congress in Geneva had often spoken?

* * *

Silberberg had lost track of time when they reached their destination.

"Raus! Alle raus!" The command came as the doors of the cars were rolled back. "Hurry up! Get out!" Raucous voices incongruously mixed with violin music coming from somewhere.

"Come on, you! Help get the dead out of here!" someone was shouting at Silberberg. He roused himself. Straightening his legs caused him terrible pain. His excrement was caked to his trousers. It was dusk outside and dark in the car. He stumbled and fell over two corpses, then tried to move them but fell again. Prisoners from the camp came to clean the car and tossed the dead to the ground like pieces of wood.

Silberberg pretended to be part of the work detail. His striped uniform and shaved head made him indistinguishable from them. "Where are we?" he asked.

"Auschwitz-Birkenau, didn't you know?" They pointed at an inscription over the main gate. *Labor makes free,* it read.

"Don't believe it. Only the Russians will make us free. Stay alive for another few weeks and you'll have a chance. They're that close."

A shrill police whistle, a snapping of whips, shouted commands, the music, and a ghastly stench. Was it burning flesh? he wondered. The night sky was bright with searchlights. The sudden confrontation with his fate hardened his will to survive.

The last corpse had been tossed down, the prisoners had cleaned the cars and were now forming ranks in front of him. He was momentarily hidden from the sight of the guards and threw himself on the ground behind the pile of cadavers. No one had noticed him. A petulant voice whined.

"Where are the damn carts?"

"Never seen so many croakers. How come?"

"Mostly older kikes. Sure don't know why they were coddled so long."

"Now what?"

"Leave 'm overnight. They won't run away and there won't be another shipment till noon."

That whistle again. "Forward march! On the double!"

The work detail trotted off into the camp, the cast-iron promise loomed overhead: *Labor makes free.* Silberberg lay among the dead.

When no one returned after an hour, he took some clothes from the dead to warm himself and crawled under the railroad carriage. He could see little and hit his head several times against the chassis. A rusty grating cut his hand and as he followed it with his fingers, he found it to have the shape of a small platform. It was a foot away from the axle, installed there for a purpose he could not discern. He wedged himself between the grating and the chassis, drew up his legs and waited. The night was cold and still. The chimneys were belching smoke into the skies.

Silberberg dozed off and was startled that dawn had broken the night's bondage. He heard them again: the whistles, the commands, the noise of feet marching, the hum of thousands stumbling into another day that might be their last.

Suddenly another sound, one that betokened death everywhere else, but here promised life: distant guns firing their lethal cargo at the enemy. The front lines were drawing nearer, the German armies retreating, the Russians approaching. What had the prisoner said? "Hold out another few weeks." Silberberg judged the guns to be no more than thirty miles away, much nearer than he had dared to hope. It wouldn't take long for liberation to arrive, he calculated. He did not know the speed of the Nazi retreat; it would depend on that.

Footfalls nearby. He saw the boots of German soldiers or guards. Probably guards, he reasoned. If they discovered him, he'd be shot and added to the pile of corpses that had not yet been moved.

He examined the grate on which he was crouching. It was about a foot above the rail and a foot and a half square. He was tightly wedged to the underpinnings of the carriage. Once the train started to roll, he would be bumped mercilessly. Still, it would be far better to be carried away. He lay still and slowly chewed his last crust of bread.

The dead were removed and for a time all was quiet. He

could see the shadow of the gate becoming shorter; the sun was nearing the noon hour. His back and knees ached miserably and the cut on his hand was larger than he had thought. He licked it. I'm like a dog, he ruminated, or maybe I should wish to be one. They treat dogs with all the love they deny us. Bastards! He fingered the broken glass in his pocket and felt better for it. What has life become when a man's confidence is reinforced by weapons like these? He said his morning prayers in a position not foreseen in any code of practice.

He dozed, then was brought back to consciousness by a sharp blow on his head. The train had begun to move with a jerk that threw him backward so that he half slipped out of the grate. He nearly lost his hold on the crosspiece, and while he grasped it with all his might, felt the cut deepen. He was bleeding profusely by the time he had clambered back; and when he could not stanch the flow, he took the rag and made a bandage. The flow slowed to a trickle and he licked the wound again. How lucky can I get? he consoled himself. The bleeding will likely wash out any infection and the licking gives me something to drink. Lucky dog, me! He laughed softly, and even the bumps on his head, which now came in quick succession as the car rolled along, seemed bearable.

The train lurched to a sudden halt. This time he was thrown forward with such force that he fell out of his cage. The ground was stony and when he unbent his knees he could not withhold a cry of agony. There was no one to notice. Instead of crawling back into his refuge, he cautiously looked about. They were in an open field, no soldiers or guards in sight. The locomotive was hundreds of yards away.

He calculated his chances for escape. There was no place to hide and he was near the camp. He remembered being tracked by dogs and did not relish the memory. Still, here no one was likely to know of him. From what he had heard of Auschwitz, they were aware only of those slated for survival, while he was clearly marked for death. For what other reason had he been shipped out of Theresienstadt? Those bound for the chimneys were not registered; they were consumed at once.

It occurred to him that at this moment the official assumption about him – if in fact there was such a thing – would be that he was dead. To be dead while alive, what a marvelous status to have!

He heard footsteps again. No time to crawl back into the cage. He lay still, fingering the piece of glass. Shiny black boots passed by. He looked after them and could see the chimneys in the distance. Seeing them helped him make up his mind: he could not leave his hiding place, not now. He would wait for the dark. Meanwhile, he wedged himself once more into the position, a feat of which Houdini would have been proud. He prayed for the ability to escape like the master.

It was quiet again. The train could be no more than a few miles from Auschwitz. Why was it standing idle instead of rolling back toward the land of those still living to gather them too into its insatiable maw? Midday had long passed and there had been no new arrivals, as expected.

Guns sounded again in the distance. They seemed distinctly nearer than earlier that day. How far away were the Russians? Survive a few days. . . His knees ached, his hand hurt and he was hungry. Yet he felt strangely exhilarated. Dusk fell and from his iron perch he said his evening prayers.

When darkness had fallen, Silberberg, erstwhile Marine major and expert at failed escapes, left his perch and peered carefully at the surroundings. The open spaces looked inviting; before morning he should be able to reach a forest somewhere. The chimneys were an easy landmark. He would at least know the direction in which to flee. Yes, he would chance it, he thought.

He heard the rhythm of heavy boots beating the road and hastily retreated to the other side of the undercarriage. The footfall slowed perceptibly until the man stopped a few feet from where Silberberg was hugging the inhospitable ground. A small flash: the man had lit a cigarette. For a moment he stood still, then decided to sit down and enjoy his smoke for a short break.

His back was turned to Silberberg who saw the camp guard's uniform and his rifle laid across his knees. A middle-aged man, he guessed, herder of human cattle to the charnel house. Silberberg wondered briefly how well the German rifle compared with the M-16, staple in the American forces. The guard was reclining now, finishing his cigarette while gazing at the edifying picture of the red sky over Auschwitz. Doubtless he would leave soon for his appointed round. But he did not. Instead, he took off his jacket, rolled it up to make a pillow of it and lay down.

Bastard! Silberberg cursed silently. Get up and do whatever you miserable son-of-a-bitch have to do and leave me alone. . . . If he sees me, I'm done. His gun against my piece of glass. Still. . . . He took the rag off his cut hand and wrapped it once more around his weapon, exposing the sharp edges. He knew that he had no chance as long as he lay prone, but how to change position without attracting attention? Patience, he counseled himself, this is but another instance, so familiar over the years, where others have the initiative and you look to avoid the blows as best you can.

The guard had finished his smoke and threw the burning stub in Silberberg's direction, underneath the carriage. It lay a foot away from the American who had a crushing desire to pick it up and taste its flavor, a luxury he had not been allowed since his abduction and incarceration.

The guard seemed to have second thoughts about the discarded stub. He decided to snuff it out and tried to reach it but couldn't. He did not see the American, who shielded his face with his sleeve.

The guard took off his cap and ducked under the carriage. As he moved, Silberberg turned slightly on his side and grasped his piece of glass. The man had still not seen him; he had his eyes on the burning remnant of the cigarette. He crawled another foot and was now close enough to reach it. He too lay prone. For a moment his hand stretched forward. This was Silberberg's chance and he used it. With as much leverage as he could muster, he raised his weapon and crashed it on the back of the man's hand and with the same motion raised himself to a semi-crouch. The guard screamed in pain and involuntarily jerked his head up, bumping it heavily into a steel rod. The collision stunned him long enough for Silberberg to pull him closer. He hit him, stunned him again and then, as the guard lay quiet, found his jugular and cut it.

He retrieved the man's rifle, coat and cap and waited for him to die. It occurred to him that if he could stuff the corpse into his old hiding place, it would be a while before it was discovered, and by that time perhaps the train would be far away.

But trying to get the dead man onto the perch was a back-breaking task. He remembered what Helga had told him about her difficulty in heaving Heinrich through the window. Ah, Hilli, he thought, what a time to remember you! You're still my inspiration. If you could do it, so can I.

He succeeded at last after he stripped the corpse of its clothing and jammed it into the same position he himself had occupied before. He put on the guard's uniform over his prison rags and, rifle in hand, ventured into the open.

There was no one in sight, and he walked away from the chimneys into the starless night, hoping to find forest cover before morning. When he found it after an hour, he continued into the thicket, marking his direction with broken twigs. He lay down and wondered what would happen to him if Russian soldiers would find him: Driscoll who became Silberberg shot as a Nazi camp guard – what a scenario! He fell asleep and dreamt of a Soviet liberator who insisted on being converted by Dr. Baeck, but the venerable rabbi refused, saying he could do it only under water. Damn you, said the Russian soldier who spoke a loud German.

Silberberg awoke with a start. German-speaking men were nearby. It was still dark and he barely saw their outlines but could distinguish two voices. They sat no farther than twenty feet away. He cocked his rifle and aimed at them. This is one time when this miserable uniform will come in handy, he thought.

"If they come after us, they'll shoot us like Jews." The voice was laden with anxiety.

"They won't come after us, they're all running away."

"The commandant is still there."

"That's what you think. Climbed into that big Mercedes of his and drove off so fast you'd think he was chasing women."

"Yeah, he liked broads. Even knocked up some Jew girls. Took them off the train and put 'em in his house for maid service. Ha! That guy's got all the luck. Last time I screwed one, I got a dried-up cow who spoke only Polish, but in the end knew enough German to say *Fünf Mark bitte*."

"Well, if we get going, maybe we'll be home soon and have all we want."

"Yeah." The worried voice again. "Are you sure our guys are clearing out?"

"Got on trucks or marched out. I thought they were going to dynamite the ovens and chimneys but I heard no explosion. Most Jews are being marched out too. Somewhere else where we can finish the job."

"You mean some of them are there all alone? What'll they do? Suppose *they* come after us? I bet they could be pretty brutal. Their God teaches them revenge. I wouldn't want to get in their way. Filthy creatures. . ."

They were silent and lit cigarettes. The first light of dawn etched the trees as silhouettes into the sky. Silberberg now had the two men in clear view. If they made half a turn, they could easily detect him, unless he lay flat, was quiet and had more luck.

I'm done with waiting for others to move, he finally said to himself. I'm done with lying down. This gun had better work.

He took aim and fired at the taller man. The silhouette disappeared.

"Russky!" Silberberg shouted. "Russky!" The shorter man jumped up in panic. Silberberg fired again; the man dropped.

He carefully crawled toward them. One lay sprawled in the surprise of death, the other moaned softly. Silberberg finished him off.

I should be glad, he thought, and wondered why he wasn't. These were the bastards who would have shoved me into the ovens. What's the matter with me? Have all my feelings flattened out? Here I am, my life is saved and I can't shout for joy! What blessing is there when one kills an enemy?

He turned away to recite his morning prayers but could not say the words. How does one speak with God at a time like this? he wondered and tried again. The prayers did not come; they were plugged up in his soul.

It was light now. He took off his German tunic. The prison stripes which so long had held him up to ignominy would soon become a shield of safety. He saw that he was covered with blood and did not mind. He stripped one man of his underwear, socks and boots, which fit him fairly well.

I fought after all, he thought, a small contribution. Still, better than nothing.

The morning sun felt good.

The dead men had water canisters and dry rations. He ate and drank and retreated further into the woods. He sat and waited.

Toward noon the first Jews wandered by, headed for somewhere, anywhere, as long as it was away from the camp. He joined them, carrying a *Luger* pistol which he had taken from the dead, an American marine ambling into freedom with a troop of survivors. He was aware that now he *could* say his prayers, and did so with a fervor that brought tears of joy to his eyes. He said them softly at first and then louder and louder, until the others joined in and chanted. A *chasid* was among them, and weak though he seemed, he danced ahead of them. *"Modeh ani,"* he sang over and over again, "I thank You, O God, I thank You, O how I thank You!"

They walked and filled the road with their prayers.

31

In February the Battle of the Bulge came to an end. Hitler's final attempt to stem an Allied breakthrough in the West had failed. From here on there would be little resistance to the advancing American and British troops. The only fighting was on the Eastern front where the Germans now tried to halt the Russians long enough for the Western Allies to take possession of the country.

It was April when Chaplain Goldberg's infantry division reached the Harz mountains in the central part of Germany. Their objective was the underground factories which manufactured the V-1 and V-2 bombs that had terrorized Britain and given Hitler hope that they would turn the tide of war.

Goldberg was riding in the Signal Corps column when a messenger on a motorcycle overtook him and gave him an urgent note from the division's chief chaplain:

> *Intelligence has learned that installation at nearby Dora-Nordhausen is in fact a concentration camp with many Jewish prisoners. Battalion A, 413 Infantry has been detailed to open camp. Suggest you accompany them.*
>
> *McDougall*

Spring was spreading its magic across rolling meadows and dark forest lanes. It had rained the night before, and now the sun had coaxed the flowers to parade all their beauty. But few soldiers in Battalion A would have eyes for nature's extravagant display, for they would come to see what until this day had been hidden from the world: a place where life and death had a meaning all their own. They were battle-hardened men; the maimed and dying were no strangers to their eyes. They would pass corpses sprawled along the roadside in postures of final agonies and not give them another look. The burying details would come and pick them up, comrades and enemies alike. Goldberg was no different. The sound of guns and the sight of death were daily companions, whom one met with a cold heart steeled against the constant urgings of compassion.

All that changed the day the G.I.s arrived at the gates of the camp. What they saw were apparitions with human shapes not seen before. Covered with striped rags, these ghost-like creatures stood immobile, huge sunken eyes staring from skeletons over which old skin had been stretched. A few were seen to amble away, trying to hide from these new arrivals who came with jeeps and trucks and shiny weapons: soldiers whom they had come to fear in their years of slavery.

Now the Americans were entering the center of the camp, and their column came to a sudden halt. Further progress was impossible. The road was littered with thousands of these apparitions. Were they dead or alive? The eye could not tell.

The soldiers dismounted and took a closer look at the ghastly scene. The living and the dead lay intermingled: those still left with a breath of life were moving their eyes to signal that they had not yet joined the drift into oblivion. Thousands were strewn about as if the wind had tossed them around haphazardly.

A terrible stench matched the eerie landscape. Many

Americans became violently ill, vomiting with their bile their illusions about the limits of man's capacity for evil. Goldberg too could not control himself, his vomit mingling with his tears.

Then suddenly they came. Recent camp arrivals, prisoners still able to work in the bomb factories, men and women marked for extinction by their masters, who had fled the day before. They saw the chaplain's flag mounted on his jeep, tablets of the Ten Commandments topped by a Star of David: white designs on a field of dark blue. They saw the flag and then the man. To those who crowded around him, Goldberg appeared to be the Messiah himself.

Tears of unbelief, a babble of cries in a half-dozen languages. And questions. Oh, the questions:

A yid? Bist a yid? Are you really a Jew? An American? You have come to liberate us? Are we truly free? I have a sister in New York, maybe you know her. How can I find my children? How can I let my family know I'm still alive? Do you have a prayer book?

A man had produced a scrap of paper. "Here, please! David Levy. You must find him right away." He cried.

"I'll do what I can," said Goldberg soothingly. "Do you have any information about him?"

"No, no!" Tears again. "I've forgotten the address. They beat it out of me. All I could remember this last year was the word 'bread.'"

"David Levy?" Goldberg asked again, trying to calm the man. "Don't worry, some place will come to mind."

"Levy in America!" the skeleton screamed. "A Jew. He wouldn't forget me, would he? Tell me, would he?"

"No, surely not." Goldberg could barely hold back his own tears. "He *will* remember you and we'll find him."

It went like that all day, late into the night. Goldberg's assistant, a young man of some learning, was indefatigable. He had food brought into camp, blankets were commandeered from the burghers in town; and the two of them set out to separate the dead from the living.

Goldberg obtained permission from the battalion commander to organize the burial of the several thousand that lay about the roads and barracks. He summoned the mayor of Nordhausen, a fat man who came with his equally well-fed wife. Goldberg looked at them with feelings of disgust and an urge for revenge.

They covered their noses and eyes.

"Schrecklich!" said the woman.

"We lived so near and knew nothing about it," the mayor added, and blew his nose.

"What about the stench?" asked Goldberg. "You couldn't help smelling it, could you?"

"Ach ja, it was bad sometimes, but we thought it came from some chemicals." The mayor waved his arms in innocence and then returned to holding his nose.

"Come with me," Goldberg ordered.

He took them to a small building with high chimneys. Two large ovens were inside, their steel doors open. Half-burned corpses still lay smoldering, the smoke wafting lazily about.

"Oh God, no!" exclaimed the woman. "Who would do a thing like that?"

"You've heard of the Nazis?" Goldberg asked in mockery.

The two tried to leave the chamber, but Goldberg made them stay.

"Well, sir," said the German, "of course we knew about Nazis. We had a few in our town, but they're all gone now. We were always anti-Nazi in Nordhausen."

"But what could we do?" his wife chimed in.

"Well, I'll tell you what you *can* do." Goldberg had formulated his plan. "Tomorrow morning at eight sharp you'll come with five hundred burghers for the burial ceremonies. Men or women, I'll leave that to you. You'll come in your Sunday clothes to pay respect to the dead."

"Yes, sir, we'll do that. Eight o'clock sharp."

"Wait, there's a small detail. You'll bring spades, shovels, anything. First you'll bury the dead and then we'll have the ceremonies."

"But, sir, that's inhuman, to make innocent people like us perform such a terrible task. I mean, look at the condition, the decomposition. . ." The mayor was horror-stricken at the prospect.

"Inhuman, is it?" Goldberg's anger was exploding. "And what happened to these human beings, what was that then? Your people killed them and now they have to be buried. Or would you just like to leave them as they are?"

The mayor did not respond. He turned aside and brought up just as his wife was fainting.

* * *

At six the next morning, on April 13, 1945, the Americans learned that Roosevelt had died. They were somber and some of them cried. On the eve of victory the President had been felled. Now a new man, untried and hardly known, would guide the nation.

In a dark and bitter mood Goldberg received the five hundred townspeople. They came with an assortment of tools. They began by carrying the dead to the field Goldberg had designed for the burial. Then they started on their labor of mercy. For three days they worked and were ill from their efforts. They hated the Americans who made them do it, but in their hearts they knew that their hatred was misplaced.

When they were finished at last, they stood at attention while the chaplain and his assistant intoned the traditional prayers. Among the mourners was General Dwight Eisenhower who had come to see with his own eyes the nature of the enemy. That day too many Americans understood for the first time why they were fighting an enemy whose outward trappings of civilization had appeared so remarkably similar to their own.

The liberated prisoners exhibited no visible feelings of sorrow. Their emotions had flattened out in years of oppression. They had seen so many die – shot, hanged, tortured, starved – that death had become commonplace. Liberation itself was a condition so extraordinary that its full impact had not yet touched their deepest layers of awareness. It was hard to feel free when bondage had seemed to be forever.

Naomi Landsmann stood in the half-mute crowd that mumbled the *Kaddish* prayer. She and the other women of her "Officer Service Unit," as the brothel was officially called, had been marched southward from Berlin. After the first hundred kilometers, the route was abruptly changed, and now day and night they walked in a northwesterly direction. They wore brief skirts only, with the black and white stripes marking them as untouchables. They possessed neither coats nor shoes and had never received underwear once their own had disintegrated from daily use and lack of washing. "Unnecessary luxury" said their supervisor, "and obviously interfering with your assigned work." Thus they wended their way through the budding spring of Germany's heartland, half-naked women attracting smirks from teenagers who were not quite old enough to fight but not so young that they were not titillated by this parade of women's flesh. Adults would stare at them or look away in embarrassment.

Of the twenty-three in Naomi's group, fifteen reached Dora-Nordhausen. Those who could walk no further were shot and left by the roadside. When the camp was liberated, Naomi had not eaten in three days. That placed her among the healthiest of the survivors.

Goldberg noticed her, for not only was she beautiful in a haunting way – despite the dirty rags she wore for clothes – she also spoke to him in a special tone. She addressed him in fairly good English, a tribute to a high school teacher.

"Are you a rabbi?" she had asked, and when he had answered, she continued: "You are a rabbi for Jewish soldiers?"

"Yes, I am. We have many of them."

"Then I too want to be a soldier. I have heard they need them in Palestine. Is that true?"

Goldberg nodded. "The Jews need settlers who can defend themselves."

"How can I get there?"

"You cannot just now. But the war will be over soon, and then ask again. You'll find a way."

"Yes," she agreed. "Yes, I will. I remember what Theodor Herzl said: 'If you will it, it is no dream.' Palestine will have one more settler willing to fight, if necessary."

The chaplain thought of the verse in the *Book of Proverbs* as he saw her walk away unashamed in her tatters. "A woman of strength. . ." And he thought of his wife, far away and so infinitely privileged, bearing their first child.

32

Hummel, assuming his own name – Hermann Gradewohl – was in luck. His Washington contact had done his work well and secured an Army commission for him, it being understood that he would soon be sent to Europe. In December 1944 he was sworn in as a Captain, Army of the United States, was briefly assigned to the Sixth Service Command in Chicago, and then detailed to G-2 at headquarters in Paris. His first assignments were routine: interpretation of German broadcasts. And when he performed with speed, intelligence and apparent zeal, he was made part of a special unit which would identify Nazi leaders as soon as the war was over. A classified directive made it clear that not all Nazis were to be treated as dangerous criminals. If they could be useful to the United States, they would be channeled to a super-secret office in the State Department for further disposition. He also learned that certain important people in the Vatican would act as facilitators, for some of the "valuable Germans" would first be sent to South America. It was clear to Captain Gradewohl that he would have a direct hand in keeping the ideas of Nazism alive through some of its important representatives. He felt he was doing well by the Fatherland.

Meanwhile, he had a more immediate task. Obviously

the good name of the Führer was to be preserved beyond the inevitable defeat. Clear him of the gravest violation of international human standards and he would in time become the rallying point of those around the world who thought him the greatest leader of the century. If yesterday the recovery of this infamous letter was politically desirable, now, in the hour of defeat, it was a supremely important cornerstone of a post-war fascist edifice.

Gradewohl found out that Sergeant Helga Raben was working in the London office of G-2, European Headquarters. She presented him with two problems: she must not see him lest he be exposed, and he had to get her to Switzerland. Keeping her in ignorance of him was obviously the more difficult and dangerous. The second problem was more manageable for he himself would control the circumstances, and it would have to wait until Germany's surrender. Gradewohl therefore played for time.

He asked for a transfer to the front, ostensibly to be on hand when German bigwigs would come into American custody. Lieutenant-Colonel Fenwick Ryan, a meticulous though unimaginative man who commanded the section, gave his permission. Gradewohl was temporarily detached for general service, given jeep and driver and went on his way the day Roosevelt died.

Gradewohl was not among the mourners. Like Germany's hierarchy (and many Republican diehards in America), he considered the President the chief obstacle to true progress, a warmonger and Jew lover whose death was a ray of hope. Truman was an unknown hick from Missouri who could only be an improvement. To be sure, he was rumored to have once been in business with a Jew, but one could not take that as a serious liability. Why not let a crafty kike share a few bucks with an honest man, as long as this kind of association was still permitted in a culturally backward country like America. Well, that too would change some day, though it would take longer now that Nazism was receiving a severe military setback. Gradewohl distinguished between the Reich's defeat – a regrettable but temporary misfortune – and Nazi ideology which would persist and eventually regain its rightful stature and irresistible attraction.

He stopped several times on the way and spent a night in Kassel. There, he summoned the city council and questioned them about their feelings toward the regime and its leaders. Perchance, he hoped, he might find one of them, surrendered by townspeople eager to ingratiate themselves with the victors. But he had little luck.

"We had hardly any Nazis in our city, most of them were superimposed on us by Berlin," he was told. Kassel was free not only of Jews – they had all gone to Palestine or America, according to the mayor – it was free of Nazis as well.

Cowards, thought Gradewohl. Yesterday they saluted Hitler as their Messiah, today they disown him. Where is the old German pride on which his father had raised him in Argentina? However, he thought it prudent to play their game.

He informed them that he would report their excellent record to the authorities, though it would be more credible if they would identify the few active Nazis in their midst. He wanted them for information only, he said; he was a one-man team and would move on tomorrow.

They consulted with each other and with obvious anxiety identified a certain Kurt Dönner, adjutant to the *Gauleiter* who had disappeared. The *Gauleiter*, he was told, was the Nazi in charge of the party apparatus in the area, a high-ranking individual with much power. No, they didn't know where he had gone.

Kurt Dönner was not the kind of prize Gradewohl was looking for. A man of average intelligence, he claimed that he had drifted into his job because of his bureaucratic background: he had been an assistant director in the city's administrative division and had joined the party "under duress," he said. "If you didn't, you lost your job or worse. I only took orders. What else could I do?" He professed not to have any knowledge of his boss's whereabouts.

Gradewohl considered him a mediocre hack whom they would interrogate in Paris to their hearts' content but without eliciting anything worthwhile. It would be good strategy, however, to run him in. Ryan would appreciate that his man was on the job.

He turned Dönner over to the troops in the city, with the request to convey this "important and possibly dangerous Nazi" to G-2 headquarters in Paris. The Kassel savants were much relieved and congratulated themselves on their own astuteness. It was apparent to them that American Intelligence was as naive as the rest of their Army.

Gradewohl left and spent the next four days in this fashion and was only moderately successful in his quest for important Nazis.

He arrived in Bergen-Belsen a few days after the camp had been liberated and entered it as the last of the dead were being buried. He had a good view of the survivors and did not like what he saw. Until now he had considered camps as mere detention centers, an unpleasant necessity. Now, when he looked at the walking skeletons who had managed to maintain a tenuous lease on life, he wondered whether the stories he had heard about extermination policies might not indeed be true. He had always denied such tales as anti-Nazi propaganda, but these camp inmates gave him pause to think. No doubt that was why the letter was of such importance. If it could be produced, it would put the Führer's responsibility for the extermination program beyond question and hamper the long-range plans for the revival of Nazism as a philosophy to which he, Gradewohl, was thoroughly committed.

* * *

Major Bernhard Toller had stayed at the hospital where technically he was now an American prisoner of war, but the Americans left him free to do his work. Before the war, he had been an assistant surgeon at a Catholic hospital, and looked forward to resuming his practice in a non-military environment. He was worried about Baumgarten. The colonel was lapsing into long periods of detachment and appeared resigned to his fate. "Do you have any relatives who might wish to be with you?" Toller asked. Yes, there was his mother, now living in Bavaria. Would he mind, asked the major, if he called her, provided the telephones were operative. "Not at all. Please do."

Miraculously, the connection was made. Frau von Bumm-Baumgarten was shocked. She had no idea how desperate her son's condition was. Of course she would come at once if the roads were still open and gasoline could be obtained. Fortunately her old chauffeur was still with her. She would leave that instant, she said, and if all went well, she might be there in a day or so.

* * *

On the day after liberation, Naomi had asked an American soldier whether the prisoners could be supplied with clothes so that they might begin to put their past behind them. The soldier took the request to Chaplain Goldberg who summoned the mayor of Nordhausen and ordered all available new clothes to be brought. The first shipment arrived that afternoon. The burghers who were not part of the burial squad were eager to comply, hoping to curry favor with the Americans.

Naomi was one of the first to be decently clothed and took a stroll outside the camp. She came to the hospital and wondered who might be inside.

As she entered, Major Toller spotted her.

"Are you one of Colonel Rolf Baumgarten's family?" he asked.

Naomi caught her breath. He's here! It's a sign from God, though she was not sure whether God was active in these terrible times. She composed herself with difficulty.

"May I see him, please?" she asked.

"Of course. Actually we expected his mother, and I don't know why I assumed that you're part of his family."

"How is he, doctor?"

"Not well at all, I'm afraid. But the presence of dear ones will be a great boost for him. He's been lonely, and his state of mind has not helped his healing process. Hope and love are great medications."

He led her into the ward. Several of the other patients had visitors.

Naomi stood by Rolf's bed and saw that his condition had greatly worsened. He was dozing. She touched his forehead, then bent down and kissed him.

"It's me," she said softly. "Naomi. I've come to make you well."

He opened his eyes and looked at her as if she was an apparition.

"Naomi! Oh, my God," he whispered, "how did you get here? And your clothes! What has happened?"

She told him of her terrible march and ultimate liberation.

"And now, Naomi, what will you do now?"

She needed no time to form her response.

"I've been thinking about it for the last few days. I have no relatives left to whom to go. So I thought I'd let time take me by the hand and lead me. Then, a few minutes ago I saw you again and you asked me what I would do. I know now. If you'll let me, I'd like to take care of you."

Tears ran down Rolf's sunken cheeks. "I'm a German officer, remember? You said you couldn't."

"That was in the dark past. I was a slave and you were the master. It's different now. We're equals, even though I'm not used to it. And I want to take care of one German officer by the name of Rolf."

"God was good to me when He brought us together again. Darling, sweet Naomi. . ."

He cried without shame. She wiped his tears and made him comfortable. After a while he dozed off again. Major Toller arranged a room for her to spend the night.

Early next morning Rolf's mother arrived. She found Naomi sitting by her son's bed, holding his hand. She had not known him to have a girl friend. Naomi gave her name but volunteered no further information.

Weak though he was, Rolf quickly discerned the tension between the two women.

"Mother, Naomi is a dear friend whom I've known for some time. If I'm alive today, it's in part because of her, and that ought to be enough. And both of us stand accused of being enemies of the regime. I'm here because the SS was carting me off to one of their famous camps, but I was too ill to be transported any further. And Naomi was over there. . ."

His voice trailed off. He was exhausted and lay silent, his eyes closed.

"My son obviously thinks the world of you," Rolf's mother said finally, "and I respect his judgment. I hope I'll have occasion to know you better."

"So do I, madame. Rolf has often talked to me about you, and with such respect that I feel I know you already. But please do not consider me as anyone except a friend who wants to help him find his way back to life."

They left it at that, each one following her own fears and hopes.

As Rolf's condition deteriorated, the two women were drawn closer to each other. Naomi discovered behind the mother's cool exterior an intelligent, free-spirited person ready to accept the young stranger on terms of human equality. Naomi had not yet become accustomed to such acceptance; long years of slavery had imprinted a pattern of inferiority on her soul. The older woman learned quickly that Naomi was a Jew who, behind her warmth and affection for Rolf, hid the memory of bitter years. She did not inquire how she had spent that dismal time or how she had first met Rolf.

33

On the last day in April Gradewohl was on his way back to Paris when he heard the news of Hitler's suicide. The Thousand-Year Reich came to an end and surrendered unconditionally. For Gradewohl this merely marked the beginning of a new challenge in a long-range struggle. Recovering the letter would be, for him, a symbol of renewal. If he could not serve the Führer himself anymore, he would serve his memory. The time to act was now.

He formulated his plan. He could obtain a Special Order for Raben, ordering her to report to the embassy in Bern. He would meet her there, also on special detached service; and disguised sufficiently so she would not recognize him, he would go to the vault with her and obtain the letter.

When he reported to his superior, he found Lieutenant-Colonel Fenwick Ryan in a foul mood.

"Captain, you may be a specialist who has friends in Washington, but the Army has its own rules which you can't disregard."

Gradewohl was nonplussed. "I beg your pardon, sir, I don't know what you're referring to."

"Captain, at your own request, you were temporarily detached. But there was a deadline and you simply disregarded it. Someone higher up asked for you and gave me shit."

Gradewohl was contrite in tone and demeanor. "I apologize, sir. It was done because I had a hot lead which fizzled, it turned out. Someone said he'd seen Bormann."

"Really! I must admit that *is* a hot one. All right, just don't do it again. Now let's get back to work."

"Yes, sir," said Gradewohl, "but I have to tell you I need another order. No transfer necessary, though, at least not for me. If Bormann was hot, this is hotter."

He then recounted the story of the Führer's letter with fair accuracy, telling Ryan enough to whet his appetite and appreciate the importance of recovering the document. He needed a Sergeant Raben, presently in London, who was the key to the recovery.

"Such a letter from Hitler will establish the guilt of the Party beyond doubt," he added. "We caught some big birds already and you told me there'll be an international tribunal to judge them. Can you imagine what *your* letter would do?"

He counted on Fenwick's vanity and was not mistaken.

"One more time, Captain, but it better be good. What you sent me so far was small fry, not worth our time. So, what do you want?"

"A detached service request for Sergeant Raben, which probably will have to be routed from G-2 to WAC. Report a week from now at the American embassy in Bern. I'll meet her there. Both of us will need visas or whatever to get into Switzerland. Also, advice whether uniforms or civvies are indicated. A couple of days later we ought to be back at our posts."

Ryan agreed. "I'll handle it, but let's make it two weeks from now. Shall we have her report here and you two go together?"

"No!" Gradewohl nearly shouted his disagreement. "No, please, Colonel. I don't want to travel with an enlisted woman. A friend of mine got into serious trouble. Please, spare me the embarrassment."

He sounded less than convincing. Ryan was not the brightest of men but he was no fool either. Gradewohl obviously had personal reasons not to appear at headquarters with this woman sergeant. Ryan resolved to have a little fun with his excitable peripatetic captain.

"All right, Captain," he said soothingly, "don't get yourself all worked up. I'll fix it. Just relax."

"Thanks, Colonel," Gradewohl responded and thought, I nearly messed it up. A good thing this guy is gullible.

Having made a mistake in showing his feelings, he now made another in misjudging Ryan who was planning his own ploy.

Ryan called Major Jack Fuchs in the Records and Personnel Division. They played cards together and saw each other at the club.

"Jack, I need a favor from you."

Fuchs teased him. "Is this an order, Fenny, or am I free to refuse?"

"Consider it an order from someone who's not your superior officer, which you are free to disobey at your peril. Seriously, I need you in a somewhat delicate matter. Is your line secure?"

"As secure as yours, which means it's wide open."

"Then let's have dinner together."

"Fenny, old boy, you've got a date. Six o'clock."

* * *

In a secluded booth at the Officers' Mess, Ryan developed his stratagem "to teach Gradewohl a lesson."

"Jack, your office is a mile away from mine. I want you to request a certain WAC from the London headquarters. Gradewohl wants her to meet him in Switzerland to get an important document from a vault there, but does not want to travel with her, which would be the only sensible thing to do. Funny business, if you ask me. He was so vehement about it that I almost think he doesn't want to see her here. So I'd like to get a line on him and surprise him. 'Dear Captain, sorry we couldn't do it your way. The lady's already working in Paris.' You get it?"

Fuchs was silent and stared at him. Memories flashed in his mind of the young woman he had met at the dock in New York, had protected and shepherded to Senator Browning's office.

"Jack, you look as if you hadn't heard a word."

Fuchs answered softly, to make sure no one overheard. "I've heard everything, Fenny, more than you think. You haven't told me the WAC's name but you don't have to. She's Helga Raben. Right?"

It was Ryan's turn to stare. "How in the hell did you know? It's her all right."

Fuchs continued: "And the document is a letter written by Hitler and is now secreted in a bank in Bern. Right?"

Ryan nodded weakly, as if suffering from shock.

"Fenny, old boy, this young woman is a pretty important person. I didn't know she was in the service. I was once assigned to protect her while working for the F.B.I. The Nazis were after her to get that letter. She has friends in high places, like Senator Browning, and even F.D.R. gave her a hearing. She's been on radio, a firebrand I tell you, cool, good looking and hates the Nazis and what they did to her people."

"A Jew?"

"Yes. And her boyfriend, a Marine major, disappeared. The latest is that the Nazis abducted him and shipped him to one of their camps. The word is out to find him, if he's still alive."

Ryan shook his head. "And all of this for that letter?"

"Yes. Now I ask you a question, Fenny. Why is this captain of yours so anxious to get hold of it?"

Ryan reported what Gradewohl had told him.

Fuchs was not satisfied. "Why then is he so jumpy? His excuse is ridiculous on the face of it. Must have made it up on the spot when you suggested they go together. Strange. The whole thing makes me uneasy. How does Gradewohl know about the letter? Is he a confidant of Raben's? If so, why doesn't he want to be seen with her at headquarters? That's what he's really saying. But in Switzerland he'll be seen with her and by her, even at our embassy. Fenny, my old F.B.I. instinct tells me it doesn't add up. This captain of yours wants the letter, that's for sure. Why? Why he?"

Both followed their own trains of thought. Fuchs said, "Let's keep our eyes open, Fenny. I'll request Raben on special detached service. I'll keep her away from your place. And you be sure not to let on. Tell Gradewohl you've made the request and all is in order. You'll be told by London when they'll send her to Bern and then he can be on his way. You tell him that and he'll be happy. And don't breathe a word to anyone."

Ryan agreed. This would fix Gradewohl's wagon. He already looked forward to springing the surprise on him.

Fuchs asked, "Do you mind if I send a wire to Washington, to the F.B.I., and ask them to do a check on your captain? The name is unusual and it rings a bell. I vaguely remember having seen it in one of our confidential reports."

"You seriously think?. . ."

"I think nothing, but a little check won't hurt."

"Go to it, buddy," answered Ryan and was amazed at himself for hoping that they could hang something on Gradewohl.

PART VII

Showdown

SPRING 1945

34

Helga was delighted when her transfer was approved. Her loneliness had at times amounted to near depression. Only her Sabbath visits to Jettie Kostler relieved her dull routine.

Now that the Nazis were defeated and their broadcasts had ceased, she was assigned to paperwork, which she hated. The transfer came as the perfect answer.

"Major Fuchs," she exclaimed with delight when she reported in Paris, "is that really you? Oh, I'm so glad to see you again! I've always been grateful for the way you looked after me when I arrived in New York. And now you've saved me from dying of boredom! I hope you have some interesting work for me."

Fuchs too was happy to work with her. He had been greatly impressed with her and was sure they would enjoy their association. That he was an officer and her superior would not stand in the way of their relationship. He then told her of Gradewohl and the planned recovery of the letter.

She was glad when she heard the news. Once the Army had the document, it would pass forever out of her life. Yes, she would be glad to go to Bern. But could the major do something for her too? Could he inquire whether Major Driscoll had been located, and was there any chance of finding Colonel Baumgarten, probably in a POW camp? She had mentioned these requests in London but had not gotten anywhere. No one was interested.

Fuchs knew for a fact, he told her, that the service was looking for Driscoll. As for the German, that would be more difficult. Hundreds of thousands of prisoners were now being processed. He would see what he could do.

"You knew him from Germany?" he asked.

"Yes, sir. We were close friends. An honest-to-god anti-Nazi and a very brave man, as I heard through a Swiss acquaintance. I would be most grateful."

She asked why Gradewohl was the man to obtain the letter.

"Actually, I don't know and have asked myself the same question," Fuchs replied hesitantly. "Certainly there's no official word through channels about this, so he's doing it on his own initiative, arising from previous knowledge. I must confess, and I speak confidentially since I think I know you, that his request puzzles me in several ways."

He told her of Gradewohl's insistence on not traveling with her.

"Why?" she asked in astonishment. "He doesn't know me, or does he?" She felt suddenly uneasy. "Major, I don't like it. I don't like it at all."

"Frankly, neither do Colonel Ryan and I. So I'm making some inquiries in Washington. Hold tight and wait. And stay away from the headquarters' central office, so you don't run into him."

* * *

Gradewohl knew that he had over-reacted and that Ryan had noticed it. He tried to repair the damage by being conspicuously industrious and attentive to the boss's needs. At the end of two weeks, he felt more secure. Ryan was unfailingly courteous and did not refer to the incident.

The scenario which Gradewohl projected was not without its pitfalls. That Raben would see through his disguise was unlikely. But what to do once the letter was recovered posed a trickier problem. She might insist on knowing where it was going, for technically it was, if not her property, at least subject to her wishes. Yet the letter had to be destroyed. Some accident would have to be arranged, one that might have to involve Raben personally. That would after all only be justice delayed, in expiation of her killing an SS officer.

He asked Ryan, in an offhand manner, when Sergeant Raben and he might be able to make their quick side trip to Bern. "I can hardly wait to see that letter," he said earnestly, and meant it.

Regrettably, the colonel's response was vague. The woman was doing important work in London and could presently not be spared. Patience, please. That document surely would not run away. "What the hell's your hurry, Captain? Why are you so damn itchy about this? Is there someone back home who's pushing you?"

Gradewohl was caught off-guard. "Yes and no," he answered defensively, trying to formulate a believable response. I've lost my expertise, he thought fleetingly. "You see, I have friends in Washington who are preparing for the trial of the Nazi bigwigs. They learned about the Hitler letter when they heard Sergeant Raben on radio and at mass meetings. Now that Göring and Speer and Ribbentrop have been captured, the trial is moving into focus. They want the document to assist them in preparing their case."

He was pleased with himself; he hadn't lost his touch after all.

Ryan accepted the explanation. Fuchs would be interested to hear Gradewohl's latest comment. They were to play poker that evening.

* * *

The news Helga received about Driscoll was devastating. He had been abducted and was traced to Theresienstadt. But when American troops had reached the camp, with specific orders to look for Driscoll, he was not there. Inmates remembered that he was among those shipped to Auschwitz. Inquiries were being made with the Russians, but that took time. As for Baumgarten, he was not on a preliminary list of high-ranking German prisoners. Patience.

Helga dreamt of her parents, her brother. They had all come back to life, their deaths had been annulled. "You shouldn't have used a feather pillow," Heinrich chided her. "It's far too small to make love on. Didn't they teach you that in school?" "Nonetheless," she told him, "you're a feather in my cap. The only one I've killed so far." "Keep trying," said Ken, who had suddenly appeared on the scene. "There are still some out there." There was a scuffle, for Heinrich tried to stuff the letter back in his SS tunic, which was full of cigarette burns. Ken snatched it from him and it tore in half. "You see, you should have been more careful with it," said President Roosevelt, whose cigarette burned a hole in her dress. Her parents stood aside and applauded, she did not know for what. Her father said, "Helga, we have made application for a visa to Auschwitz. They welcome Jews there, we hear." "Oh no!" she screamed and awoke.

* * *

Helga liked Fuchs and his professional ways. He treated her without regard to rank, as a co-worker whom he respected. They were analyzing captured Gestapo files and she helped him interrogate high-level Nazi officials. Fuchs was well aware of the trial plans, and the two of them carefully collected incriminating materials.

Fuchs thought more highly of Ryan as a human being

and enjoyable companion than as an intelligence officer. He felt Ryan's quick acceptance of Gradewohl's explanation to be naive. It was too pat and sidestepped his true motives. His own instincts made him persist. With Helga involved, another plot was plausible. He decided to have a chat with Gradewohl, to find out how he reacted. So far no word had come from Washington in response to his inquiries.

He telephoned Gradewohl and asked for a meeting. An important question had arisen. Yes, lunch at the club would be fine.

Fuchs was slightly delayed and found the captain reading a newspaper in the lobby. He had a strong face and light eyes framed by glasses. When he looked at the figure, something stirred in his mind; he had a photographic memory which stood him in good stead as a professional sleuth. He felt uneasy and did not know why. He had seen this man before in a situation with unpleasant associations, but could not recall the occasion. Do I know him from my F.B.I. days? Fuchs wondered. He found Gradewohl's eyes penetrating in an unsettling fashion, especially after he had learned that his proposed expedition to Bern was the subject of the discussion.

"You see, Captain," said Fuchs, "all detached service in G-2 is run through my office. London sends the request down to me and I process it. So I thought the easiest thing would be to find out what this is all about. Your request is unusual: separate travel, bank vault in Bern. Unusual and mysterious. So please fill me in."

Gradewohl recounted the outline of the story, wondering why Fuchs was suddenly in the picture. Channels, he supposed. Probably Ryan's doing, typical of the mentality of the man. But he wasn't sure. Besides, this fellow had an inquisitorial manner he didn't like. Perhaps the conversation would reveal his background.

"I'll admit," Gradewohl said, "my request is a bit out of

the ordinary. I'm doing it for a friend in the State Department who's working on the upcoming trials. He could have applied to the Army, but this appeared to be simpler since I'm assigned to a special task in G-2 related to Nazi bigwigs. Colonel Ryan can fill you in if he thinks it's essential. That'll be up to him to say, of course."

Fuchs found Gradewohl's tone condescending and wondered whether the man had a managerial position in civilian life. If so, he would not like to work for him, he concluded. I don't like this guy.

"Of course, Major," Gradewohl continued, "if you see any problems, forget it. I'll write my friend and tell him to go through channels. It'll still end up with Sergeant Raben, and I'm sure someone will have to go with her for security's sake. That is, if that letter is really all that important, which I can't judge."

"Well, Captain, neither can I, of course. But knowing the people I work with, they'll balk at having this sergeant go there by herself. Someone will have to go with her, so why not you? Forgive me, I'm a bit puzzled by your request for separate travel."

Gradewohl responded with a sheepish grin. "Just an odd personal hang-up, Major. Maybe I need a shrink. Once had a most embarrassing experience and ever since have been allergic."

Fuchs thought that Gradewohl had told Ryan that the embarrassing incident had happened to a friend and not to him. Small discrepancy and then maybe not so small. Unless Fenny didn't tell it right. He decided to probe further.

"I don't really care too much, but I know the guys in London, and don't forget it has to go to the chick's WAC superiors. Some of them are sticklers of the worst sort, go by the book. So I think the best way of handling this is to request detached service to Paris, say to my office, and we don't mention Switzerland. Then, when she gets here, you two arrange for your rendezvous and I'll write the transportation order for separate travel. What do you say?"

He was watching Gradewohl closely and saw his eyes cloud and his head shake slightly as if to ward off the idea. He would have missed it if he hadn't paid attention. Long training and experience convinced him that this captain opposite him had another agenda. He had also barely touched his lunch. A troubled man, he decided. He doesn't want to see Raben here, but in Bern it's okay. Has he seen her before? Or maybe she knows him?

"Major Fuchs," Gradewohl broke into his speculation. "I'm coming to find this whole thing a bit distasteful. I'm trying to do someone a favor, which is apparently in the interest of the country, and I learn that with all the convolutions of the service, the request can't be handled straightforwardly. So what do you say I withdraw it and forget it? Let the guys in Foggy Bottom do it by themselves."

Gradewohl didn't want Raben in Paris, and this major was gumming up the works. He'd have to wait for another chance, although he wasn't clear how that would occur. My luck to run into this hound who's got his nose into the wind. What was he doing at home? Where did I see him? Behind a desk? Walking? Yes, walking. Carrying something. Damn it, where?

* * *

Word came from Washington. The F.B.I. reported that from time to time they had had Gradewohl under surveillance. He was known to have adopted another name: Dr. Cohn. For what purpose was not clear. His source of income was vague, though I.R.S. records were in order. He had immigrated with a certain George Snyder, a friend from

Argentina, who was suspected of being a German contact. That association had led the F.B.I. to look at Gradewohl. Nothing further on him, nor could anything be pinned on Snyder.

A postscript followed: While it was customary to get F.B.I. clearance when assignment was made to Intelligence, no such clearance had been requested by the Army. Unusual. Apparently someone important had vouched for G. and the usual check was skipped. *Repeat: unusual. If you have something, let us know.*

Fuchs went back to his office and, as was his habit, put his facts on paper. He started with the latest information.

> *F.B.I. has at times suspected him – of something. Army commission without F.B.I. clearance. Seen with Snyder, suspected German contact. Has used one alias (Dr. Cohn), maybe others (unknown).*
>
> *Source of income vague.*
>
> *Intensely interested in Nazi document – reason given is plausible.*
>
> *Knows* about *Raben – possibly knows her or she him.*
>
> *Excuse for separate travel unsatisfactory. In any case, does not want to see R. in Paris. Withdraws request when that possibility arises.*

When he looked at the chart, his old professional suspicions hardened into conviction: this man, whose Army records showed him to be of Argentinian background and whose name testified to German origins, had a German connection of some kind. If he wanted to adopt a cover, a Jewish name would point away from his designs. But "Cohn" was so patently Jewish it was either clumsy or adapted to special circumstances. Probably the latter. The man was not stupid.

DR. A. COHN. Fuchs scrawled the words in large letters and called for Sergeant Raben.

"I think I'm making progress, and you're my likely key to success."

"Always me," she said. "I'm tired of it, Major. Some day I just want to be Helga Raben, nothing more than that."

Fuchs comforted her. "Bear with me just a little longer, and if I can prove what I suspect, you'll be the first to be happy."

"So?. . ."

"So get hold of yourself, trust me as you once did when you were in my care and. . ."

He paused suddenly and stared at her.

"My God, Helga, I've got it! I've got it!"

In his excitement he forgot Army formalities.

"You remember your first day in New York? You checked into the Gotham Hotel and then you checked out and we left for Washington? Do you remember a man sitting in the lobby buried behind a newspaper?"

"No, I don't, but you spoke about it in Senator Browning's office. You thought he trailed me."

"Yes, ma'am, that's what I thought at the time."

"And now?"

"Now I know. When I saw Gradewohl here in Paris, I knew I'd seen him but couldn't place him. But it's him all right. By God, it's him!"

"You mean this man who's a captain with G-2 was trailing me back then? Why?"

"Just wait, dear lady. Now comes the clincher. Are you ready?"

She nodded and trembled with anticipation.

"You know Dr. Cohn by any chance?"

Helga opened her eyes wide.

"Don't tell me. . ."

"It's obvious you know him. Would you kindly describe the gentleman."

As she spoke, Fuchs realized he was perspiring profusely.

"It's the same man?"

"You bet."

She was trembling. "He's been after me for a long time. Employed me, even trailed me to Camp McCoy. He's a cold fish who leads some sort of hidden life. Gives me the creeps. Talked about the letter when I worked for him. He's been after it for a long time. Maybe he had something to do with Driscoll's disappearance?"

Fuchs looked at her admiringly. "Yes, it had occurred to me too."

"Is that why he came after me, the bastard? I'd like to get my hands on him and choke him to death."

"Maybe you'll have the chance. I'll have to submit this case to someone in the military hierarchy. I want this bird under lock and key before he does more damage. But first let's work out a little surprise for him."

"It'll be my pleasure," Helga said with fervor.

* * *

Fuchs visited Ryan in his quarters that night and told him of his suspicions.

Ryan was dumbfounded. "My God, Jack, you're making the most serious charges. You're dealing with an American officer, not some POW, and if your case isn't foolproof, it can backfire badly." He thought a while. "I think you and I ought to go to the top."

"Bramson?"

"Yes. Just got his second star. I don't think you ought to move another step without him."

It was Fuchs's turn to mull things over. "Guess you're right. A jury wouldn't convict him perhaps, but by the time we see the general I'll have enough on him or maybe spring a surprise. Meanwhile, Fenny, please be very natural with him, correct, nice. Nothing has happened. Okay?"

"Don't worry. Does the Raben gal go along with you?"

"She's the clincher. I think after we get home, I might persuade her to join the Bureau. She's got the goods."

Ryan smiled. "My, my, Jack, you seem to have taken quite a shine to the girl. Is it purely professional?"

"You double-digit s.o.b., you lecher! Keep your dirty mind out of my business. Really, Fenny, I like her, but this has nothing to do with it."

Two days later they saw Major-General Montgomery Bramson, career officer, West Point, expert in psychological warfare. He listened carefully, without making notes. Fuchs had requested a preliminary informal session and purposely postponed mentioning Gradewohl's name.

Bramson let Fuchs build his case. When he had finished, the general asked: "What are you suggesting we do? The unnamed party has not broken any law we know of, unless of course he's the one that abducted Major. . ."

"Driscoll, sir."

"Yes. If you can't pin that on him, what can you? That he went under an alias in civilian life? It's odd, but not against the law. He's after a piece of paper, you say, but maybe he's really after the girl, I mean amorously. He could be, couldn't he?"

"I've thought of that, General. And I also know that if Sergeant Raben surprises him and says 'Hello, Dr. Cohn!' and it throws him, he's still not proven to be what I think he is. So I would suggest a bit of old-fashioned melodrama."

"I hope it's not too far out."

"Well, sir, if he's the man I think he is, then he knew the whereabouts of Major Driscoll. Therefore I'd like to spring the major on him – I mean, pretend to. I'd like to tell him, in your presence, that Driscoll has turned up from Theresienstadt and requested to meet with him. I'd like to do that after he's had a surprise from Sergeant Raben. He can stand the latter but not the former. And not both of them together as a one-two punch. He's pretty good, but it'd be a miracle if he's that good and can tough it out without blinking an eyelash."

Bramson looked at Fuchs with a mixture of admiration and worry. This thing could blow up into a nasty affair if Fuchs was wrong and an even nastier one if he was right. He wasn't sure F.B.I. men should be in the Army. Choice between two negatives, he thought. He asked Ryan for his opinion.

"I'm not sure, General. Guess my work isn't sleuthing. I will say, though, that the man's unwillingness to see the woman here, while agreeing to see her in Bern, is puzzling."

Bramson got up, paced the room weighing the odds. "Look, Major, my expertise lies elsewhere. You happen to stumble on this case, and your professional instinct tells you to pursue it. Let's then. Give me the man's name, the whole thing."

Fuchs and Ryan described Gradewohl in detail; the way he was commissioned without F.B.I. clearance; his interest in the letter, and Raben's connection with it and Dr. Cohn.

"If he is a spy," Bramson said finally, "I hate to even think about it, but if he is, what's the letter to him now that the Germans are kaput?"

"Wish I knew, sir. Maybe there's money riding on it. The general may have heard that a few months ago large amounts of gold were shipped to South America by submarines. There'll be Nazis around with money, lots of it. How the letter fits in with that, I don't know. Maybe they'll just want it destroyed, but that's mere speculation."

"When do you want to set it up?"

"Give me a week, sir. I'll phone personally if I may."

35

"My son calls you Naomi," said Rolf's mother, "please let me do the same."

"Of course, ma'am, it will be an honor. I only wish he were better. I pray for him day and night."

The older woman bit her lips, trying to hold back her tears. "I wish I were more religious and could pray," she said. "I haven't done it for years, I'm afraid. I feel hypocritical doing it now."

Naomi was firm in her answer. "Please pray anyway, for his sake. He may not live, but at least our common prayer will lighten his burden and ours."

"You're as wise as you are beautiful," said the mother. "I'm only sorry these were the circumstances under which we met."

* * *

The doctor who had been examining Rolf sat down with them.

"The news is not good, I'm afraid. Only a miracle will keep him alive. But he's very lucid, and he wants to see you. Both of you together, he specified."

They went in, instinctively clasping hands. A deathly

pallor made Rolf's eyes appear almost luminous. They shone large from cavernous sockets, his breathing labored, his voice weak but clear.

"Naomi, I would like to pretend that I'll live, though I know I won't."

The women uttered a weak demurrer, but he waved it aside with a shake of his head.

"I would like you to marry me. Now."

Naomi bent over and kissed him gently, then both women broke down and wept.

"Yes, Naomi? Will you say Yes?"

She nodded her head and wept on his mother's shoulder.

An hour later the clerk of Nordhausen's City Hall arrived, witnessed their vows and entered their marriage into the Registry.

"Who would ever have guessed you would acquire a Jewish daughter-in-law!" Naomi could not help saying.

"It must have been in the cards all along," was the answer delivered with a wry smile. "Rolf's father had Jewish antecedents, which is one reason my family was not keen on the match. He was a marvelous man. Kind and generous. Just like our Rolf."

She kissed his forehead, which was covered with beads of perspiration.

He looked at her and smiled. "Thank you, Mother. Take care of my wife."

Those were his last words. He died that night.

* * *

Silberberg was housed in a refugee camp east of the Elbe river two weeks after the last guns were fired and the war in Europe was over. The Russians halted opposite Delitzsch where the Americans were bivouacked. The collection of displaced persons was as large as it was diverse. Jewish women from Hungary, survivors of various camps, political prisoners who had escaped, Gypsies and others who spoke a dozen languages and had one aim in common: to go home, or what was home before the war.

For more than two months Silberberg had wandered through Poland, first in advance of and then behind the Russian lines, living with other former Auschwitz inmates in the woods, requisitioning food here and there. In the end, the Russians collected them in camp compounds. Silberberg had tried several times to explain to various Russian soldiers the particular nature of his status, but could not communicate meaningfully with anyone. One day a Jewish chaplain from the U.S. forces crossed the river and visited the camp. Though he spoke some Russian, he too faced difficulties when he presented himself to the Soviets. To an officially atheist Army, the military function of a priest or rabbi was an anachronism. When at last Chaplain Aaron Stern was allowed to proceed and was spotted, with the Star of David flying from his jeep, he was instantly surrounded by wildly shouting survivors. Not only was he the first American whom they had encountered, he was also the first Jew from the West. And he spoke Yiddish, their language.

They were exuberant when he suggested holding a thanksgiving service. They prayed and sang with fervor. Afterwards when the chaplain asked what they needed, they requested ritual articles, mezuzot, phylacteries and prayer books. Silberberg spoke up suddenly and with a loud clear voice addressed the American: "Sir, permit me to speak on behalf of everyone."

He had not uttered an English word in a long time. The very sound felt good to him. "We are deeply grateful that you have come. You've brought us home again. God bless you!"

The chaplain, a young man from New York, was startled.

"You speak like a native!" he said.

"I am, Chaplain. I'll explain it to you, if I may."

They sat together in a corner of the compound. Silberberg-Driscoll told him his story. Slowly at first, then in a torrent of pent-up memories. Three years of agony poured into the span of an hour. Chaplain Stern rarely interrupted, only a question here and there when it came to people he knew, like Rabbi Baeck. He sat looking at the bearded man and tried to visualize the Marine major.

"Chaplain, do you think I'll be able to leave here and go with you to our own troops?"

"I'll try, Major. But the Russians are always suspicious and may balk."

Stern talked to the officer in charge and explained that prisoner 457400 was a member of the American forces who had been abducted by the Nazis. When he finally made himself understood, the Russian refused to give the permission. Superior authorities would have to be consulted. As Silberberg, liberated prisoner, the man was harmless; in his new/old identity as Major Driscoll, he was a question mark.

After the initial joyful joining of the two Armies at the Elbe, the friendly contact had ceased. Allied guns were now pointing at each other. The cold war had already begun, though the participants in the field were but dimly aware of it.

Driscoll's knowledge of Russian was negligible, and there was no one in the front line unit who spoke English or German. For several weeks he was held under guard. None of his captors – junior-grade Soviet soldiers – knew for what reason he was their ward. At last word got through from the Americans to Soviet divisional headquarters where a U.S. liaison officer was stationed.

He visited Driscoll, and the next day had him delivered back across the lines. Driscoll was grossly underweight but otherwise in fair health. The medical officer who examined him suggested that a week's stay in the field hospital would be advisable. Meanwhile, the authorities would be informed that he had been found. Divisional G-2 sent a message to Paris, from whence it was forwarded to Washington and sent to the Army instead of the Marines. A clerk placed the information with the massive files of missing persons, where it rested while the nation was turning its attention to the war still raging with Japan.

Chaplain Stern visited Driscoll regularly. The man's physical and spiritual odyssey fascinated him and he shared the tale with his friend Goldberg, the chaplain of the division stationed nearby.

Goldberg too was intrigued.

"You know, I once heard of an American who had been abducted. The story was told to me by the woman who was planning to marry him. You may remember a Helga Raben who spoke at Madison Square Gardens and on radio about Hitler's Final Solution. Even saw Roosevelt. She joined the WACs and we became very friendly at Camp McCoy. Eventually we both went to Europe together, and the last I heard of her was from London. You know, I have an uncanny feeling that this may be her man."

Chaplain Morris Goldberg became Driscoll's miraculous link with his past.

"Please help me get out of here, Chaplain, if not for my sake, then for Hilli's. I want to contact her," Driscoll pleaded. "And if you can help me to be accredited with our lovely Army, I'd be eternally grateful."

The two chaplains at last convinced someone in the adjutant's office to issue temporary papers to Driscoll. Sorry, they could not give him a uniform. After all, he was not an Army officer and Marine gear was not found on this side of the ocean. They procured civilian clothes and gave him a document which stated his name, rank and serial number, and that he had been declared missing for three years and was now on his way to rejoin the force. The document did not attempt to explain how an American Marine had been found missing behind the Russian lines.

Driscoll wrote letters to his sons, in care of Senator Browning, and he appended a warm note to the Senator, asking him to kindly expedite his entry into the world of the living. And he wrote to Helga, pouring out his heart. He filled ten pages and ended only because a messenger from division headquarters was waiting for the mail to Paris.

> *Write me c/o G-2 in Paris. I hope to be there in two weeks or less. As soon as they pronounce me fit to travel. I may have to walk, but I'll be there. Anything to see you for whom I have prayed day and night.*
>
> *Ken Driscoll*
> *alias Abraham Silberberg*

* * *

Paris was bathed in the glory of spring. The boulevards were green; happy customers congregated in the cafes. In June 1945 life was returning to the capital.

Gradewohl hadn't seen Fuchs since they had met for lunch, which was just as well. The man gave him the creeps. Ryan, on the other hand, continued to be unfailingly polite.

A note lay on Gradewohl's desk when he entered his office.

> *Major Fuchs advises that Sgt. Raben will* not, *repeat* not, *be required to travel to Paris first. London WAC and G-2 agreed to dispatch her directly to Switzerland. You will leave here a week from today, June 12, for Bern. Travel allowed: two days each way. Driver and jeep from carpool authorized. Sgt. Raben will report to American embassy, Bern,*

on June 13 or 14, depending on travel arrangements, and will report back to London thereafter. Fifteen dollars per diem will be authorized for you. London will fix per diem for Sgt. Raben.

Glad it worked out.

(Lt.-Col.) Fenwick Ryan

P.S. Major-General Bramson wishes to be advised of your mission. You are to report to him before and afterwards. The general will see you June 11, 1000 hrs.

Gradewohl was elated. Ryan was a good soul after all, though a bit simple. Perhaps it went so well because the two of them had managed to identify some important Nazis whom Washington wanted in America, to help in its expanding nuclear research. Also, there were German experts in Communist ideology who could be useful to the U.S. Some had already left for South America. There was talk that Martin Bormann was among them, but that was speculation. Gradewohl had certainly not seen him, though he had devoutly hoped he might be the one to interview him.

* * *

After reading Ken Driscoll's letter, Helga had an overpowering urge to find a place for prayer. She had cried and laughed and cried again. A small church stood nearby and she entered it, clutching the precious letter. In the dim light she perused it again, until it became moist with her tears and kisses. She knew the words of the *gomel* benediction which one was supposed to utter after being saved from danger. She said it for Ken, not precisely the way it was meant to be said, but God would understand.

A moment later she raced back to find Major Fuchs. "Ken's alive!" she fairly shouted as she burst into his office, forgetting all formalities. "We must catch him before he starts hitting the road. We can get him here for June 11. And I know he too will want to be here," she added, her eyes filling up again.

Fuchs knew that here was a woman in love, a love repressed by the horrors of past years but as alive again as if it were burgeoning for the first time. He felt a slight tinge of regret and reprimanded himself.

As she stood there aglow, Fuchs felt the impact of the news returning to him: Driscoll was no longer a pretense in a melodrama as he had planned. He would be there and Gradewohl would be unmasked. Perhaps the whole spy apparatus of the Nazis would unravel through this man. His instincts would have paid off and he would have contributed enormously to America's future security. If he couldn't win Helga, he would win Gradewohl's conviction.

"Marvelous, marvelous!" he congratulated Helga. "You deserve this break and I'm happy for him. My God, what he must have gone through!"

His professional judgment came to the fore. He got on the telephone and asked to be connected with the hospital of the 69th Infantry. Was Major Driscoll still there?

"Major Driscoll? Just a moment, sir. I'm not sure about anyone by that name."

The hospital chief came on the line.

"Sorry, he left here yesterday. Hoped to hitchhike to Paris, I believe."

It took Fuchs's initiative and Bramson's authority to locate Driscoll the next day as he was ready to cross the Rhine to Mannheim. A staff car had been dispatched. He reached Paris at night and Helga was waiting for him.

* * *

"Major Driscoll," said Fuchs in the morning, after hands had been shaken all around, "as Sergeant Raben has no doubt told you, we hope to snag the man who abducted you. Have you a clear picture of him?"

"Clear enough to identify him behind a hundred disguises. I'll never forget that bastard as long as I live. He owes me three years of my life. I'd love to work him over."

"I understand. But first we must make sure it's the same man. Would you describe him, please."

Fuchs was satisfied with Driscoll's picture.

"Two more days till the unveiling. Why don't you and your friend go out on the town. No, on second thought, it might be our luck that he'll run into you. Take a trip into the country. Colonel Ryan will keep him close to the office and I have two men assigned by the general who'll keep an eye on him, so he doesn't skip town if he smells a rat. Sergeant Raben has two days off. Here's fifty bucks. Guess you haven't seen any money for a while."

* * *

General Bramson was most expansive. "Sit down, gentlemen. This won't take long."

Gradewohl, Fuchs and Ryan took their seats.

The general opened the session. "I'm much interested in your mission, Captain Gradewohl. I have advised Washington that we intend to send you, and they approve heartily. Is there anything you need or any problem that you think you might have?"

"Thank you, sir, not that I can think of. Except in Bern, perhaps. The sergeant deposited the letter under another identity. She was escaping from Germany at the time. But I think the embassy will be helpful."

Fuchs entered the conversation. "Captain, I take it you don't know the sergeant?"

"No, I don't. But if she'll be at the embassy, there won't be a problem."

"To be sure. But with the matter so important we can't afford a slip-up. Of course, we'll respect your desires about travel. So, the best thing for you is to meet her and then go your way."

Gradewohl wiped his forehead and began to protest.

"Please, Captain," Fuchs said sweetly, "the general too thought it was important." He went to the door and whispered to the soldier guarding the entrance.

A moment later Helga entered. She took one look at Gradewohl, then exclaimed with feigned shock: "Dr. Cohn, I mean Captain Cohn! I had no idea!. . ."

"Cohn?" General Bramson asked. "What's this, Sergeant?"

"Beg your pardon, General. I've worked for the captain in civilian life."

Gradewohl had jumped to his feet but managed to regain his composure.

"But you said you didn't know her!" the general said severely.

"May I explain, sir?" he asked.

"By all means."

"As for Miss Raben, I never made the connection."

Helga looked disgusted and was about to speak, but Fuchs motioned her to be quiet.

"As for the name Cohn," Gradewohl continued, "I had many Jewish clients in my work, German refugees, and I thought a Jewish name would be useful in my trade. Quite harmless, I assure you."

Fuchs turned to Helga. "Any comments, Sergeant?"

She stood in front of Gradewohl and spoke to him with barely suppressed fury. "You didn't make the connection? You pestered me about the letter when you employed me, and you couldn't make the connection? You pursued me to Camp McCoy, and you couldn't make the connection? Why *did* you hire me except to get the letter! And why did you come to McCoy? Maybe you wanted to abduct me?"

Profusely perspiring, Gradewohl turned to the general.

"Sir, do I have to take this abuse? This enlisted woman

is making libelous allegations. I will have to prefer charges against her to clear my character."

"Why, sure, Captain, you should do that," Fuchs said. "Would you call a certain George Snyder as a character witness?"

Gradewohl blanched and sat down heavily. "Snyder? What does he have to do with it?"

"He's told us some interesting things about you," Fuchs invented with gusto.

"What would he have to say except that he's a childhood friend of mine?"

"Don't be so sure, Captain," Fuchs continued. He was now in full flight, pursuing his prey relentlessly. "Mr. Snyder told us of your involvement with Major Driscoll."

"He what?. . ."

Gradewohl had lost his composure. The walls were caving in on him. "Driscoll? I know of no Driscoll."

"Let me refresh your memory. Major Driscoll happens to be in Paris and he's much interested in meeting you. Or shall I say, meeting you again."

Gradewohl stared at him.

Fuchs went to the door again and motioned to the guard in the outer office. Everyone had risen except Gradewohl, who sat transfixed, his eyes on the door where suddenly Driscoll stood framed as if in a picture. He had been given an Army uniform and looked very fit.

Driscoll took one look at the frozen figure and turned to the general. "It's him, all right," he said and spat in Gradewohl's face.

Gradewohl covered his eyes.

"You are under arrest, Captain," said the general. "Major Fuchs, the man's in your care. Talk to Washington and see whether they want him back right away or whether we should warm him up with a court-martial first."

"Yes, sir. It will be a pleasure."

The day after the atom bomb exploded over Hiroshima, in August 1945, an International Military Tribunal was established and charged with laying the ground work for the forthcoming trial of Nazi war criminals. A lawyer for the planning commission asked Helga, who was still working in Paris, to go to Bern and obtain the famous Hitler letter. She would be accompanied by Kenneth Driscoll, now a Lieutenant-Colonel in the marines.

Their first visit was to Dr. Bertha Klaus, at this time living in a nursing home. Her mansion in Oberhofen had been sold, but her reputation for generosity and the pursuit of justice had made her name a household word in the capital.

Dr. Klaus greeted Helga as a mother would welcome a long-lost child. Their embrace was long and ardent, their tears of joy flowed amply. As the hours wore on, the woman's physical condition was forgotten as she became submerged in the rush of memories.

When Helga and Ken went to the embassy to obtain the keys to the safe, no one had knowledge of the circumstances. They would search the files, they promised, but held out little hope. What had not been destroyed would probably be found at the National Archives in Washington. Sorry, they could not even give any supportive testimony should it be necessary to have the box opened.

The Berner Landbank and Savings Society – the words proudly displayed over the front portals – had not visibly changed. Of course the management would extend every courtesy to the Americans, they were told by a youngish clerk who spoke with a mixture of deference and authority.

"I have a savings account here and a box in your vault," Helga informed him. "I know the number but I do not have the keys. They were left at the American embassy four years ago, where unfortunately no one can find them. Will you help me?"

"You must appreciate that there are some rules we observe," the clerk informed her. "They function for everyone alike so that everyone is equally protected." He consulted the file. "Yes, an account was opened in December '41, and a box rented on the same day. May I inquire under what name?"

"Emily Byrne."

"Quite so. I don't think then the keys will present a problem. All we will need is your passport, ma'am, and a matching signature."

Driscoll explained the circumstances: the passport was a forgery to enable Raben to escape from the Reich. He himself had been military attaché in Berlin, and the passport was produced there, at his direction. If necessary, testimony of a certain Corcoran, who had actually made it, could be obtained. Perhaps the Swiss police still had it in their files. Also, Dr. Bertha Klaus would give testimony about Emily Byrne being identical with Sergeant Raben.

"The famous Dr. Klaus?" the clerk inquired. That might be acceptable, he explained with some reserve, but it would be far better if the police could find the document.

The visit to police headquarters turned out to be fruitless.

A quick search of their records revealed no trace of the passport. One official remembered Helga's difficulty and recalled that the passport had been delivered to German authorities for verification.

The next day when they returned to the bank, the clerk at the vault was not alone. At his request, the bank's vice-president had joined him. He confirmed that all the precautions and conditions with which Helga had been made familiar the previous day were indeed in force.

"However, I have good news for you," he said. "Testimony from Dr. Bertha Klaus will probably be accepted by our directors. So, if you will fill out this form and sign it Emily Byrne, I will submit it to the board who have the final say. If they rule as I think they will, we shall then together call on Dr. Klaus who I believe is at the Helvetia Nursing Home and, all being well, we will have a new key made. There will, of course, be a special opening charge. I hope you understand."

"I am most grateful for your courtesy. You're making a contribution to history. The box contains the most valuable information about certain aspects of the last six years. You will have had a hand in making it available to civilized humanity."

"Thank you, ma'am," said the vice-president. "We try to do our share."

The clerk produced the forms ready for signature.

Helga signed her name.

"No, ma'am, you must sign the name under which the box is rented. Emily Byrne."

"I was Emily Byrne for only a very short time. I haven't the vaguest notion how I signed it."

"I am sorry," said the director, "on that score our bank is inflexible. The signature must match, except where the client has had a stroke or something similar. No match, no opening."

Helga tried three or four signatures, the way she imagined she might have signed. All fell far from the mark.

"Damn it," Driscoll finally exploded, "isn't it clear that the lady will *never* be able to reproduce that fake signature from a fake passport? Will you then hold on to the money and box indefinitely?"

"I'm sorry, sir, our rules operate for the benefit of all."

"Is not the important thing to establish that this *is* the Emily Byrne who rented the box in December 1941? Having established that beyond a doubt, why does a fictitious signature matter?"

"That signature goes with our records and protects us," the vice-president explained. "The signature is essential. There's no relief on that score. Unless a court ordered us to open up, of course."

"A court?" asked Helga.

"Yes, ma'am. A long procedure and not usually successful."

They argued for another half hour without any further progress. The Americans stressed the importance which Allied governments gave to the matter. The banker remained firm.

"What happens to the deposits of people whose whole families were wiped out by the Nazis? Who will claim these billions?" Helga could not help asking.

The banker smiled thinly. "Large deposits are no different from small ones. We will hold the money. . ."

"And use it?" Driscoll interjected.

"And use it, yes. Until someone comes with a knowledge of the number and a certificate of inheritance. The monies were deposited with an agreement to all conditions. We cannot be held responsible for other people's fate or erroneous judgments."

Helga rose to leave.

"Good-bye then. I suppose I shall not come again. You

keep what is mine, is that it?"

"I'm sorry, ma'am. It would appear that way."

Helga and Ken shared their frustration with Dr. Klaus, to whom they paid a farewell call.

"The system is devised to protect the depositor as well as the bank," she said, "and in a case of difficulty, it's always the bank that has the last word. It has the money, and possession is nine-tenths of the law. We Swiss are a rich people because we know how to manage other people's money."

"Including the millions of the dead."

"I'm afraid so. I'm glad I was a dentist, not a banker. There's something about money that inevitably invites corruption – if not legal, then moral."

"I don't care about my few francs," said Helga. "It's the letter. The world deserves to know the truth."

"Don't you think it knows by this time?"

"No, ma'am," Driscoll responded quickly, "it doesn't. The war in Europe has been over for three months, and around our headquarters there is hardly any comment about the extermination program. A few times I've tried to speak to co-workers about Theresienstadt and Auschwitz."

His eyes filled up with bitter memories. "My God, I can't sleep nights without having nightmares, and when I tell others just a fragment of what happened to me, they say 'terrible' and either aren't interested or think I'm exaggerating. And on more than one occasion they've told me that Hitler wasn't really so bad, and maybe he was right and we should have fought the Soviets together. A few more turns of the screw and the Führer will be considered a saint."

"I think that's why this creep Cohn-Gradewohl wanted the letter," Helga said. "The Nazis are defeated, but they haven't gone away. Now they're whitewashing first themselves and then their dead leader."

"I hope you're wrong," Dr. Klaus said without much

conviction. "People won't forget."

"May God hear you," Helga said fervently. "And if they do forget, I'll come back here and blow up the bank personally and get the letter."

"If you do, dear, don't forget to visit me first. Or even better, don't wait that long. Come back soon. Remember, there's an old woman who loves you."

Her eyes had a luminous quality. She had almost forgotten how fond she was of Helga.

"I didn't realize how much I had missed you. You were like a daughter to me and I'd like to think you still are."

Helga and Ken embraced her warmly.

Dr. Klaus looked affectionately at her two friends.

"Since you are like family to me, may I ask what your plans are?"

"I've learned I am divorced," said Driscoll. "We're on our way to London. There's a rabbi there who was my teacher in the concentration camp. Dr. Leo Baeck will marry us."

"We want you to come too," Helga insisted. "It wouldn't be right without you. We want you to be the guest of honor. We'll see that you get there."

Dr. Klaus smiled. "I've never been able to resist you," she said. "Maybe I will come."

When they left she wondered what life had in store for them. Two human beings thrust together, torn apart and united again. How much would it take to make both of them whole? Some wounds keep festering while others heal in time. Like the letter which had shaped their fate, their future was written in a book which, for the time being, was inaccessible.

Afterword

The setting of this novel is historical and the major political figures and events are drawn in accordance with attested records. Though all conversations have been freely invented, they are meant to reflect the known personalities and policies of the speakers.

The principals of the novel – Helga Raben, Rolf Baumgarten, Ken Driscoll, and their families and associates – are entirely fictional. No resemblance to any person, living or dead, has been intended.

About the Author

Trained for a career in law, W. Gunther Plaut left his native Germany as a refugee from Hitler and turned to theological studies, serving as a rabbi in the United States and Canada, and as a soldier participating in the conquest of Germany during World War II. His books earned him a world-wide reputation as a biblical scholar whose lectures are in demand in many countries. He has been president of national and international organizations.

In his latter years Plaut has given his time to writing and public service, filling special assignments by the Canadian and Ontario governments. His volume of short stories, *Hanging Threads* (entitled *The Man in the Blue Vest and Other Stories* in the U.S.), appeared in 1981. *The Letter* is his first full-length novel.

The author has been an outstanding athlete since his youth and continues to play tennis and golf. He and his wife Elizabeth, a genealogist, live in Toronto.